FATAL CHOICES
AND
SECOND CHANCES

Book Three of The Untangling Tale Series

Adda Leah Davis

ADDA LEAH DAVIS

ISBN: 978-1-4834-3875-7 (sc)
ISBN: 978-1-4834-3874-0 (e)

Library of Congress Control Number: 2015915835

Lulu Publishing Services rev. date: 10/13/2015

DEDICATION

THIS BEING THE THIRD BOOK IN this series I feel it would be unfair if it was not dedicated to all my precious readers. Only a writer knows how important it is to have people love one's writing.

I have tried to write what my heart feels about many issues that we face today even though the books are set in an earlier period of time. Time has no relevance when it comes to honor, integrity, faith, hope, charity, family, and love of one's country.

For those who have read my books I feel a special kinship. It is a mutual caring about the same issues that draws people together and from the messages I have received I now have many, many more friends. I thank each of you and especially those who have sent messages of love, caring, and the desire for more of my work. You have my undying thanks and appreciation.

Without readers there would be no need for writers. The human need for knowledge and expression has been there since the beginning of time and will endure as long as time lasts. Therefore my deepest and most cherished desire is that from my books you, the readers will find something in each of my characters that will help you in some way.

May the blessings of the Lord shine on each of you and may your days be filled with joy and gladness.

CHOICES OR A CHANCE

Choices are daily made on subjects of every hue
Some are wrong in the making
Varying with the chooser's view
Or
Unwise choices often occur by simple happenstance
Not thoughtful and life advancing
But leaving everything to chance
Or
Some choices are compulsive causing much distress
From lack of wisdom in the choosing
These bring no peace or rest
Or
A measure of the choices that one foolishly selects
Is how much suffering one withstands,
From the darkness they inflict
Or
Fate steps in to alter choices made in haste and without thought
And steers us from disaster's pathways
Bearing chances yet unsought.

ACKNOWLEDGEMENTS

As it is written in Ephesians, Chapter 5, and 20 verse, 'Giving thanks always for all things unto God and the Father in the name of our Lord Jesus Christ,' I hope I'll be found doing that in all that I say and all that I do in this life. With this fervent wish I acknowledge that God has given me the gift to write and I must never neglect to give my God the praise and glory for every word.

In this past year, through the divine purpose of our God, my dear, dear husband was called from this life, but I'm left with enduring and precious memories. Many people are not that fortunate and therefore I have another precious blessing for which I am so thankful.

Our wonderful children, daughters and sons-in-law, and grandchildren as well as our precious church family, have huddled close and helped to smooth the biting edges of grief. I pray God blesses them with the strength and courage to carry on the wonderful legacy of love and caring left by my husband.

Each of them in some way has encouraged me to continue my work as a writer and I have. The gift of Jonathan, my beloved grandson, has been a 'nail in a sure place' since he is always by my side. Through such encouragement how could I stop using the gift given by the Lord? So, I first thank my Lord and then each of you who have been by my side and been my mighty arm of strength.

"A people that values its privileges above its principles soon loses both"
Dwight D. Eisenhower

CHAPTER 1

"I'LL BE HAPPY IF I NEVER have to be involved with a trial again," said Hannah Larkin. She was mentally and physically exhausted. Sergeant Keith McCauley, her companion in the front seat of her battered old Ford Escort station wagon, looked at her and smiled.

"I think the human spirit can only take so much anguish before needing a breather. Today has been enough to last a long, long time hasn't it?"

"You people don't seem one bit happy that I've been freed. I thought Mom would be walking on air," said Freddie Larkin from the back seat.

Hannah turned to look at Freddie, her eyes misted with tears of thankfulness. From the morning his father had been found dead, Freddie had been the center of her daily and nightly prayers.

She smiled. "How would you have acted if I had jumped up and down in the court room and cried like a baby?"

Freddie grinned as he leaned up and kissed her cheek. "I'm kidding, Mom. I know you're happy about me, but worried about Mar . . . my grandmother right now."

"Yes. It's been pretty awful, but wonderful at the same time," Sergeant McCauley said, as he turned and smiled tenderly at Hannah. "You, Freddie, were released from jail, were freed of guilt, and gained a grandmother who may go to jail, all in one day. That's high emotion on both ends of the spectrum. It's no wonder your mother is worn out."

The three of them had gone to Shoney's to get lunch after Judge Wilson had proclaimed Freddie innocent on all charges and said he was free to return home. His newly acknowledged grandmother, Margie Meadows, however, was taken to the hospital in an ambulance.

They wove their way through the heavy traffic on the way to Pike Lane without talking at first, each involved with his or her own thoughts. Images of the ups and downs of her life ran like a kaleidoscope through Hannah's mind, beginning with her wonderful childhood on the farm in Mullens, West Virginia.

"Keith, did Freddie ever tell you about our farm in Mullens? The house sits on a knoll above the Guyandotte River and is still in pretty good shape. It could use a little fixing up, but the structure is sound."

"A farm? Do you own a farm? I've always dreamed of living on a farm, but don't imagine I ever will." Keith looked wistfully ahead.

"I think I'll sell our house on Pike Lane and move to the farm. Pike Lane is nothing like it was when we first bought our house, but Bill never liked the farm, did he, Freddie?"

"God no, he hated it. He didn't even like to go camping, but he would go when I was young."

"How old are you now, Grandpa?"

They all found that funny, but Freddie leaned to the front and said, "I'll have you know that I'm a man now. I'm twenty-one years old."

Keith pursed his lips. "Twenty-one, yes sir, that makes you a man, but it takes a lot of living to give many of us adult wisdom."

Hannah looked at Keith. "That's certainly the truth. There's no way someone Freddie's age could know how to react to events in life, but then does anyone ever really know?"

"I like to think I'm wiser now than I was at twenty-one, but as you say, who really knows? Even with the same circumstances we will all act differently since we are all different. I used to think it was either black or white, but I've certainly learned that isn't always the case."

After a few miles of silence, Keith asked, "Hannah, at what age did you leave the farm?"

Hannah smiled. "My heart never left. It lived on that farm beside the Guyandotte River even when my eleven-year-old body was moved to the state of Washington."

Keith turned fascinated eyes to her dreamlike expression and was again captured by her beauty. "Why did your parents go that far away? Did you have someone living out there?"

Freddie piped up from the back. "Yeah, Uncle Cam went there to work and he begged Grandpa Fred to move out there, but he probably wouldn't have moved if it hadn't been for Aunt Betty."

"Freddie!" Hannah gasped giving her son a warning glare.

"Mom, it doesn't matter anymore. Aunt Betty is dead."

Hearing the censure in Hannah's voice, Keith quickly asked, "Did your dad work out there? I mean he was a farmer back here, wasn't he?"

"Yes, he was, but he knew all about trees and timber and they were glad to get him at the saw mill where he went to work. He scaled logs, appraised timber, and graded lumber along with other odd jobs until he retired," replied Hannah.

"Was he still working when he died?"

"No, he had retired. Dad, Mom, and I were in the garden picking beans when a telegram came about Junior being killed in a plane crash. Dad fell over with a heart attack and died."

They rode along in silence for a few more miles and then Freddie spoke up again.

"Mom met Dad when she went to college in Seattle. I'm sure glad she did because I wouldn't be here if she hadn't."

Hannah said in a dreamy voice as her thoughts went to that magical time of first love. "It was the second semester and I had been so bored all during the first semester that I dreaded each new day. That all changed when I saw this handsome young man looking at me. He was so good to look at that I think I did some staring myself. Anyway, we married and I thought I could forget the farm and West Virginia, but I didn't."

"Yeah, Uncle Cam said that when Dad complained about not liking his job Mom jumped onto that like a dog with a bone. Uncle Cam said she never let Dad rest until he agreed to move her back to West Virginia." Freddie laughed at Hannah's startled expression.

"Mom, I swear that's what Uncle Cam told me."

"Well, Cam was wrong. I didn't nag your dad. I was afraid he'd get one of those moo . . ." She stopped and looked back at Freddy, who rolled his eyes and sighed.

"Mom, everybody will know anyway, before they find out who really killed Dad, so we may as well tell Keith." Hannah dropped her head and sat inspecting her nails.

"Keith, Dad had some kind of problem. He would sometimes go into some kind of dark mood and wouldn't talk or do anything but work and eat. Mom and I learned to work around it and recognize the signals that indicated a mood was coming on."

"Freddie, I'm sure that Keith is not interested in our life history. We don't need to bore him with our problems." Hannah turned to look out the window.

"It's all right, Hannah. Freddie knows that I won't tell anyone what he tells me. Don't get upset. We're back at your house anyway." Keith pulled to a smooth stop in the driveway.

Keith got out and went around to help Hannah out of the car while Freddie went ahead to unlock the door. Keith looked up at the house. "Did you buy this house new, or did you build it?"

"No, it wasn't new when we bought it. We had only been back in West Virginia about a month and Bill had drawn a couple of paydays when we bought the house. It was really a nice neighborhood back then."

"Was your husband's first job with Civic Enterprise Endeavors?"

Hannah smiled as she remembered how happy they were when he was hired. "Yes. The job required someone with training in business management and that was what Bill had studied in college. We were so happy, and it stayed that way most of the time for a little more than eighteen years."

Suddenly Freddie said, "I guess I came along and messed it all up. They'd only been here about six months when I surprised them. I'm surprised Dad didn't get one of his moody spells and refuse to acknowledge me."

"Freddie, you know that you were your dad's pride and joy," scolded Hannah.

"Yeah, everything was great until I got big enough to know he wasn't God. In fact, I really can't remember him having very many moody spells when I was in school. Were they as bad during that time, Mom?"

"No, Freddie, he didn't have as many during that time. He had some, as you know, but not like the past three years. We had eighteen years of mostly peace and contentment."

They had all gone into the living room and taken seats, but Hannah rose suddenly. "Keith, I'd like a cup of coffee. Would you and Freddie like some?"

Keith rose to his feet. "You don't need to be waiting on us. Freddie and I will make the coffee."

He turned to Freddie. "Lead the way, Grandpa."

Freddie laughed. "I'll take you over to the farm one day and we'll see who is the most like a Grandpa."

They left and Hannah went back to her chair and sat thinking back over the last few years. *Bill was such a good father and faithful husband until Freddie graduated from high school. Then Freddie met Sam Henson's daughter, Nicole, and that seemed to be the starting point for everything that's happened since. Bill was put over that Blennoc Project and he had to take the Draper woman as his assistant.*

5

Hannah was jerked out of her reverie by the return of Keith and Freddie bringing a tray with coffee, creamer, and sugar as well as slices of cake.

Keith put her cake and coffee on a low table in front of the sofa and took a seat beside her. He pointed to the cake.

"I hope you don't mind me cutting your cake. It looked so good that I couldn't resist. Freddie said you wouldn't mind."

Hannah grinned. "I'm upset. I planned to eat the whole thing by myself."

Freddie chuckled and so did Keith who was so pleased because Hannah seemed to be accepting him as a friend that he was fearful of doing something to change this progress.

"Hannah, I'm not asking this just to be nosey, but do you know what changed your husband so much in the past few years?" Keith questioned with an intent look on his face.

Hannah thought he needed that information to help with the trial and she wanted to help.

"Well, when Freddie started dating Nicole Henson he soon started staying out late and got into drugs. Then one night Freddie stayed away all night and the next morning Bill found him and Nicole Henson locked up in jail. I don't know if that was the cause, but that's when the change became so obvious."

"Did he not try to understand and help Freddie? I know you've both said that he seemed to adore Freddie. A sudden change like that doesn't make sense unless something else was going on," said Keith in a softly questioning voice.

Freddie spoke up. "You're sharp, Keith. A person can't love someone one day and then hate them the next unless they're using that to hide something they're doing themselves."

"Freddie, you know your dad was working so much that he couldn't have been doing anything else. I think he just loved you so much and thought you were perfect and couldn't adjust to you being different from the vision he'd always had of you as an adult."

"Hannah, don't you think that's an awfully heavy load to drop on your son?" Keith was looking very serious.

"Yeah, Mom, it's been hard enough to be jailed for suspicion of killing Dad without you saying I started him on the path he's taken for the past three years. Do you really believe that I caused all our troubles?"

Hannah turned white. "No, no, Freddie. I don't believe you caused your dad to do any of the things he's done for the last while. I just meant that it seemed to be his reaction at the time, but he was worse after you came back home. You know he was."

Hannah was very upset and agitated. She looked at Keith. "I said that all wrong. I guess you think I'm a terrible mother and human being."

Keith started to speak, but Hannah went to sit on the foot stool in front of Freddie's chair. "Freddie, I'm so sorry. I really didn't mean it the way I explained about your dad. He just couldn't give you a chance to explain or defend yourself. I thought it was because he saw it as a flaw in himself and wouldn't admit it." She turned to look at Keith.

"Does that make sense?"

"Yes, it does and I think Freddie understands what you were trying to say. Don't you, Freddie?" Keith gave Freddie a direct look and Freddie leaned over and hugged Hannah.

"I hadn't thought about it in that light, but I suppose he possibly reacted that way. I didn't like him for a while, but the night he died I saw a glimpse of the old Dad that I loved so much," said Freddie.

Hannah still stayed on the foot stool, but sat as if puzzling about something. "Freddie, while you lived away, your dad stayed away more than he stayed here. He took the check book, and yelled and fussed about every move I made. Sarah is the only person who knew what was going on and I didn't tell her for a long time. The night you came wanting that money, I really didn't have any. Your dad gave me so much a week for groceries and that was all."

Keith's muttered damn went unnoticed. Freddie and Hannah seemed to be caught up in reliving the drama they had gone through.

"Mom, did Dad give you any excuse for staying away weekends and nights?"

Hannah shook her head. "He always said there were meetings he had to attend. I believed him, but I started having all those stomach problems and didn't go to the doctor."

"I think Mom was being slowly poisoned, Keith." Freddie didn't get to continue because of the reactions from Keith and Hannah.

Hannah sat in a pale-faced, round-eyed gaping stare as if frozen in place, but Keith was very alert.

"What? Why do you think she was being poisoned?" Keith sat forward in his seat.

"Well, she had been taking Mylanta, and felt it helped, but it hadn't. One morning as I came down the stairs to go to work I found Mom passed out on the floor beside the stove. She was in the hospital for several weeks and had to have blood transfusions. So, when Dad died and he had also taken Mylanta it made me suspicious."

CHAPTER 2

KEITH ASKED FREDDIE ABOUT EVERY DETAIL of the night his dad died. He only stopped when he got a call from Steve Hammer, a special investigator on the case, and had to leave. Later he learned that Hannah had been in the hospital two weeks because of stomach problems with pain and bleeding. Now, with Freddie's suspicion he realized that she had good reason for being so weak and unsteady on her feet.

In the following trial testimonies he also learned that Hannah hadn't been out of the hospital a full month when Bill was found dead in the living room floor by Freddie when he arrived home from work. This led to Freddie being arrested for murder since he had set out a glass with what he thought was milk for his father before he had gone to work. The contents proved to be Mylanta laced with cyanide poison. This had started the untangling of a web that shook the foundations of the business world in Beckley and the surrounding areas.

Hannah and her closest neighbor as well as best friend, Sarah Preston, had gradually grown to like Sergeant Keith McCauley, the officer who had arrested Freddie. They liked him even better when he had gotten Freddie released to attend his father's funeral.

During Freddie's bail bond hearing and at the trial of Sam Henson, Margie Meadows admitted to giving out the Mylanta that had poisoned Bill Larkin. She claimed she didn't know the samples she handed out contained poison, but she gave them to Sabrina Draper even though she knew they had been doctored with something.

Margie wanted to get back at Sam Henson and became so emotional during her statement that she blurted out that Bill Larkin was her son, and that she had given him up for adoption when he was born.

It was the evening of that revelation that Keith drove Hannah and Freddie home after the trial ended for the day. When they pulled into the Larkin drive Keith called the hospital. They would not tell him anything about Margie Meadows, but before he left that evening he again called Steve.

Steve answered on the first ring. "Keith, I'm glad you called. She is sedated right now, but the doctor thinks she will be all right. She went through Hell today in that court room, didn't she?"

Keith asked if he had worked out a plan for security. "Well, I'm staying here, but that means I can't take a shift guarding Sabrina Draper. David Shortt said he had another deputy that was completely honest and reliable that will work with him guarding her, though. I worry that we may not be able to keep other people from being sent in," said Steve.

"Steve, you may have to use that doctor . . . what was his name? Yes, that's right, Zimmer. I think we can tell him our situation and he will run a cover for us. He could say that Sabrina is still in a coma, even if she isn't, until we need her. Do you think he will go along with us?"

Steve promised that he would talk it over with the doctor and get back to him. "Where are you now, Keith?"

"I'm here at Hannah's house. I brought her and Freddie back from the trial." Steve hung up thinking, *So it's really Hannah now, since he's talking in front of her.* Steve smiled with satisfaction, knowing Keith had been alone for ten long years.

Keith stayed another hour with Hannah and Freddie. The three of them discussed Margie's surprising admission that Bill Larkin was her child.

"It had to be hard to admit something like that. She was just so torn up over Freddie, I guess. She had never gotten to really be with her son and today she saw her only grandson in trouble and just blurted it out before she thought," said Hannah.

Freddie grinned. "I think when she made that slip and no longer had anything to hide she was so relieved that she just threw caution to the wind."

Keith nodded his agreement. "It must have been hard keeping such a secret for so long. Can you imagine someone leaving everything they knew to follow someone who didn't even know they existed? I guess only a mother could do that."

Hannah smiled reflectively. "A good mother would, Keith, but there are lots of women with children who are certainly not good mothers."

That's another good quality she has, thought Keith as he rose to take his leave.

"I'll check with the hospital tomorrow, and if Margie is allowed any visitors, Freddie can drive you out there, Hannah. I can't. I'll be at Henson's trial all day."

"That's all right, Keith. I know you can't chauffeur me all over town. Freddie can drive me out there," said Hannah.

"Hannah, you may not be allowed in, anyway, unless Steve or I can be with you," said Keith, explaining about security.

"That's why I want to check with the hospital before you make the trip."

Freddie walked out to the car with Keith. "Keith, I'm worried that some of the people Margie mentioned may try to get to her. Whoever it is could kill again," said Freddie with a worried frown.

Keith clapped him on the shoulder and assured him that he and Steve had already thought about that. "We have to watch Miss Draper also, but we have worked out an arrangement in which either

Steve, David Shortt, or I will be in one place or the other at all times, regardless of who visits."

Freddie didn't know it, but several attempts had already been made to get into Sabrina Draper's room. Thankfully, she was still in ICU, but in a secured setting rather than an open ward with curtains, and a twenty-four hour guard was on duty. Security had reported that first a man claiming to be Sabrina's uncle and second a woman, wearing dark glasses and a wig, had tried to gain access. When the nurse questioned the woman she made some excuse and hurriedly left.

Knowing this, Keith, Steve, and David Short kept their phones set so that each of them could be easily reached and one of them was always on duty.

When Margie awoke the following morning, after her breakdown, Steve was sitting in a chair beside the bed working a crossword puzzle.

"What are you doing here?" asked Margie.

"Waiting to see if you would talk to me," answered Steve, closing his crossword book and standing up.

"How long have you been here?"

Steve looked at his watch. "Since five o'clock this morning, but Sergeant David Short was here from twelve last night until I came."

"Are the police afraid I'll leave town or try to harm myself?" asked Margie querulously.

Steve grinned. "We just want you to know you have friends in this town, whether you trust us or not."

When she started to pose another question, Steve came to the side of the bed and looked down directly into her eyes. "Margie, we are trying to protect you from the deep-voiced man and that other fellow, whoever they are."

"Oh. Well, thank you. I had forgotten about that. What did I say, Steve, besides blurting the secret I've held inside for over forty years?" asked Margie.

Steve told about her saying that she had overheard a conversation between two men, one with a deep voice. "Since you never saw either man, we want to make sure that you will never have to see them nor they will ever see you."

Tears welled up in Margie's eyes. "What difference will it make? I'll go to prison anyway for giving that Mylanta to Sabrina thinking she would give it to Sam Henson. I can't believe I did that."

Suddenly she began crying and reached out to grasp Steve's hand. "I did something else too."

Steve held her hand gently. "Margie, are you able to be going into this now? Maybe you should wait until you feel better."

"No, Steve, I want to get it all out. I'm ashamed, but I was just so torn up. You see, I found out that Bill was having an affair with Sabrina. That made me angry because I knew that Bill had always been faithful to Hannah from the time he married her." Margie gulped and swiped her hand across her eyes.

"When I heard that Bill was dead, I nearly died too. Then I heard he had been poisoned with Mylanta and it all fell into place. I knew then that the 'doctoring' that those men were talking about was poison instead of just something to make someone sick for a few days. They had put it in the Mylanta that I gave Sabrina. She gave it to Bill. I know that by giving that to Bill, she killed him, but I also had a hand in it. Sabrina enticed Bill to cheat on his wife and I really wanted to make her pay. I put a handkerchief over the phone and I accused her of killing Bill and she either hung up or dropped the phone."

Steve stood holding her hand and now he leaned over and wiped the tears from her face with a Kleenex.

"Margie, don't you think you're being awfully hard on yourself? Sabrina is very ambitious, and whatever it took to get her to a higher position she did it. She may not have put the poison in the Mylanta, but neither did you. However, I'll bet Miss Sabrina knew who did it."

Just then a nurse came in and Steve backed away from the bed. "Good morning, Miss Meadows. How do you feel?" she asked.

"I'm weak and weepy, but otherwise all right."

"Do you think you can get up?" The nurse bent over to get Margie's shoes. Steve's eyes widened as he saw the hem of a flowered skirt below the edge of the nurse's uniform. His reaction was swift. He grabbed the nurse's arms and pulled them back behind her.

"Who are you? You're not a nurse, that's for sure," said Steve in a voice of cold steel.

The woman turned white and started babbling. "I told him I couldn't do this but he made me."

"Who made you?" asked Steve, adding pressure to the arms.

"I can't tell, or I'll get my throat slit," blurted the woman, wincing in pain. Steve handcuffed her, and holding the chain between the cuffs, he opened his cell phone and punched a number.

When Keith answered, Steve said, "The first one has arrived. How soon can you get here? Good. This one is a woman."

Steve ended the call and backed the woman into the chair. "Sit there and keep your mouth shut," he ordered.

"I haven't killed anybody, so don't look at me as if I'm dirt," the imposter snarled.

"But you were going to kill somebody, weren't you?" He spat the words at her and she winced at the venom in his voice.

In a few tense moments the door opened and Keith walked in. He stopped as he saw the woman dressed as a nurse. "Well Velda, it seems you can't keep a promise. You promised me that you would have nothing else to do with Sam Henson, but here you are doing his dirty work again. You were in a cell the last time I saw you. That time you were caught peddling drugs. This time you've moved up to the big time . . . now it is attempting to murder someone. You could get life for this."

Velda Arnetta, sat trembling in wide-eyed fear.

"Where did you get the uniform? Did Sam Henson bring it to you?"

The woman sucked in her breath. "It ain't just Sam Henson." Realizing she was talking too much, she clammed up and sat in mulish silence for a few moments and then blurted, "If you had any love in your heart you'd do the same as me to keep your child safe."

Then she clamped her hand over her mouth and slumped lower in her seat. Keith looked at her with compassion and shook his head.

"I'm sorry, Velda, but you should have come to me a long time ago," he said as he motioned her to her feet. She arose and walked stoically beside Keith through the hospital and got into the patrol car.

CHAPTER 3

AT THE STATION, THE WOMAN WAS booked on attempted murder. Stopping back at the desk, Keith told David he had to be in the Henson trial, but to be on the alert in case Steve needed him. He started out the door, but looked back at the Chief's office. Seeing no lights on, he asked, "Where's the chief? Is he not working today?"

David shrugged. "I don't know, but I'd say he's at the courthouse. When he talked to me yesterday he seemed awfully interested in what Sam Henson had to say."

Keith left the station and hurried over to the courthouse. He knew the trial wasn't scheduled to begin until nine o'clock, but he wanted to talk to the prosecuting attorney. Kyle Swann was nowhere to be found. Keith went down the street to Meg's Diner to have breakfast. After eating he dialed the Larkin's.

Hannah answered and Keith was surprised. "Hannah, I expected Freddie to answer. I didn't know you got up this early."

"I've been up since six o'clock. I had a bad dream about Margie and I couldn't go back to sleep. Have you heard from her this morning?"

"Yes. She's fine. Steve is with her, but I'm afraid you won't get to see her today. No, she isn't. Honest, she's feeling all right, but there's nobody to escort you in to see her. I have to be in court all day, and Steve can't leave Margie and nobody can get in to see her without one of us," Keith explained.

Keith had already given the prosecuting attorney the investigative report, but he wanted Swann to know about the Arnetta woman trying to get to Margie. As soon as Swann's car pulled up Keith walked to meet him. He was surprised at Swann's response to his information. "Well, we know that Sam Henson didn't send her."

"I wouldn't be too sure about that," replied Keith. "Sam Henson has connections in many places. He could have gotten word out to somebody."

"That's possible, I guess, but I still don't think this was his doing,"

"If not him, then who do you suspect?" asked Keith.

Swann looked at Keith in a speculative manner. "Is there any way you could get Margie Meadows back here in ten minutes, if I should give you the sign?"

"I don't know if the doctor would allow it; nor do I know whether she should. Remember, she broke down yesterday," replied Keith.

Mr. Swann shifted his weight from his left foot to the right and taking his left hand pressed the edges of his lower lip together from the sides. He stood like that for a few minutes.

"Well, see what you can do. I have a little experiment that I'd like to try. It may give us some revealing answers if Miss Meadows can get here."

"You mean you want me to go to get her now?" asked Keith.

"No, not right this minute. Sometime during the proceeding I'll look at you and do my lower lip like I just did. That will be the sign that you should go get Miss Meadows."

"What if I call Steve and let him clear it with the doctor and Margie, uh, Miss Meadows before I go?" said Keith.

Swann nodded his agreement and left Keith standing on the sidewalk, deep in thought.

Keith put in his call to Steve. "I'll talk to the doctor and Margie and get back to you," Steve promised. "Don't forget to put your phone on vibrate, Keith. You don't want to be kicked out of the courtroom."

"Oh, Steve, I almost forgot. If you get everything cleared, will you call Hannah and Freddie? Tell them to meet you and Margie here at the courthouse."

"I didn't think Hannah wanted to ever go to a trial again," said Steve.

"I know that's what she said, but she also said she wanted to come if Margie was involved."

Keith entered the courtroom just as the bailiff shouted, "All rise. Judge Nathan Wilson, presiding."

The case of the state against Sam Henson was reconvened. Jacob Stern, lawyer for Henson, and Kyle Swann, the prosecuting attorney approached the bench. After a brief discussion, Kyle Swann repeated the charges against Sam Henson.

Keith's eyes were trained on the actions in the courtroom. Sam Henson had been sitting stoically, but now began looking around him furtively until his eyes fastened on Chief Donaldson. Keith switched his gaze back toward Sam Henson and was puzzled by his expression. It was a mixture of disbelief, chagrin, and anger, which he was trying hard to control but not succeeding.

Sam sat as if he hadn't heard one word of the charges against him. His face became pale and then turned a mottled red as he glared at Donaldson. In fact, he was concentrating so much that he gasped in startled surprise when Swann called Bertram Briscoll to be his first witness.

Bertram Briscoll was a tall slender, handsome, but effeminate man. He tried to ignore Sam Henson's vindictive glare as he walked past the table where Sam was seated. Keith sat watching all three men.

There's some kind of connection there, that's for sure, thought Keith as Chief Donaldson jerked as if to protest when Bertram Briscoll was called. Now, the chief had such a look of dismay on his face that Keith almost felt sorry for him.

Bertram Briscoll took the witness chair and was sworn in. He constantly pushed his hair back from his forehead and wiped his face as if he felt something on it. As he waited, he coughed nervously until the bailiff brought him a cup of water. This helped and the prosecuting attorney walked to the side of the witness seat.

Again the witness was asked for his name, address, and information as to how long he had lived in the area and then, almost out of left field, Swann asked, "Mr. Briscoll, how well do you know Chief Harry Donaldson?"

Briscoll jerked himself into a statue-like posture. "I know he is the chief of police for the city of Beckley."

Kyle Swann smiled. "We all know that, Mr. Briscoll. Are you personally acquainted with Chief Donaldson?"

Keith's eyes were kept busy judging the reaction from the chief and from Sam Henson. Both men were leaning forward on the edge of their seats, glaring malevolently at Bertram Briscoll. Keith's eyes swung to Briscoll. Now he was not only rubbing his face, but plucking at his tie as if it was constricting his breath.

Kyle Swann stood patiently waiting, and finally Mr. Briscoll spoke. "We are friends."

"Friends? Do you mean friends that you visit, have lunch with, or . . . vacation with?" asked Swann intently.

"I've never been on a vacation with Ha . . . uh, I mean Chief Donaldson."

A snicker was heard here and there in the room and the judge tapped his gavel.

By this time Briscoll was perspiring, and gulping the water. He actually became strangled at Swann's next question.

"Mr. Briscoll, how long have you known Sam Henson?"

Henson half rose from his seat and Chief Donaldson gave a quick twist from looking at Briscoll to glare at Henson. They reminded Keith of two dogs warring over a prized bone.

"I've known him since high school. We graduated together," replied Briscoll.

"I know that your family owns the Briscoll Pharmaceutical Company and that you work there. Have you done business with Henson?"

Briscoll looked at Sam, raised his eyebrows and answered. "Yes, the company has done business with Mr. Henson."

"What kinds of things does Sam Henson purchase from your company?" asked Swann.

"He purchases films, chemicals, frames, and all sorts of things for the various businesses that CEE is involved with."

"Where are these materials sent when Mr. Henson purchases them?"

Jacob Stern, Henson's lawyer, jumped to the floor. "Your honor, I object to this type of questioning?"

Judge Wilson looked over his glasses and asked, "On what grounds, Mr. Stern?"

"Where something is delivered is irrelevant in establishing a relationship with Mr. Henson's business," replied Stern.

Kyle Swann stepped back to his table. He extracted a folder from his briefcase and presented it to the judge. "Your Honor, I think this evidence will prove that delivery is more than relevant to this case."

Judge Wilson sat looking over the material and the attached notes by Swann and then looked up. "Objection denied. Continue, Mr. Swann."

Swann turned back to Briscoll. "Again, Mr. Briscoll, where were the materials purchased by Mr. Henson sent?"

Briscoll at first dropped his head and then lifted it, and looking directly at Sam Henson, he said, "Warren Wholesale and Distribution Warehouses."

Pulling a sheet from the folder, which the Judge had returned to him Swann placed it in front of Briscoll. "Is this your signature, Mr. Briscoll?"

Out of the corner of his eye, Keith saw Henson sink lower in his seat and then turned back to the witness. His eye, however, was caught by Swann's seeming thoughtful pose. His left hand had pressed both sides of his lower lip into a ridge in the center. Keith quietly rose from his seat and left the courtroom.

CHAPTER 4

SOON STEVE, MARGIE, HANNAH AND FREDDIE arrived at the courthouse. Hannah and Freddie entered the courtroom and took an aisle seat in the middle of the room.

Margie was taken to a room adjacent to the courtroom. The walls of this room were not well insulated and voices from the courtroom could be easily heard if the door was cracked.

Margie was seated in a chair with its back to the separating wall. Keith quietly opened the door and reentered the courtroom leaving the door slightly ajar. He took the aisle seat beside of Freddie Larkin, making sure that Kyle Swann knew that he had returned.

Bertram Briscoll was still in the witness chair, but was now a disheveled caricature of the debonair man who had been sworn in earlier. Looking around Keith noted that Sam Henson's usual florid complexion now had a pasty hue.

Just as Keith was seated, Kyle Swann walked to the jury side of the room and turned. "Mr. Briscoll, you stated earlier that Sam Henson bought chemicals and other things from your company. Is that correct?"

Briscoll swallowed as if choking and replied, "Yes, that's correct."

"Who in your company processed those orders, Mr. Briscoll?"

"The shipping department processed the orders, but I always inspected them," Briscoll replied.

"Did Henson ever buy cyanide poison from your company, Mr. Briscoll?" asked Swann.

Bertram Briscoll gulped, jerked at his tie and muttered something. "Speak up, Mr. Briscoll. Did Sam Henson ever buy cyanide poison from your company?"

Sam's lawyer, Jacob Stern, jumped to his feet. "I object. Mr. Swann's questioning is intimidating the witness."

"Objection denied. Mr. Briscoll, answer the question," ordered Judge Wilson.

Bertram Briscoll bowed his head and answered. "Yes."

Sam Henson jumped to his feet. "They're not going to pin that on me. I gave that . . . ." He didn't get to finish since his lawyer and the bailiff both grabbed at him. The bailiff took his arm, but Stern stepped in and pushed Sam back into his seat. He stood over Sam with such a threatening look on his face that Sam subsided.

Everyone in the courtroom reacted loudly. Judge Wilson rapped his gavel several times until they quieted down.

Kyle Swann stood quietly for a moment then walked to the judge's bench and picked up a folder. Taking some sheets from the folder he placed them in front of Briscoll.

"Mr. Briscoll, is this your signature?" he asked, pointing to three different sheets."

Briscoll visibly jerked and then mumbled. "Yes."

"These orders are dated three months apart. You signed off on them, but only on the orders coming in about every three or four months from the Blennoc Project. Did you personally fill or supervise the filling of these orders?"

This question came seemingly out of left field and for a moment Briscoll seemed stunned and then paled.

There was complete silence as everyone waited for Briscoll to answer. Finally without raising his head, he replied. "I didn't personally fill them, but I did sign off on them."

"Did you know that the orders were not complete, Mr. Briscoll?" Swann rose to his tiptoes and then settled down again.

Bertie Briscoll stiffened. "The orders were all complete, when they left our company. If they were short somebody besides me did it," he stated emphatically.

Everyone in the courtroom realized that Sam Henson had just been caught up in some kind of unprofessional activity and Briscoll's testimony had confirmed what Bill Larkin had found before he died.

Kyle Swann said he had no further questions for Briscoll for the present and Jacob Stern had none either, so Briscoll was allowed to return to his seat.

Henson stared daggers at him as he made his way back to his seat. Briscoll kept his head down, never looking at Sam Henson.

Just as Keith took his seat, Swann called Chief Harry Donaldson to the stand. Every eye in the room opened wide in astonishment. Surely, the Chief of Police couldn't be involved in all the deals that Briscoll had revealed, was the prevailing thought.

Donaldson hoisted himself from his seat and blundered his way to the witness box. He passed Kyle Swann, looking at him as if to say, I've got your number and I'll remember you.

When he was sworn in, Swann began the questioning. The chief gave abrupt answers in a belligerent tone. Swann looked around the courtroom as if he was looking for someone and then turned back to the chief. He walked back and forth a few times and then abruptly stopped.

"Chief Donaldson, is there a big problem with drugs in this county and city?"

Donaldson sat up tall and straight, showing the full six-foot stature of his Law and Order persona. He bit his lip as if in deliberation.

"If you mean are there any drug arrests, then yes, we do have a minor drug problem," he stated as if to end this kind of questioning.

"What is done with the drugs confiscated in arrests?" asked the prosecutor, peering narrowly at Chief Donaldson.

"The deputies and policemen dispose of them," stated the chief. Many raised eyebrows and negative nods were noted from many places in the room.

Swann walked back and forth a couple more times and then turned. Standing at the side of the witness seat facing the jury, he asked, "How well do you know Sam Henson?"

Jacob Stern hit the floor. "Your Honor, I object to this line of questioning. Who he knows has nothing to do with his job as chief of police. After all, he needs to know as many people in the area as possible."

Judge Wilson turned to Swann. "Is your question relevant to this case?"

"Your Honor, I intend to prove that Chief Donaldson was a willing partner in the many deals made by Sam Henson, if you will bear with me," replied Swann.

Again, loud talk burst out all over the courtroom and the judge banged his gavel loudly for the crowd to settle. One man had to be forcibly removed who was still yelling as he was forced through the doors. Keith smiled at the man's last words. "That's how the sons-a-bitches tricked me."

By this time the chief was showing unease but still blustered. "I've not been in on any deals, and anybody that says I have is a damn liar."

"Chief, one more outburst and you will be cited for contempt of court," said the judge.

Keith had seen Kyle pull his lower lip together from the sides again and look at him. He realized that was his signal to bring Margie into the courtroom. He eased himself around the back of the room and out the side door.

"Chief Donaldson, have you ever bought any drugs or poison from Briscoll Pharmaceuticals?"

There were audible gasps from many areas of the courtroom and a loud whoosh of seeming relief from the section where Sam Henson was seated.

"I don't know what you are talking about. Why would I want to buy poison from anybody?" asked Chief Donaldson in a disdainful tone.

"You tell me, Chief," shot back Kyle Swann.

Chief Donaldson worked his lips back and forth and turned in his seat before answering. Finally he said, "No. I've never bought poison from Briscoll Pharmaceuticals or anyone else."

Swann said, "Chief Donaldson, you are aware that you are under oath, aren't you?"

"Hell yes, I'm aware. I said I have never bought poison from that company and I haven't," stormed the chief.

Sam Henson started up again, but was again shoved back by Mr. Stern who was looking haggard himself.

The chief was allowed to step down after Swann said he had no more questions for him at the moment. Stern said he had no questions.

Donaldson walked back to his seat and sat staring as Margie Meadows was led into the room by Steve Hammer. Steve had answered Keith's call and escorted Margie from the hospital.

Swann stood waiting until the effect of seeing Margie Meadows eased and said, "I call Margie Meadows to the stand."

Steve led Margie to the witness chair and helped her into it. Swann stepped close to her and asked if she was all right. Margie nodded.

"Miss Meadows, you testified in yesterday's hearing that you heard a conversation between two men while at a conference sponsored by CEE. Do you remember that testimony?"

"Yes, sir, I do," answered Margie.

"As I recall, you said one of the men had a deep, rough voice. Is that accurate?" asked Swann.

"Yes, sir, that is correct."

"Would you recognize that voice if you heard it again?"

"I didn't think I would, but I heard it again, today."

"Where did you hear it, Miss Meadows?" asked Swann.

"I was just on the other side of that wall," said Margie as she pointed to the wall on her right.

"Did you see who the voice belonged to, Miss Meadows?"

"Yes sir. I came to the door and peeped in and the voice was coming from Chief Donaldson," stated Margie in a very firm voice.

"That's a damn lie," shouted Donaldson, jumping to his feet.

Judge Wilson looked at Donaldson and pointed his finger. "As promised, I sentence you to thirty days in jail for contempt."

"So, Miss Meadows, you recognized the voice of the man who asked if the Mylanta was doctored as coming from Chief Harry Donaldson. Is that correct?" asked Swann slowly.

"Yes sir. It's the same voice I heard at the conference," replied Margie. Again gasps of amazement and anger were loud in the room.

CHAPTER 5

JUDGE WILSON'S GAVEL BEAT A RAPID tap-tap for minutes before the exclamations of surprise and anger settled down. Kyle Swann stood quietly looking at some notes, but when the rear courtroom doors suddenly opened, all heads turned to look. The doors were held open and Sergeant David Shortt pushed a wheelchair through the door. A faded and defeated Sabrina Draper sat in the wheelchair.

When the chief recognized who was in the chair he seemed to shrink in size as well as lose all color. He became almost as white as the uniform shirt that was his daily attire.

Hannah was shocked to see Sabrina Draper. "I thought she was in intensive care," she whispered to Freddie as Sergeant Shortt propelled the wheelchair down the center aisle to stop before Kyle Swann. Freddie looked at Hannah and put his finger to his lips denoting silence.

Kyle looked at Sabrina with compassion. "Miss Draper, are you able to testify?" Sabrina nodded yes.

Kyle walked back to the witness box and told Margie she could step down. "I call Miss Sabrina Draper to the stand."

Sergeant David Shortt wheeled Sabrina over to the witness seat and lifted her into the chair. Kyle motioned to the bailiff, who brought Sabrina a glass of water. She slowly drank several sips.

Sabrina was weak, but seemed calm and assured. As usual Swann asked the identifying information and she answered. He then told her to rest a moment. She sipped her water again and sat waiting.

"Miss Draper, you know most of the men who work or worked for CEE. Is that correct?" asked Swann.

"Yes, I do."

"In what capacity?"

Sabrina swallowed and wet her lips then lifted her head. "In whatever capacity my immediate superior described as needful."

"Miss Draper, did the capacity in which you worked involve business or was it also personal?" asked Swann.

In a toneless voice, Sabrina said, "Business and personal, but not in all cases."

"Miss Draper, did you have a personal relationship with Sam Henson?"

Sabrina swallowed. "Yes I did, but he sent me to Bill Larkin when he wanted to get rid of the Blennoc Project."

"Was that a good move for you?" Swann asked.

"Yes and no. I received a huge raise, but my job was to keep Bill busy with things other than work," said Sabrina wearily.

"Did you have an affair with Bill Larkin, Miss Draper?"

"Yes, but I didn't put poison in that Mylanta."

Hannah and Freddie had been listening intently. When Sabrina said she'd had an affair with Bill, Hannah rose to her feet. "That's not true! Bill wouldn't be unfaithful to me."

Judge Wilson had been struck by the beauty of this grieving widow and now her protection of her dead husband's honor touched him deeply. *I didn't think there were any women like her still left in this crazy world*, he thought as Hannah's voice rang clear and every head turned in her direction.

Freddie stood as well and put his arm around her, and whispered. "Mom, let me take you home."

Hannah wouldn't leave, but she did sit down. She dropped her head into her hands too hurt to cry anymore. Bill was the only boy she had dated. She married him thinking that he would never use her as all those men had used her sister, Betty. Although shocked and disillusioned, Hannah couldn't leave. Her life had been a sham, but she wanted to hear all of it.

"Are Henson and Larkin the only CEE personnel involved in this, Miss Draper?"

Sabrina sat in deep thought. "I'm not sure what Thomas Mitchell wanted, but he took me out to dinner and dancing. It never got any further than that, but I knew he wanted something."

Sabrina had gotten very pale and Swann asked her if she was able to continue. Sabrina crimped her lips in a determined line and nodded yes.

"Miss Draper, have you had any dealings with Chief Harry Donaldson?"

"Not personally, but I know all about his drug dealing and most of the other things he's involved with. Sam Henson talks a lot at night, especially if he's had a drink or two. If you want to find out about corruption in this city take a look at Chief Harry Donaldson."

Donaldson rose from his chair and made a dash toward Sabrina but Keith and Steve were too quick for him. They had his arms twisted behind his back in seconds. He was handcuffed and escorted back to his seat. The entire courtroom sat briefly stunned as if all the air had been sucked out of the room. Then the silence was shattered with furious voices, raised fists, and people trying to move about, only to be halted by policemen. Just as the judge rose to call a recess, the room calmed down.

Swann looked around and seeing that people were calmer he turned back to Sabrina. "Miss Draper, you just stated that Chief Donaldson sells drugs. Do you know this for a fact?"

Sabrina drew a long breath. Looking directly at Henson, she said, "Yes. That's where Sam Henson gets all the drugs he uses to get people to do his dirty work. He was always bringing a bag to me, and I used it. I got poor Bill Larkin to use it, too. I didn't kill Bill, but I was helping Sam to set him up so that all the shortages caused by Sam would be blamed on Bill. James Harrison knew about Sam's underhanded deals and asked me to help him get the information he needed to confront Sam. I couldn't find it because somebody had taken that part out of the files."

Sabrina stopped. She was gasping for breath. Swann poured her more water. After a few minutes he asked if she wanted to go on. She took another drink of water and said, "Yes."

"I want to get it all out. I guess I'll burn in Hell for all eternity for what I've done, but I hope some of these people can forgive me. I know I'll never be able to forgive myself." Sabrina was crying but gulped and took another sip of water.

Swann said, "Miss Draper, do you want to tell the rest of this story?"

Sabrina nodded in the affirmative, and he told her to proceed. He added that if she missed something that was needed he could ask when she was finished.

Taking another calming breath, Sabrina began. "James Harrison and Bertram Briscoll had been a couple ever since I came to Beckley, but they kept a low profile. Sam Henson knew it, however, and Sam stores that kind of information. I think he threatened James Harrison with a revelation of his lifestyle and James committed suicide.

"James Harrison was an honorable and upright man, who never harmed a soul in his life, but Sam Henson knew about his lifestyle and Beckley has lost a good man. He is dead today because of the twisted and devious mind of a person like Sam Henson. Mr. Harrison would have found out anyway, but Chief Donaldson had somehow gotten Bertram Briscoll involved with Sam's underhanded schemes. Then Donaldson used this to try to get Bertie to begin a relationship with him. I know all this because I also know a lot of things on a lot of people."

"Good God Almighty" and I wouldn't have thought a thing like that about Mr. Harrison," and "What's the world coming to," were phrases heard throughout the room. The judge pounded his gavel and the room became quiet.

Sabrina leaned on the side of the chair, trying to keep erect, but nevertheless motioned that she wanted to go on.

"The two men Miss Meadows heard talking were Chief Donaldson and Bertram Briscoll. You see, Bertie supplied the poison and the Chief used it wherever he wanted to, but Sam Henson gave me the Mylanta that almost killed Hannah Larkin. Chief Donaldson sent the poisoned Mylanta that I gave to Bill. I did not know what was actually in it, but I knew it had been doctored. I thought he just wanted Bill to become ill. Then Sam could charge him with falsifying the books on the Blennoc Project."

Sabrina looked around. The people in the courtroom saw a picture of total dejection. Her eyes looked as if all life had been removed and only a shell was sitting in that chair.

"I'm so sorry. I wanted to make men pay. I did make men pay, but I didn't want to make men like James Harrison and Bill Larkin pay. They were both good men. Chief Donaldson has been bilking the people in this county in every way possible, and Sam Henson has been his willing partner. I don't know who really poisoned the Mylanta. I wish I did," Sabrina finished. Before anyone could get to her she toppled from the chair onto the floor.

Gasps were heard from all over the courtroom and several voices said, "Poor, poor woman." And a louder voice said, "She sure don't have much to look forward to, does she?"

An ambulance was called and Sabrina Draper was soon on her way back to her secure room at an unknown hospital.

During Sabrina's testimony, Beatrice Mitchell turned pale as a ghost and turned to look at her husband.' She shivered and shrank away from him. Thomas had drawn in a quick breath and whispered,

"Beatrice, please wait until we get home and let me explain." Beatrice sat in stoic silence.

Now all eyes were on Hannah Larkin, who still sat stunned in disbelief. Her lips quivered and her face became more ashen than her usual pale shade. She reached out with trembling hands as if to keep something away. Covering her face with her hands, she dropped her head. Freddie put his arm around her shoulders and tried to console her.

Margie sent a silent appeal to Steve. She wanted him to take her to Hannah. Steve slowly rolled her to Hannah's side. Margie leaned over and put her arms around Hannah.

"Don't cry, dear. We'll talk later and I think you will understand and not be so hurt."

Chief Harry Donaldson, who already had to serve thirty days for disrupting the court proceeding, was now put under arrest, but no date was set for his bail bond hearing. Sam Henson's trial was still in progress and after a discussion between the judge, the prosecuting attorney, and Jacob Stern, court was adjourned until the next morning at ten o'clock.

CHAPTER 6

WHEN SABRINA PITCHED FORWARD, ALMOST EVERYONE in the room had risen from their seats in a concerted and compassionate moan. What would start a beautiful young girl on such a path was the prevailing thought running through the room.

One of the people not feeling very compassionate was Freddie Larkin.

"I don't feel sorry for her," Freddie mumbled quietly to Margie.

Margie leaned close to Freddie and whispered. "I didn't either, Freddie, but after the way I've acted, I can't help but wonder what led her to act the way she did. People react in different ways to pain and hurt."

Hannah was now sitting as stiff as a stone statue, not batting an eye nor making a sound. Her mind was very active, however. Like a kaleidoscope the events of the last three years began flitting through her mind. She heard Bill exulting about Sam Henson promoting him, she watched Bill's unmerciful handling of Freddie's conduct, she heard Bill hurling scorn and blame at her, and again she felt her disillusionment and sadness at Bill's move from an occasional beer to mixed drinks or gin. She remembered her worry over Bill's many late nights of work and his overnight or out of town trips, and recalled her dismay when Bill took the checkbook from her while spending money on a new Cadillac. Now she winced as she recalled his complaints and disparaging remarks about her being too thin, not dressing right, and so many things that she should have thought were strange.

She had forgiven it all, telling herself that he worked too hard with his new job and also his worry over Freddie. Still weak, Hannah thought about how ill she had been for so long. She had thought she would die from stomach cancer since she hurt so badly. She had desperately wanted somebody to talk to. Before Bill had taken the new job she could talk to him, but afterward she had nobody.

Mylanta had played such a role in this murder and mayhem, and Hannah remembered that Bill had started her taking the stomach medicine. Now, she knew the Mylanta came from Sabrina Draper. Hannah had been so pleased that Bill cared so much. Believing he was trying to help her, she would have done anything he asked, but now she knew that either Bill or this Draper woman wanted to get rid of her.

Hannah sat wondering why Bill couldn't have just asked for a divorce. Maybe Sam Henson planned her death so he could accuse Bill of murder. Steve or Keith could find out if this was so, but they didn't know about it.

She reached past Margie and plucked at Steve's sleeve. When he looked down, Hannah motioned him nearer and whispered, "Steve, I took Mylanta for over six months because my stomach hurt all the time. Finally, I passed out and was taken to the hospital. I almost died. I had to have a blood transfusion and was in the hospital for two weeks. They said I had an ulcer, but she . . . that woman said the Mylanta I took had poison in it also," whispered Hannah.

Steve grasped Hannah's hand, squeezed it, and in sotto voce said, "Hannah, I want to talk to you, but not here. Keith and I will come by your house later," he promised.

She became so engrossed in her reflections that she didn't notice Freddie and Margie. Margie touched her arm and whispered, "Hannah, I'm sorry. Are you all right?"

Hannah turned bewildered eyes to Margie and Freddie. "I . . . I don't know how I am. I never dreamed that anything like this was going on. I never once in my life doubted Bill's honor and integrity. I guess I must be stupid." Hannah was still keeping her voice low, as were all the others since it was a courtroom.

Margie leaned closer and talked softly as she patted Hannah's arm. "Hannah dear, I hope you won't think too badly of Bill. Both he and Sabrina were pawns in Sam Henson's evil scheme. Bill didn't want an assistant, but Sam insisted. Sabrina was put in that position so she could set Bill up. Sam already had enough against Sabrina to insure that she followed orders."

Hannah didn't even notice Sabrina being transported out of the courtroom. She was too shocked to notice much of anything. Freddie, however, noted every move made. Chief Donaldson and Bertram Briscoll were in custody, and Sam Henson was marched out to return to his cell. Most of the people had soon vacated the room.

Steve let go of Hannah's hand and looked at Margie. "I promised the doctor to bring you back in two hours, so we'd better go. I don't want him to send a patrol after us."

Margie tried to rise from her wheelchair by using the seat in front of her. She smiled weakly. "I guess you're right. I feel weak as a kitten."

Hannah stood also since everyone else did, but leaned over to Margie, who gave her a hug. Hannah's motions were automatic for she was in such a state that it didn't register. Margie grasped Steve's arm and motioned toward Hannah. "When can Hannah come to see me again? Can she come tomorrow?" she asked.

Keith walked over. "I'll call in the morning and if the doctor approves, Hannah can come tomorrow."

Steve soon had Margie settled more comfortably in her wheelchair. He pushed her up the aisle toward the double doors in the back. Hannah, still numb with shock, was supported by Freddie and Keith as she walked up the aisle and through the doors.

"Keith, will Margie have a trial for her part in this mess?" asked Freddie as they walked out the door.

"I don't know exactly how Jerome Judson will proceed. He may do some kind of bargaining with the prosecuting attorney, the other lawyers, and Judge Wilson. Of course, Margie did know there was something in the Mylanta she passed on to Sabrina Draper," explained Keith.

Freddie frowned. "I hope Margie doesn't have to go to jail. I've just found my grandmother, and I want her home with us. Don't you, Mom?"

Hannah made no reply. She had tried to distance herself from any more pain and disillusionment. Freddie gave her a curious look. Keith shook his head briefly.

Freddie nodded and said, "Well, for my part, Margie is the one good thing that has come out of this whole nasty, horrible mess."

"I'll wait here with Hannah until you bring the car around, Freddie," said Keith and Freddie nodded before walking briskly down the street. Keith stood holding onto Hannah's arm. He knew that she was still weak and looked very tired.

As if suddenly waking from a long sleep, Hannah looked up at Keith. "Will Jerome Judson be Margie's lawyer?"

"Yes. If anybody can free Margie of charges, Judson can. Margie can afford him now that James Harrison left almost everything to her," explained Keith.

Hannah shivered and Keith was instantly alert. "Are you cold, Hannah? You're trembling."

"No not really. I think I hurt so much for Margie that it just makes me feel shaky inside."

Keith eased his arm around her. "Please, don't misunderstand. I feel that you've been under a lot of stress lately and it's made you weak. I'm just lending you some support until Freddie comes with the car."

In her weak state Hannah sighed inwardly and gladly leaned against Keith's sturdy strength. It was then that she realized how alone she had been feeling for the past two and a half years. To have somebody who truly wanted to help felt so good. Without meaning to do so, she nestled closer to his warmth and Keith's arm drew her closer and she didn't draw back for a moment. Suddenly she remembered Bill's utter neglect and cruelty and pulled away just as her car pulled to a stop at the curb.

CHAPTER 7

HANNAH REALIZED THAT SHE NEEDED KEITH'S body to lean against, but she resented having to lean on a man. After what she had learned today, she felt men could not be trusted. She had completely trusted Bill Larkin from the first day she met him, and look what that trust had gotten her.

Her battered Ford Escort was certainly welcome as it stopped in front of her. Keith helped her inside and closed her door with the assurance that he and Steve would be out later.

"I'll check in the morning about getting you in to see Margie," he promised as he turned to leave.

"Do you think the trial will end tomorrow?" Freddie asked from the driver's seat.

"Well, they haven't discovered who actually put the poison in the Mylanta or in the cocaine, so the trial will go on until this is all cleared up. I think someone will be convicted of murder," said Keith, stepping back onto the sidewalk.

"I'd like to sit in on the rest of the trial, but I don't want to leave Mom. I think she'll want to go back, though, if Margie is involved."

"I'll try to find out if Margie will be there and let you know," Keith promised.

"Be sure to call if you can't come out tonight," said Freddie as he raised the window. Keith watched the car roll out of sight down the street. He stood thinking about his attraction to Hannah, which grew stronger every day.

He felt uneasy, however, for he sensed her withdrawal, especially after Sabrina Draper's testimony.

He dwelt on this withdrawal or whatever it was, as he walked up the street to the parking lot behind the courthouse. It wasn't that Hannah had ever acted as if she had an interest in him, but until today she had been relaxed and seemed to consider him a friend. Hannah had allowed him to put his arm around her, while they waited for Freddie, but only because she was so weak. He felt that she resented having to lean on him.

Keith pulled into the driveway of his dark and lonely looking house. "I don't know why I have stayed on here. It isn't a home anymore. Actually it had never been the home he had dreamed of as a youth and now there was a dread for evening to come, since I know I have to go home," he chided himself as he hit the button on the opener and the garage door slowly lifted.

The phone rang when he stepped into the kitchen. He lifted the receiver and said, "Hello."

"Keith, can you take an early shift of security?" asked Steve.

"You want me to come back now?" asked Keith, wondering what had happened.

"Well, I can wait an hour. There are some things I want to check on and sooner rather than later, if you know what I mean," Steve said as if it was something urgent.

Keith said he would be there in an hour and they hung up. After showering and donning a clean uniform, he went into the kitchen. He looked in the cupboard, opened the top freezer in the refrigerator and finally, he picked up his hat, strapped on his gun holster and left again.

Living in the house he and Ursula had shared was keeping him depressed. He thought that he might feel better if he ate something, so he pulled into Wendy's and stepped out of the car. As he turned to go into the restaurant he saw Thomas Mitchell walking toward the restaurant. Thomas didn't look at Keith, but walked like he carried the weight of the world on his shoulders.

Keith reached the door about the same time as Thomas and stood waiting to allow Thomas to enter ahead of him.

"We meet again, Mr. Mitchell," said Keith in greeting.

Mitchell looked up with an angry glare. "Yes, and I wish to hell I'd never laid eyes on you, Sergeant." He passed through the door and walked straight toward the restrooms in the back.

Keith was taken aback. He couldn't understand Mitchell's animosity. He went on into the restaurant to take his place in a long line of other people wanting to order food. While making his way to a table with his food, Keith glanced to the side and saw Mitchell pass on his way out the door.

Mitchell's actions made him more depressed or something. Keith knew that everybody he met wouldn't like him, but he had never done anything to Mitchell. In fact, until he and Steve had questioned him and Sabrina Draper, he only knew his face and didn't know his name.

Keith had almost finished eating when Steve called again. "Where are you now, Keith?" asked Steve impatiently.

"I'm leaving Wendy's as we speak," said Keith as he emptied his tray in the receptacle. "I should be there in seven minutes unless traffic holds me up. What's up anyway?"

"I just need to be somewhere within the next half-hour. I thought you weren't going to make it in time for me to get there. No, I can't tell you what it is right now. I will later, good buddy, so put the pedal to the metal," urged Steve jokingly, yet his tone indicated he was dead serious.

Keith hurried to his car and headed for Raleigh General Hospital. He parked near the entrance and was soon on the second floor. He knocked on the room door, and it opened so fast Keith knew Steve had been standing close to it.

"Were you getting ready to leave before I arrived?" asked Keith, stepping inside and closing the door.

"No, but I wanted to be ready to run as soon as you did. See you later, good buddy," said Steve, going swiftly through the door.

Keith walked into the room and found Margie awake. "What was that all about? Did he get a call or something?" asked Keith.

Margie frowned. "I've been asleep. I don't know if he did or not. When I woke up he was on pins and needles about something."

"Well, I guess he'll tell us when he comes back." Keith smiled as he pulled up a chair close to Margie's bed and sat down.

"How are you feeling, Margie?"

"I'd feel a lot better if you would crank this bed up to sitting position. I don't understand why they won't let me up to walk around. Why can't I walk down the hall? You could go with me, couldn't you?"

Keith grimaced. "I'm afraid not until this trial is over. We still don't know who may take a notion that you know something that could be used against them."

"But aren't they all in jail? I think Sam Henson is the one who had my house and Hannah's trashed, but now he's in jail. Besides, there's nothing else that would make it worse than it already is, is there?"

Keith didn't know and didn't really want to talk about the case this evening. He wanted to talk about something that would make him feel better. He looked at Margie and grinned. I don't want to talk about murder and mayhem tonight. Let's talk about something else . . . something like Hannah."

Margie's eyes widened and then she smiled. "That sounds good to me."

Keith hesitated for a moment then sighed. "Well, I think you know that I am fascinated by your daughter-in-law. I find it hard to believe she grew up here. Her accent is hard to pin down. She doesn't sound like the rest of us hillbillies. I guess she could be an educated hillbilly though." Keith chuckled.

Margie laughed also. "I think she has the sweetest accent and voice, but to tell the truth, I don't know for sure where she grew up. I think she lived around here until she was in her teens, but I don't know for sure."

"She did. She said she was eleven when her parents moved," said Keith just as there was a knock on the door and Keith went to answer.

"I have two dinners here. Do you want to take them like that other feller does, or do you want me to bring them in?" asked a smiling black woman.

Keith smiled. "I'll take them if you'll hand them to me one at a time, or better still just leave them there on the table. I'll bring the whole thing in."

The woman shook her head. "It's okay by me. Who you all guarding in there? Somebody important, like the governor or some such, I'll bet."

Keith raised his eyebrows. "It's somebody important and you are playing an important role in getting to serve them."

A big smile spread across her face. "That's right, ain't it? I hadn't thought of that." She left the table and went down the hall, still smiling.

Keith brought the table just inside the door. Then he called the nurse's desk and asked to speak to Margie's doctor. He hung up and turned to Margie.

"I hope you aren't hungry because I don't think we should eat this food. I know I'm not and you can't get to it," he said with a grimace.

Margie looked surprised. "What's wrong? Do you think there's something wrong with the food?"

Before Keith could answer, the doctor knocked on the door and Keith let him in. Expecting to see Margie in worse shape, the doctor acted disgruntled.

"Why did you call me? Miss Meadows seems the same as she did yesterday," the doctor stated in an aggrieved tone.

Keith walked over to the food. "I think you need to have this food tested. I'm fairly sure that you will find that it has poison in it."

The doctor's eyebrows rose in amazement. "What makes you think that?"

Keith explained that the woman who brought the food knew that Steve was gone and there had been nobody around when Steve left.

"The kitchen help would not have known we had changed places unless someone from the outside gave them a signal," he explained.

The doctor nodded in agreement and using the room phone called the lab. While they were waiting he asked, "Did you know the woman?"

"No, I didn't know her, but I think I would recognize her if I saw her again. Keith and the doctor agreed that when Steve returned they would go down to the kitchen and see if she was there.

The man from the lab arrived and after explanation from the doctor pushed the table, with the food still on it, out of the room. The doctor left saying he would personally check into this if the food was poisoned. Margie let out a long sigh.

"Keith, when is this all going to end? It makes me almost afraid to drink water or anything brought in by anyone but you or Steve."

CHAPTER 8

KEITH WAS WORRIED. IT WAS EIGHT o'clock at night and Steve had left at two that afternoon. "Margie, did Steve talk to anybody before I arrived?"

Margie shook her head. "I was asleep most of the time, but I woke up just before he called you. I could tell he was anxious or something. If you remember, I told you that he paced around a lot."

"Well, I'm going to give him another thirty minutes. If he hasn't shown up or called by then I'm going to call Dave Shortt," said Keith, looking down into the parking lot again.

Margie flipped on the television anchored in the wall opposite her bed. The news anchor was reporting a fire. Keith turned and stood listening.

"Fire fighters were in time to save most of the main house, but Sabrina Draper's apartment was completely destroyed," announced the newsman before going on to interview the fire chief and several bystanders, who all claimed it was arson.

Margie shivered. "Keith, you don't think Steve was there, do you?"

"I hope not, Margie," replied Keith just as his phone rang.

"Steve, where are you? You've had us worried. Yes, I mean Margie too, you moron."

Keith stood listening and occasionally saying yes or no until he finally said, "Well, you come on back here. I have some news for you, too. No, I'm not telling you over the phone. Sure, I can stay another hour, but no later. You've been gone six hours and you said a little while," chided Keith but in a light-hearted tone.

Keith had given up on hearing from the doctor, but he arrived at nine o'clock that night.

"You were right, Sergeant. Cyanide was found in the food that was brought to you. The day shift has gone home, but tomorrow you and I can go to the kitchen. I hope you'll be able to identify the woman who brought that food," said the doctor as he went out the door.

"Gosh that doctor sure earns his pay if he works these hours every day," said Keith, smiling at Margie. Margie didn't return the smile. She wore a worried frown.

"I'd be safer at home than I am here, Keith. Even the medicine they bring me may be poisoned," said Margie with a quaver in her voice.

Just then there was a knock and Keith admitted Steve, but a much different Steve than the one who had left. His hair was gapped in front, he had a black eye, and the rest of his face and neck were really red. He laughed at the reactions from Keith and Margie.

"I wish you two could see your faces. I didn't know you both had such big eyes. Have you never seen anybody with their hair singed before?"

"Steve, were you in that fire that destroyed Sabrina Draper's apartment?" asked Margie.

"I was and I wasn't. I was hiding under the stairwell in the foyer leading up to her front door. I got into a skirmish and almost didn't make it out before the stairwell collapsed."

"You may as well tell us all of it. You've only told us enough to whet our appetite," said Keith with a wry smile.

Steve explained that he'd gotten a tip that someone was going to burn Sabrina's apartment. He was suspicious because the caller wouldn't identify himself.

"I suspected that it was a set up, but I still wanted to go. I called Dave Shortt to be alert, in case I needed him."

"Did he come and help you?" asked Margie.

"He sure did. If he hadn't knocked that fellow in the head, I'd be more than singed. I'd knocked one guy down the stairs, but the other one came from behind and we were wrestling right in the middle of the fire when Dave came on the scene."

Keith and Margie listened with bated breath. "We have those men stashed away. We'll put them on the stand and see how Chief Donaldson wriggles out of this one."

"Do you mean that the Chief of Police for Raleigh County had this done?" Margie had such a shocked look on her face that Keith tried to explain.

"Margie, that makes sense. The chief had the apartment burned since he knew Sabrina had a lot of information on him, but he also wanted you there, didn't he, Steve?" said Keith.

Steve grinned. "He wanted my body found there. The fire could be blamed on me, but his plan didn't work. He doesn't know that, though."

Margie sat listening. "How could Chief Donaldson send those men? He's in jail, isn't he?"

"Margie, Donaldson has been in power in this county for fifteen years. A lot of people owe him favors, and a lot rely on him for other things all over this county. He could tell one of the guards that he needed to see somebody, and most of those guards would get to that person just because the chief wanted him to," explained Steve.

"Well, he doesn't need to be the chief of police. That's almost like the Mafia," stated Margie.

When Steve's adventure had been thoroughly discussed, Keith said, "Well, we had an adventure too, didn't we Margie?"

Margie rolled her eyes. "We certainly did, and I'm scared to even take a drink of water because of it."

Steve looked puzzled. "What happened?"

Keith told him about the food having cyanide in it. Steve sat stoically listening as Keith explained that he was going with the doctor to identify the woman who brought the food.

"That doesn't feed us now, though, and I'm hungry," stated Margie.

Keith looked startled. "That's right. We never did get any food, did we? I'm sorry, Margie. I think I was worried about my buddy here and forgot about food."

Steve pulled up a chair and sat down. "Well, I'm here now. You go down to Long John's and bring us three fish dinners and a thermos of coffee."

Keith picked up the thermos that Steve always kept with him and went out. Steve sat studying Margie. "How are you feeling, Margie?"

Margie was sitting up in bed. "I think I'm able to go home, but I'm scared, Steve. So many things have happened and I don't know who to trust." Seeing Steve's look of astonishment she reached out toward him.

"Don't look like that. I trust you and Keith, but you can't stay here night and day. I'm just so tired and it seems like this is never going to end."

Steve nodded in understanding. "I know. It must seem to you that everybody is dishonest, but there are still a few good people left."

There was a knock and Steve cracked the door open to see Keith loaded down with food from Long John Silver's.

"Open up. I can't hold this much longer. My hand is cramped." Keith shook his hand when Steve grabbed the thermos.

Margie sat on the side of the bed and so did Keith. Steve sat in the chair so they could all share the small bedside table, while they devoured the fish, coleslaw, hush puppies, and fries. When they had finished and stowed all the receptacles in the garbage can Steve went into the bathroom.

When he came out he said, "Margie, could you walk out of the hospital by yourself?"

Keith's eyes blared in astonishment and Margie perked up. "You say the word and I'll run out of this place," she stated emphatically.

Steve looked at Keith. "Margie is afraid to eat, drink water, take medicine, or anything else. I don't blame her since this is the second attempt to get at her since she's been here. The problem is where could we hide her?"

"First, we have to decide how to get her away without someone seeing her," said Keith.

They sat huddled close together for the next hour with Steve and Keith making calls to others for help. Soon there was a knock at the door and Keith admitted David Shortt.

"Here's the uniform you asked for, but I'll have to get it back tonight. Little Joe Green would take a fit if he knew someone had taken his uniform," said David.

"Who's going to wear it anyway?"

Twenty minutes later a short plump policeman walked out of the room beside David Shortt who threw up his hand in salute as he passed the nurses desk. The shift changed and about twenty minutes later Keith opened the door and stepped into the hall. Seeing the nurse looking at him, he stuck his head back around the door and said, "You two behave yourselves. I'll see you in the morning."

Thirty minutes after that a nurse knocked on the door. Steve cracked the door but didn't open it. "She's asleep," he whispered. "Let me have the medicine, and I'll give it to her when she wakes up."

The nurse looked agitated. "I'm supposed to give this to her and see that she takes it, Doctor's orders."

"I'll take responsibility for it." He reached out his hand and stood waiting. The nurse looked back to the desk and finally handed him two little cups with pills in them. Steve took the cups and quickly closed the door. He quickly took out a pad and wrote the name Naomi Rutherford on it.

CHAPTER 9

IN THE MEANTIME, DAVID SHORTT TOOK Margie around the corner to Keith's car, which was parked in a dark area behind the hospital. Very few people parked there, so they were not seen. Soon Keith showed up and David got into the police cruiser and drove away.

Still in uniform, Keith turned his car and drove Margie toward his house. When he arrived the house was dark, by his instructions. He hit the garage door button and drove inside. In the other space was Hannah's battered Ford Escort.

Keith helped Margie out and they went through the garage, using only the overhead lights that had automatically come on. When he reached the kitchen door, he flipped the switch and there sat Hannah and Freddie. Keith glanced toward the windows and saw that they were uncovered, also per his instructions, since that was the usual procedure when he came home at night.

"Did you see anybody out as you came in?" Keith asked.

"There wasn't a light in any of the houses, and no cars came down the street. Are you sure there are people actually living on this street?" Freddie said with a grin.

Hannah got up and hugged Margie, but both she and Freddie laughed hilariously at the plump but lumpy policeman with Margie's head, before pushing out a chair for her to sit in. Keith smiled at Margie also.

"Some of your stuffing is a little awry, and I'd say it's a good thing you were traveling at night, Margie."

Margie tried to look around to see, but without luck. "Oh well, I'd have left in any disguise just to get away from that hospital before somebody killed me."

"Killed you? What happened?" asked Freddie.

"I'll tell you two about that later. Right now I want to get out of this stuffed suit."

"Did you bring Margie some clothes, Hannah? She needs to change and let me get this uniform back before it is missed."

Hannah smiled. "Yes, I did, but do you two want something to eat? I brought some of the roast we had for supper," Hannah offered.

"We ate from Long John Silver's tonight since the supper they brought was suspect," said Keith. He walked to the sink and looked through the windows above it in an alert manner as he surveyed the street.

Feeling along the walls Hannah took Margie into the bedroom, and soon returned with the uniform, folded neatly. Keith put the folded garment in a kitchen trash bag and prepared to leave.

"Margie, you and Hannah take that first bedroom and Freddie and I will bunk in the other room. Oh, I forgot to tell you this house has a security system. If it goes off, I, as well as the closest police station, will know immediately. I wanted to warn you so these two women won't be scared out of their minds." Freddie looked at Hannah and Margie and nodded his thanks as Keith opened the door to leave.

"Before I leave it would be best if you all went into the bedrooms. If you're there anyone passing won't see anything except a dark house." Keith left taking the packaged uniform with him.

Margie, Hannah, and Freddie gathered in the first bedroom. Margie took the easy chair. "You'll have to excuse my selfishness, but I've had to stay in bed so much that I can't bear the thoughts of another one right now," she explained.

Physically, Margie had been able to be out of the bed for several days, but to keep the impression that she was really ill, she sat or lay on the bed. When she had complained, Steve explained that even though people knocked before they were admitted she wouldn't have time to get from the chair to the bed and still look ill.

"I don't know what the judge will do to me, Hannah," said Margie with a worried frown. "I did do wrong. I knew that something was wrong with that Mylanta, but I gave it to Sabrina Draper anyway. I would have gotten it back later, but I didn't know how. I really can't complain, no matter what I have to pay."

Freddie got up and hugged her. "Grandmother, you didn't kill anybody, nor did you think there was anything lethal in the Mylanta. I don't see what they could do except perhaps fine you. After all, it was your testimony that brought out the shenanigans the Chief of Police was involved in. This county should thank you."

Margie hugged Freddie, and when he stood back he saw the tears in her eyes. "Just to have you hug me like that and call me grandmother is worth anything they want to do."

Hannah got off the bed and hugged Margie also. "I wish Bill could have gotten to know you, Margie. He would have loved you, too. Freddie and I feel that we've been given a precious gift."

It was now three o'clock in the morning and they were all sleepy. Freddie went down the hall to the other room, and soon the house was not only dark but also quiet.

Keith tiptoed in at eight o'clock the next morning, but it still roused Hannah from her sleep. When she jerked up it also woke Margie.

"There's someone in the house," whispered Hannah as she eased out of the bed. Margie crept out behind her.

Hannah quietly cracked open the door and smelled coffee brewing. She turned and looked at Margie. She walked around Hannah and through the door leading to the living room and kitchen. Keith stood at the sink gazing out the window. The kitchen windows were high narrow windows above the sink and outsiders couldn't see in, but they could see if lights were on. Keith knew his neighbors wouldn't notice anything about his house unless it was unusual. Before he'd left the night before he'd covered the windows. He knew Hannah and Freddie would be coming and the lights would be seen. The neighbors knew he was on duty.

"You scared us to death, Keith," said Margie walking toward him. She forgot that she was in her pajamas. Hannah, however, turned back and quickly donned her robe.

When Hannah came into the kitchen the coffee was done. Keith was still standing by the sink, but now turned to her with a smile. "Good morning, Hannah. Did I scare you too?" he asked.

"Yes. I jumped up so quickly that I woke Margie. " She grinned as Margie hurried past her. Seeing Hannah's robe made her realize that she only wore pajamas.

"Do you want coffee?" asked Keith. "I make good coffee, or so I'm told."

"Which one of the women who visits you here told you that?" asked Freddie coming through the door.

Keith didn't grin. "Freddie, your mother and Margie are the only women who have stayed at this house since my wife died ten years ago."

"You have a nice house," said Hannah, fearing that Freddie had touched on a sore nerve.

Keith came to the table and sat down across from Hannah. "It's all right. It's just a house. I'm thinking about selling it and moving."

Hannah looked at Keith speculatively. "Would you retire from the police force?"

Keith sat thinking. "I've always wanted a small farm in the country. You know, a few sheep, some chickens, a dog, and a stream," he said and then grinned sheepishly. "It's been a long time since I've thought about that old dream."

Hannah had been listening and now she said in a dreamy voice, "I was raised on such a place. I still own it. Do you remember me telling you about it? It is between Sophia and Mullens. I wanted Bill to take me there so many times, but he was always too busy. Freddie and I went, though, didn't we, Freddie?"

Freddie's face broke into a wide smile. "We sure did. We went there so many times that I could find my way blind-folded.

Margie had returned and now reached across the table and patted Hannah's hand that lay on top of the table. "When all this mess is over, and if I'm not in jail, we'll go live over there if you want to, Hannah. Keith may even want to go with us. Would you like that, Keith?" asked Margie, giving Keith a sly grin.

"I'd be awfully happy to be given that opportunity, but that's not likely to happen, Margie. I haven't been over that way in a long time myself," Keith replied from a very red face.

Changing the subject, he explained that the medicine that the nurse, or whoever she was, had brought to the door for Margie, was poisoned.

Hannah and Freddie gasped in amazement. "Does Steve know which nurse it was?" asked Freddie.

"Steve wrote down the name pinned on her uniform. It was Naomi Rutherford," said Keith, but they all agreed that the uniform had probably been stolen.

"I was scared to death in that hospital. I couldn't have stayed if Steve hadn't . . . well, if you and Steve hadn't been there, Keith," stated Margie.

Keith got up again. "Well, I have to get cleaned up and be at the courthouse before ten o'clock, so I'll have to leave this good company. We will go look over your farm soon, Hannah. Like Margie says, though, we need to get past this mess first."

"It can't be too soon for me. This 'cloak and dagger' existence is getting on my nerves," said Hannah.

"Nobody likes to live like this, Mom, but I sure don't want to take the chance of one of those villains getting to my grandmother," said Freddie.

CHAPTER 10

SAM HENSON'S TRIAL RESUMED AT EXACTLY ten o'clock and Keith had barely made it in time. Judge Wilson came striding purposefully through the door behind the judge's bench as the bailiff called "All Rise. The Honorable Nathan Wilson presiding."

Kyle Swann and Jacob Stern approached the bench, and after a brief conference, Stern called Martha Henson to the stand. She was sworn in and took her seat. When she looked back at Sam her eyes were hostile.

Stern asked how long she and Sam had been married.

Martha didn't answer for a few moments and Stern waited patiently. "We've been married thirty years," she stated in a flat monotone.

"Is your marriage a happy one, Mrs. Henson?"

Martha looked at Sam for a moment. "About as happy as any marriage is, I guess."

"Would you say that Sam Henson is a good husband?" was the next question.

"He provides well for me and our daughter and is not abusive," Martha replied.

"Is Sam Henson the kind of man who would deliberately murder someone?" asked Stern.

"No, he is not," stated Martha.

"Ladies and gentlemen, who would know a man's character better than a wife who has been with him for thirty years? She says Sam

Henson is not the kind of man to murder anyone," stated Stern to the jury. Then Stern said he had no further questions.

Kyle Swann walked to the front of the room. He looked at Henson and then abruptly turned to Martha.

"Mrs. Henson, has your husband ever been unfaithful to you?"

Martha gasped and sat as if struck dumb. "Remember, Mrs. Henson, that you are under oath," cautioned Swann.

Martha drew in a long breath and looked at Sam. "Yes," she spat.

"Was your husband unfaithful with any particular person?" asked Swann in a soothing voice.

"Yes. He almost allowed that Draper woman to break up our marriage. His dalliances have nearly destroyed our daughter."

"Is he still seeing Sabrina Draper?" asked Kyle.

"No, he made her move when he gave the Blennoc Project to Bill Larkin. If he hadn't, I was going to take everything he had."

Kyle walked back and forth across the room stopping in front of Martha. "Would you say that your husband is an honest man in his business dealings?"

Jacob Stern hit the floor. "Your Honor, I object to this line of questioning. A wife doesn't have to testify against her husband."

Judge Wilson looked at Stern and a smile flickered briefly about his lips. "Her testimony may not be against her husband, Mr. Stern. What makes you think it will be? Objection overruled."

"He's been with CEE for thirty-five years and I think he would have been in trouble before now, if he hadn't been honest," said Martha.

"Mrs. Henson, do you know why your husband wanted to give Bill Larkin the Blennoc Project?

Martha didn't look at Sam, but grimaced and drew in a long breath. "It was the only way he could get rid of Sabrina Draper without having a discrimination suit filed against him."

Quickly, Swann came back with, "Was that the only reason?"

Martha declared that she knew of no other reason. She explained that it would mean a move up for Draper and a raise for her as well as for Bill Larkin. Then she was allowed to step down.

Bertie Briscoll was then called to the stand and Kyle Swann was first to question him. Within twenty minutes everyone in the room heard about how he and Sam had been bleeding the Blennoc Project. Briscoll told of Sam's schemes with every project in which he had been involved on behalf of CEE. Everyone in the courtroom was raptly listening and thought that Sam Henson deserved a long time in jail. They hadn't heard it all however.

Kyle Swann walked back and forth for a few seconds and then stopped in front of Briscoll. "How long have you and Sam Henson been using cocaine?"

Jacob Stern jumped up to object, but Judge Wilson ordered him to sit down.

Bertie Briscoll seemed to wilt, and his answer came out as a soft mumble.

"Sam was a user when I met him again after high school. I had never used cocaine until then. He got me started. Once I was hooked he used that knowledge to keep me in line."

Briscoll looked as if he was about to cry. "He has forced me to do things I never wanted to do. He has destroyed my life, and I helped him."

Swann saw that Briscoll needed to be calmer in order to answer any more questions and allowed him to step down.

Judge Wilson called a recess until one o'clock, and the prisoners were led back to their cells. Henson was led out a defeated man. Bertram Briscoll looked not only defeated but ravaged and beaten.

At the outset of the trial Briscoll had been a handsome, neatly dressed man, who had won the sympathy of the court. Now he had a haggard, unkempt appearance. With blaring eyes he looked wildly around the room as if trying to find a way out.

Chief Donaldson had not been allowed to sit in on this session, and many people wondered why. Henson walked with his head down, looking neither to the right or left.

Soon the courtroom was empty. Keith walked outside and dialed Steve's cell phone. "Steve, did you find that boy?" Keith asked.

"I sure did, and I'm bringing him with me this evening. He's scared to death, but I told him we'd protect him and his family. You call me ten minutes before the court meets after lunch," said Steve and rang off.

Keith called his home but used Freddie's cell number. "Are the women all right?" asked Keith.

"Do you mean both of them or one in particular?" Freddie wanted to know.

Keith didn't know how to truthfully answer that so he said, "Both, of course, since they are both in my house and are neither in the best of health right now." He already knew that Freddie had picked up on his attraction for Hannah, but he didn't know what Freddie really thought about it. He stood waiting for Freddie's response.

Freddie laughed. "That put you on the defensive, didn't it?"

Keith relaxed and tried to laugh. "I didn't know what you were asking, and it sort of threw me."

"Are you waiting for my approval?" When Keith didn't answer Freddie laughed and changed the subject.

"Everybody here is in good shape "We've received no phone calls or visitors. Of course, we feel like we're in jail since we're living under 'black-out' conditions, except for these small kitchen windows that are so high we can't see out of them. I'm not complaining, though. I know you are acting to take care of all of us, and we do appreciate it. How's the trial going?"

Keith told him about Martha Henson's testimony and of Bertram Briscoll's breakdown. "I fear that Mr. Briscoll will have to be institutionalized before this is over."

"I thought he looked kind of pitiful when we were there that first day," said Freddie and then quickly asked about Sabrina Draper. "Is she still in the hospital? I'm surprised that someone hasn't tried to get to her like they did Mar . . . I mean, Grandmother."

Keith explained that nobody knew where she was. Everyone had been told she was in Raleigh General, but she wasn't. "If certain people knew where she was, she wouldn't last long."

CHAPTER 11

THE TRIAL RESUMED AT ONE O'CLOCK. It started off in a similar fashion to the morning session except for a tension that permeated the atmosphere. Everyone gave suspicious glances at the room partitioned off to the left since there had been surprises from there earlier in this trial.

It was noted that Chief Harry Donaldson, in prison garb, was led in by a policeman. His lawyer, Harold Slater, was also present at this session. Most of the people present today had also been in the courtroom when Margie Meadows testified. This had led to the arrest of Chief Harry Donaldson for murder since Margie named him as the man she heard talking about doctoring the Mylanta that killed Bill Larkin. This knowledge contributed to the atmosphere of suspense and baited anticipation pervading the courtroom.

Keith picked up on this as soon as he entered the room. All eyes seemed to be centered on the chief, but Keith only concentrated on him briefly. In that short time he noted that the chief seemed very troubled, but was sitting with his chin thrust out and his brows raised as if inquiring why he was in this position.

The three lawyers approached the bench and had a lengthy discussion with the judge. When it was over, Donaldson and his lawyer were ushered out of the room by Keith. The chief whirled around with a scowl of vehemence when Keith grasped his arm.

"Get your hands off me, you two-faced, lying, bastard," snarled Donaldson. Keith only tightened his grip and propelled the police chief forward.

Sam Henson was called to the stand. His lawyer, Jacob Stern, was to question him first. Stern went through a lengthy dissertation eulogizing Henson's merits as a major contributor to the economic welfare of Raleigh County and the surrounding areas. When this was accomplished to his satisfaction, he then turned to Sam.

"Mr. Henson, during these trials we have heard various people testify that you have manipulated and used the businesses that CEE allowed you to help set up. Are these allegations true?"

Although Sam looked worn out and appeared to have aged ten years during this trial, he leveled a penetrating stare straight at the jury. "There is not one person who can prove that I did anything illegal in my business dealings."

Mr. Stern looked around the room then turned back to Sam. "We heard Bertram Briscoll state that you used cocaine and that he used it through your influence. Do you agree with his statement?"

"No, I do not. Bertie Briscoll had been doing some things that he didn't want James Harrison to know about. He came by my place one evening in a terrible shape. I thought he was going to collapse, and in trying to calm him down, I told him cocaine sometimes helps to alleviate stressful situations. He was really tense and said he'd like to try it. I had a small amount that someone had tried to get my daughter to use. I didn't sell it to him, but I did let him try it. He left my place in a much better frame of mind. That is the only time cocaine was ever mentioned between us," related Sam.

"Did Bertram Briscoll also work for CEE?" asked Stern.

"No. CEE bought chemicals and other supplies from his family's pharmaceutical company."

"If Briscoll did not work for CEE, why was he concerned about upsetting James Harrison?"

Sam acted as if he really did not want to answer. He looked around the room and twisted in his chair. Judge Wilson turned a stern eye at him and ordered, "Answer the question, Mr. Henson."

"It was a personal matter, between Bertie and James Harrison," said Sam in an almost inaudible mumble.

"I think you said, 'a personal matter,' Mr. Henson, and if you did, please tell this court what you know about this personal matter," stated Stern.

Henson pulled at his shirt collar, wriggled in his seat, and cleared his throat. He finally said, "According to Bertie Briscoll, he had upset James because he was seeing someone else."

There was no reaction from the jury section since Sabrina Draper had already mentioned the relationship. "It's already been stated that Briscoll and James Harrison had a relationship. Is that the only way Briscoll feared he would upset James Harrison?" asked Jacob Stern.

Sam Henson saw that he wasn't shifting any blame and dropped his head after mumbling, "I guess."

"Mr. Henson, you said earlier that Briscoll had told you that James Harrison was upset because he, Briscoll, was seeing someone else. Did he tell you who the, 'someone else' was?" asked Stern.

Sam didn't raise his eyes, but blurted out defiantly, "Chief Harry Donaldson."

From the many snickers and smothered guffaws heard around the room, Jerome Judson and Keith surmised that Chief Donaldson didn't have nearly as many friends in the area as he was purported to have.

Jacob Stern was now almost swaggering. He knew that he had established an idea in the minds of the jurors that Henson was being set up since he knew about this misalliance. Now he almost strutted back to stand beside Sam Henson. "Is it possible, Mr. Henson, that neither of these men wanted their relationship revealed and are making you the scapegoat?"

"I think so, since James Harrison came to see me and so did Chief Donaldson," stated Sam, sighing heavily. Stern then said he had no further questions.

Kyle Swann almost sprang from his seat in his eagerness to cross-examine Sam Henson. He addressed the jury. "Ladies and gentlemen of the jury, you have heard Mr. Stern's questions and Sam Henson's answers, but I believe there is more to this than his questions brought out."

Swann looked at the judge and then walked to a spot near Sam Henson, making sure that the jury could see Sam's reaction to his questions.

"Mr. Henson, you stated earlier that CEE did business with Briscoll Pharmaceuticals. Was Bertram Briscoll the man from that company that you dealt with?"

Henson mumbled in the affirmative and Swann came back with, "Did you ever order any chemicals from Bertram Briscoll?"

Again Sam's answer was yes, but he was getting tense. He was beginning to perspire and was nervously wiping his face with his handkerchief.

"Did you buy cyanide from Bertram Briscoll?" asked Swann as he leaned a little closer to Henson.

Henson turned red and then grew pale. He looked wildly around the room as if checking for an escape route. Finally he looked at the jury and said, "Yes, I bought some cyanide, but not for my own use. I bought it for somebody else."

"Who was this person you bought cyanide for, Mr. Henson?" Swann shot back.

Sam gave a shuddering sigh. "I bought it for Chief Harry Donaldson."

Keith looked around and saw three men arise from the back and walk quietly out of the courtroom. He walked over to the side of the room and quickly sent a text to Steve Hammer. When that was completed he went back to his seat intending to concentrate on the trial. This didn't happen, though. Sam Henson had also seen the three men get up and leave and he was trying to get out of the witness seat.

"Let me go. Somebody has to stop them. They'll kill my wife and daughter," he cried, struggling with Swann who was trying to calm him.

Keith asked permission to leave from Judge Wilson. With his approval, Keith hurried out of the courtroom just in time to see the men drive away in a Subaru Outback. He rushed to his patrol car and followed them, keeping several cars behind them. Soon he saw Steve's unmarked car slide into traffic right behind the Subaru, and was thankful for texting.

Back in the courtroom, Sam Henson had gone ballistic and two officers had to restrain him. When he was calmer they led him out. Judge Wilson called a recess until the following morning at ten o'clock. The jurors were sequestered in The Honey in the Rock Hotel and gladly climbed into the van that shuttled them from the courthouse to the hotel on a daily basis.

Steve phoned Keith, saying the car bearing the three men was on the road to Sam Henson's house. Neither of them thought the men would try anything in broad daylight, but Steve continued to follow them. Sure enough, they passed slowly by the house. They stopped on the street in front of the next house. One man got out, walked back to the Henson home, and rang the doorbell. Getting no response he returned to the car and it sped away. Steve followed it until it went completely outside of town on the road leading to Pinecrest Hospital. Steve wondered why they were going there, so he called Keith.

When Keith was told, he immediately asked, "They couldn't possibly know that Sabrina Draper is there, could they?"

"Nobody but me, you, and David Shortt is supposed to know. They're pulling into the parking lot anyway. I'll try to get a closer look at them and get their license number," Steve said as he ended the call.

CHAPTER 12

CHIEF DONALDSON WAS FIRST IN THE witness chair the next morning. He denied any connection with Sam Henson's business deals as well as refuted everything that had been said about him. Keith was itching for the call from Kyle Swann asking for the witnesses he was holding in the side room. All that was forgotten, however, when Steve Hammer came through the rear doors with the three men he had followed yesterday. Steve marched them up the aisle stopping only when he reached Kyle Swann.

Kyle talked to Steve and the men briefly and then approached the bench. Before he could utter one word, Chief Donaldson jumped to his feet.

"What are those men doing here? They've all three been in jail. How did they get out anyway? Are you going to take the word of three criminals?" His tone was belligerent.

Neither the judge nor Swann paid any attention to the Chief's diatribe. They called Harold Slater, Donaldson's attorney, to the bench also. The judge rose from his seat and motioned for Swann, Slater, Steve and the three men to follow him into his chambers.

Chief Donaldson was no longer blustering. He sat in glaring silence, but his eyes roamed the courtroom as if searching for help from someone. When the entourage returned, Swann told the chief to step down. He was led, still handcuffed, to his seat behind his lawyer's table.

Swann then called Steve Hammer to the witness chair. "Mr. Hammer, will you tell the court in your own words what you discovered today."

"After the noon break yesterday I received a call from Sergeant Keith McCauley. The sergeant told me that three men had hurriedly left the courtroom after Sam Henson's testimony concerning Chief Donaldson. The sergeant wanted me to follow them. I followed them to Sam Henson's home. They rang the doorbell but got no response so they drove on to Pinecrest Hospital. One man got out and went in for a few minutes and then came back out. They then returned to Sam Henson's home. They again were trying to gain entrance to the home, this time through a rear window, when I apprehended them. On questioning, they confessed that Chief Donaldson had sent word that they were to pick up Mrs. Henson and her daughter," Steve explained.

"What did they say they were to do with Mrs. Henson and her daughter?" asked Kyle.

"They said they were to take them to a warehouse right off of Route 16 toward Oakhill and leave them there," replied Steve.

Kyle stated that he had no further questions for Inspector Steve Hammer and he could step down. Harold Slater, Donaldson's lawyer, said he had no questions and Steve left the witness chair.

Kyle Swann addressed the jury, telling them that a lot of circumstantial evidence was cropping up against Chief Harry Donaldson. "Chief Donaldson is not on trial here today, but he is a witness in Sam Henson's trial. However, from what we have heard it appears that Donaldson may have committed murder. We won't know that until he is brought before this court. However, I ask that this jury pay close attention to the next witnesses."

The jury members nodded their heads, but nobody asked any questions. Swann then asked Sergeant Keith McCauley to bring in the witnesses sequestered in the adjoining room.

Keith hurriedly left the room and soon came back with Naomi Rutherford, the nurse who had tried to bring poisoned medicine to Margie Meadows. He also had Yolanda Johnson, who had brought the poisoned food to Margie Meadows. The two men Steve Hammer had arrested after they burned James Harrison's house came in also, and last, Jerry Willis, a young boy who looked to be around twelve years old. They were all seated, but they were all nervous and would not look toward Chief Donaldson.

Swann called Naomi Rutherford to the stand, and she stated that she had never met Donaldson. "Sam Henson gave me my 'stuff'. . . I mean medicine. He kept saying Chief Donaldson sent it, but I don't know. All I know is Sam Henson said I'd be turned over to the chief if I didn't do what he told me." Naomi shivered as she shot a quick glance toward Donaldson.

"We all know what happens when the chief gets a hold on you. He sent my friend Peggy Farley to Moundsville last year."

Donaldson scowled and leaned over to talk to his lawyer. He must not have gotten the answer he wanted, for he raised up out of his seat with his fist drawn. Steve Hammer hurried over to intervene. Donaldson sat down again, but still glared menacingly at his lawyer.

Then one after the other, Kyle Swann called those brought in from the side room to the witness chair. With each new voice the case built against Sam Henson but also Chief Donaldson. The young boy, Jerry Willis, was called and it was found that he was actually eighteen. Kyle Swann asked him about being present when the Mylanta was handed out at the seminar presented by CEE.

"Sam Henson told me to help Bertie Briscoll. Briscoll went outside, or somewhere, and brought back a brown paper poke with two bottles of Mylanta in it. He gave it to me and I carried it to the woman waiting in the hall. I don't know whether he put poison in the Mylanta or not, but if he did the chief probably forced him to," said Willis without looking up.

"Why didn't you tell Margie Meadows that it was poisoned when you took it to her?" asked Swann.

Jerry Willis had a stricken look on his face, "Cause he would have killed me and my mother and sister. If he gets free he'll kill us all." Jerry Willis was almost in tears and shaking like a leaf.

"Who is he? What's his name?" asked Swann.

"Chief Donaldson," whispered Jerry, looking fearfully to see if Keith and Steve were there to protect him.

"How did Chief Donaldson get all these people to do what he wanted?" asked Swann.

Willis heaved a heavy sigh. "I don't know about everybody else, but he threatened to kill my mother and put my sister in a whore house to get to me, but I don't know about Bertie Briscoll."

"Did he do anything personally to you? I can see that you are afraid of him," said Swann quietly.

Jerry Willis then began to cry. "He likes men . . ., and he does nasty, filthy things to them. He didn't do that to me. I guess it's just men, or maybe it was because I'm small for my age, but I knew about it. I was scared all the time. I wanted to run away, but I stayed and helped him because I didn't want anything to happen to my mother and sister."

Jerry Willis was shaking like a leaf in the wind and Swann asked if he was all right. When the boy nodded, Swann asked, "How did you get involved with Chief Donaldson?"

"I needed a job and had been working at Henson's Drug Store, but one day Henson asked me if I'd like a better job. Of course I did. My mom, my sister, and I lived hard and Sam Henson took me to the chief saying he had a job for me. He hired me to work around the house, the yard and anything else he demanded; even lying and stealing."

By this time, Jerry Willis was sobbing wildly and couldn't seem to stop and Steve helped him into the side room and stayed with him.

Chief Donaldson jumped to his feet. "That boy is a damned liar!" he shouted, but Keith stepped toward him and he settled back into his chair just as Farley Chase, one of the men Steve Hammer had arrested, leaped to his feet.

"No, that boy ain't lying. That man right there ain't no man. He is a dirty, filthy, nasty piece of horse shit," he yelled, only to be silenced by Keith before he could utter any further obscenities.

There was a hushed, shocked silence in the courtroom. Every eye that was on Sam Henson at first was now focused on Donaldson.

Chief Donaldson must have told his lawyer that he wanted back on the witness stand, for Slater walked to the bench and held a conversation with the judge. The prosecutor was called to the bench and soon he nodded and went back to his own chair.

Slater called Donaldson to the witness stand again. This time there was no pretense. The chief knew he was going down, but he intended to take as many down with him as possible.

The story that came from Chief Donaldson was hard to listen to, but everyone thought he told the truth. His mother had been a prostitute and she had farmed her son out from the time he was eleven years old. Men and women used him in any way they wished, and he had no option but to submit.

"We lived in Cleveland, Ohio then and finally I killed the last old slut that my mother sold me to. She'd kept me tied to her bed for days. You may think men are bad but women are much, much worse. I hate the damn sluts," Donaldson stated.

He continued to tell how he had run away, changed his name, dyed his hair and almost starved to death before meeting a Robert Maxwell, who took him in. Maxwell was a drug dealer, but he didn't abuse boys. The chief loved him and did anything he was asked to do in the drug trade. He soon realized that money was power and learned the ropes well. At twenty-five he left Maxwell, who was dying with cancer anyway, and started his own operation. Then he met Sam Henson, and together they worked out a deal. He was to run for Sheriff of Raleigh County and do a really good job in order to get the elected officials behind him. Henson was to supply the money and get him elected as sheriff, which he did.

When they had everything the way they wanted it, the chief and Sam Henson had started their own drug operation. Chief Donaldson stopped and asked for water, which was quickly supplied.

"Almost everyone in CEE except James Harrison and Thomas Mitchell had something going on. The only trouble with Harrison was that he had as his friend the person I wanted for myself."

"What about Thomas Mitchell and Bill Larkin? Were they involved in your schemes?" asked Slater.

"No, they weren't involved, but they would have been. Thomas Mitchell wanted James Harrison's position. He wants to be a Senator and he would have come around in order to get elected. He was already taking Sabrina Draper out," said Donaldson.

"What about Larkin?" Slater asked.

"He was just a middle-aged man who got taken in by a young woman and used by Sam Henson. Sam got Sabrina into cocaine and she got Bill Larkin into it, but Bill Larkin wasn't so far into it that he wouldn't have blown the whistle on Sam Henson"

It was suddenly as if a dam had ruptured and the chief just kept talking. "Sam came to me and I gave him some cocaine to use on Larkin, but something happened; he didn't die or Sam didn't doctor it. So, it now looks like Bertie. . ., I mean Mr. Briscoll, got somebody to doctor the Mylanta and get Sabrina Draper to give it to Bill Larkin. She gave it to him and that took care of Bill Larkin. I have not personally killed anyone since that old slut in Cleveland, Ohio," finished Chief Donaldson.

Harold Slater said he had no further questions and started to tell Donaldson to step down, but Kyle Swann said he had some questions.

The chief gave him an unbelievable stare as if saying, 'I've spilled my guts, what else do you want.'

Kyle walked over to stand beside the witness chair. "Chief Donaldson, you've just stated that you have not personally killed but one person. You intended to kill Sabrina Draper though, didn't you? You put the poison in the cocaine she used?"

"I didn't give her that cocaine. Sam Henson is the one who got to her," he smirked.

CHAPTER 13

A BLAST OF AIR SEEMED TO sweep through the courtroom as the side-door burst open and Jerry Willis came charging in. From a red face and wild eyes, he yelled,

"He's lying! I saw him hand something to Bertie Briscoll and tell him to mix it with cocaine and take it to Sam. Mr. Briscoll went into a bathroom and when he came out he gave whatever it was to a man in a dark denim jacket.

"'Take this to Sam Henson and tell him it is from Chief Donaldson,' is exactly what he said, and I heard him."

Jerry was calmer now and seemed in a daze. "I guess Sam Henson is bad, but he couldn't be any worse than him," said Jerry, pointing at Donaldson.

"I hope they hang you, and I get to watch you and hear you scream like you make other people scream." Jerry Willis held up his left arm and shoved back his sleeve.

"I'd like to make you scream the way I did when you twisted my arm into this shape," yelled Jerry, thrusting his misshapen arm up to be seen.

"You ain't nothing but trash." Jerry glared at the chief, stumbling as he turned to make his way out of the room. Keith McCauley helped him out and closed the door behind him.

"Well, Chief, what do you say to that?" asked Swann grimly. "You may as well tell us who the man in the dark denim jacket is."

"I don't know who he is. He's probably one of Sam's minions. Besides, that Draper woman ain't dead yet, or I don't reckon she is," said the chief as if suddenly remembering something.

With the Chief's revelation the courtroom was stunned. This was Sam Henson's trial on charges of unethical business conduct, but so much had been revealed that the judge felt some clarification had to me made since Donaldson had said that Henson had poisoned Sabrina Draper.

The jury was admonished to adhere strictly to the charges against Sam Henson and not allow Donaldson's revelations to interfere with the evidence on Henson.

"Chief Donaldson will be bound over to the grand jury and if he is indicted his trial will come later," stated Judge Wilson.

A long-suffering jury would again be transported back to their hotel. This had been a trying day and they each knew that the next day might reveal much more.

Everyone knew that Sabrina Draper would be brought to trial if she ever got out of the hospital and also that Margie Meadows would have a hearing on her part in the Mylanta situation. Both Sam Henson and Chief Donaldson were to be transported back to the county jail to await further developments. The chief's charge that Sam Henson planned to murder Sabrina Draper would have to be proven before a verdict could be reached.

Chief Donaldson had to await a bail bond hearing, but everyone knew he had confessed to killing that woman in Cleveland, Ohio and knew that if he got bail it would be extremely high.

The people who had carried out Sam Henson and Chief Donaldson's orders were also to be incarcerated, except for the man in the dark jacket who had not yet been identified.

Just as the judge raised his gavel preparing to adjourn the court, the back doors opened and a deputy came through. Everybody stopped and waited.

The deputy went straight to the judge's bench and said, "Somebody got to Sabrina Draper. They pulled the plug on her oxygen and when the nurse found her she was gone."

Now, they all knew that Chief Donaldson's comment about Sabrina Draper was due to his knowledge that someone was trying to murder her. Keith looked over at Steve Hammer and nodded. They both felt that they had dropped the ball by missing some clue. They had thought that once all these other people had been caught and they had Sabrina hidden, that nobody else would be hurt. Judge Wilson tapped his gavel and court was adjourned.

People began pouring out of the courthouse. News reporters were speeding away to their cars while talking on their phones and the jurors were walking with relief to the shuttle. They were to be taken back to the hotel for what they had hoped would be the final time, but now they knew they'd probably be kept over for the other trials.

Steve and Keith drove back to the station and just as they arrived, Dave Shortt drove up in his patrol car. In the backseat was a handcuffed woman in a white nurse uniform. Dave parked the patrol car and got out. When he opened the door the woman got out and walked in front of him into the police station.

"This is Velda Arnetta. I was going to check on Sabrina when I met this woman hurrying down the stairs from the third floor. I detained her. I don't know why, but I just had a feeling that she was running away from something and she was. I think she had just killed Sabrina Draper. She was scared out of her wits when I caught her, but she didn't confess. She claimed she was there with someone else, but an orderly said she was the nurse he had seen outside the door of Sabrina's room just a few minutes before I arrived."

"I guess Chief Donaldson had something on you too, didn't he?" asked Steve.

"No, he didn't have nothing on me, but that Sam Henson had something on somebody else. I didn't kill that woman, but Sam Henson will tell the chief I did," replied the woman.

"Well, you don't have to worry about Sam Henson or Chief Donaldson for a long time. They're in jail," said Steve.

"I hope they don't send me to the same jail, then. They have ways of getting to people. In this town you can't tell who is working for the chief. By the time you find out it's already too late." The woman's voice was filled with fear

She was soon booked and placed in a cell to await a hearing. Keith asked Steve if he wanted to go out to his place.

"I've got Margie Meadows out there. I don't know if they are still looking for her or not, but I don't think they've found her if they are. Freddie would have called me if anybody had been seen nosing around," said Keith.

Steve declined with the excuse that he was too tired and grimy. "I'll be out tomorrow, if they are still there."

As Keith finally pulled into the road that led to his house he saw that all the drapes were closed and the house looked as if it was vacant.

God, I hate this place. It's been nothing but sorrow for me. As soon as I retire, I'll sell out or just move as quickly as I can, thought Keith as he hit the garage door opener.

When he opened the kitchen door a wonderful smell wafted toward him, perking up his senses.

"What is that I smell? Whatever it is I want the first bite," he said as he walked into the kitchen where he found Hannah stirring something on the stove.

Hannah turned and smiled. "I guess you smell the peach cobbler I'm baking. Smells good enough to eat, doesn't it?"

Keith was entranced by the sight of Hannah in an apron and with all that glorious hair falling in waves down her back. He thought she was the most beautiful woman he had ever seen and didn't hear a word of what she had said.

Hannah went back to her stirring, since she thought Keith did not want to talk. Keith, however, just stood savoring the feeling of contentment that had stolen over him when he had stepped into the kitchen.

This is the way a home should feel, thought Keith, still watching Hannah. Finally Hannah turned away from the stove and stopped dead in her tracks. She looked down to see if she had spilled something on her apron. Not seeing anything, she looked up.

"What are you staring at? Did you not want us to cook while we were here?" she asked in a puzzled voice.

"I was staring, wasn't I? I didn't mean any harm. It's just that this feels so like home. It seems like the way it was when I was little and could be in Mom's kitchen. Smells always remind me of home."

Hannah smiled. "That's all right then. I thought I had done something wrong."

Keith grinned. "More like you're doing everything right." He started to say something else, but just then Margie came through the door.

"I was wondering about the trial. How did it go today?"

"Well, we thought the trial was over for Sam Henson. He was convicted for aiding and abetting a criminal in murderous conduct, unlawful business practices, and dealing in illegal drugs and now there is more evidence and there may be charges of murder later. We'll probably find out tomorrow and even though Chief Donaldson wasn't on trial today, he confessed to murdering a woman in Cleveland, Ohio.

"Why would Chief Donaldson confess to that if he wasn't on trial?" asked Margie.

"I think he knew he was going down and wanted to take as many with him as he could," replied Keith.

Keith went on to tell how somebody had sneaked in and killed Sabrina Draper by unplugging her oxygen.

"Sam Henson either doctored the cocaine used by Sabrina or he had someone do it for him, but we don't know if she was poisoned or her oxygen was unplugged by a woman pretending to be a nurse. Either way, she's dead." Keith looked at Hannah who had dropped her head as she gasped in shock.

Seeing Hannah covering her face, Margie went to her. "Hannah, what's wrong? Why are you crying?"

"I'm not crying, but I feel so sorry for that poor woman, already in the hospital and then for somebody to do that . . . it's just too cruel. I wish I had gone to see her. You know she did come to the house when Bill died. I believe she was sorry."

"Well, she probably was sorry. Poor soul, but it is probably for the best that it happened. Steve told me that the doctor feared her brain had been damaged from the poison anyway," said Margie, trying to console Hannah.

Freddie came in from the living room. He, of course, had to be filled in on the whole proceeding. By the time Keith had finished, Margie had the table set and Hannah was dishing up.

Both Keith and Freddie went back to the bathroom to wash up and when they came back Margie told Keith that Steve Hammer wanted to talk to him. Keith picked up the phone and stood listening.

"Oh! Well, I guess that is possible. Do you want me to come back in?" Keith didn't want to go back in and was very relieved at Steve's negative reply. "Okay, I'll see you in the morning."

CHAPTER 14

KEITH HUNG UP. "I GUESS YOU all knew that Bertie Briscoll was out on bail, didn't you? When he had their attention he continued. "Steve just told me that the police were called to the Briscoll home by the father. Bertie was found dead in his room about four o'clock this evening."

"Who poisoned him?" Hannah turned startled eyes to Keith.

"Poisoned? I don't know how he died. I can understand you thinking that though, since poison has been used so often in this tangled case."

"Oh, his poor parents, I know they must be heart-broken. Isn't it sad that so many people have died?" Hannah was looking at Keith.

"It still seems like my begging Bill to bring me home is the cause of all these people dying. I've always loved West Virginia so much and felt so safe here. I never dreamed that this kind of corruption could reach my mountains. It did though, and I helped it along by begging so hard to come home," Hannah said sadly.

Keith looked at her with compassion. "No, Hannah, don't put the blame on your love of West Virginia. It's still a good place to live. I wouldn't want to live anywhere else, except maybe on a farm."

He had such a pleasant look as he talked about West Virginia that Hannah's eyes widened. She had always felt the same way.

Margie saw the look and smiled. "I like it too, but ambition, greed, and passion will corrupt anybody who will allow it to and the place has nothing to do with it."

Keith nodded. "That's so true. All three of those things, plus drugs, gradually spread like a giant web and a lot of people got caught in its tendrils."

Margie sighed. "Well, I don't know what will happen to me, but even I got tangled. Many of the others probably never intended to get in this mess. They are just like me. I was in the wrong place at the right time, I suppose."

Hannah reached over and patted her hand. "Margie, you had no idea that poison was anywhere in that building and especially not in that Mylanta."

"She won't be sent to jail, will she Keith?" Freddie asked.

"I wish I could say an unequivocal no, but I can't say for certain. I don't believe she will be sent to prison, but I'm not the judge and jury."

Keith looked at Margie and shook his head sadly. "I'm sorry, Margie."

"Don't worry about it Keith. I admit that I'm scared and don't want to go to jail, but look what I've gained; a grandson and a daughter-in-law who is exactly like my own daughter," said Margie, looking first at Freddie and then Hannah.

"Let's make sure she treats us with the proper respect, Mom. Christmas isn't too far off and we both like expensive gifts." Freddie crossed the room and threw his arms around Margie, who turned a glowing face to Hannah as she encircled Freddie in her arms.

Margie looked at Keith with misty eyes and smiled. "They're going to have me crying and I'm hungry. Come on everybody, let's eat."

Keith McCauley looked over the table with a satisfied gleam in his eyes as Margie and Hannah dished up the food. He sat down at his own table and sighed with content, savoring the sight and smells that he'd always connected to mother and home. There were homemade biscuits, fried chicken, gravy, creamed potatoes, green beans and the best looking peach pie he had ever seen or smelled.

When everyone was seated he automatically reached out to Hannah on his left and Freddie on his right and clasped their hands. Hannah was startled for a moment.

In all of her married life to Bill Larkin, asking a blessing aloud had never been done. The first morning after she and Bill were married she had bowed her head and Bill hadn't known what she intended, so he said, "Pass the butter."

From then on she had silently thanked the Lord for his bounty and had reminded Freddie of God's goodness.

"But Mom, Dad works and makes money to buy what we eat," Freddie argued when she said they needed to thank the Lord.

"Freddie, the good Lord gives us health, the ability to work, and even jobs for us, but we have to use the gifts God gives us to be able to do all those things," Hannah explained.

Freddie sat contemplating this and finally said, "Yeah, that's what Preacher Seth said, so I guess it must be right." Preacher Seth Adair was very kind and gentle to everyone and especially to the children, and his congregation, young and old, truly loved him.

Hannah reached out for Margie's hand on her other side and soon all hands were joined as Keith asked God to bless the food and all those present and to put HIS loving arms around Margie.

When Hannah raised her head she saw tears in Margie's eyes as she dabbed her own. Both women looked at Keith and nodded their approval.

Nobody talked, but sat waiting patiently for the plates to be filled as they were passed around the table. Keith smiled in nostalgia as he looked on.

"This should be the evening meal in a farmhouse kitchen with kids all around the table."

"How many kids? Some farmhouses have large kitchens and huge tables so you'd better not have big dreams. Most women don't want more than two children." Margie gurgled with laughter when Keith's face turned a mottled red.

"I was just remembering Uncle Ben's farm when I used to visit him each summer. There were three of us and Uncle Ben had six boys and two girls so their table was always full," Keith reminisced.

Hannah recalled a similar mealtime in their old farmhouse. "I'm surprised we didn't all get fat since we all loved gathering around Mommy's table."

"Was it like that at your house, Margie? Keith asked as he passed the potatoes to Margie.

"No, I was an only child," replied Margie with a somber expression.

"I bet all your friends came to visit about dinner time, didn't they?" questioned Freddie, since, in his eyes, Margie was so sweet that she would have had lots of friends.

They were all surprised when Margie hurriedly rose from the table and left the room. Hannah looked at Keith and then Freddie. "Her childhood must have been awful. She never talks about the past."

Keith looked troubled. "Other than what she blurted out in the courtroom I don't think anyone knows much about her, but I thought she might have talked to you, Hannah."

"No, she hasn't," said Hannah, pushing back her chair. "I'm going to see if she's all right." Just as she turned to leave, Margie came back into the room.

Hannah took her seat again and so did Margie before turning to look around at each face. "I'm sorry. I thought I had strong control, but being in such a caring, loving group brought back all those wretched years of loneliness and agony."

Freddie jumped to his feet, toppling his chair backwards and flung his arms around Margie. "I'm so sorry, Grandmother. Stay with me and I'll see that you're happy for the rest of your life."

Margie hugged him close and then pushed him back to look into his face. "You would, wouldn't you? You can't do that though, Freddie. The judge and jury will have to make that decision, but it makes me feel good to know you love me."

Simultaneously Keith and Hannah spoke. "We all love you, Margie." The two of them looked at each other and Margie burst out laughing.

"I wish you two could see your faces. You're shocked that you both said the same thing at the same time. Maybe that's a sign. You two may be soul mates."

Hannah's eyes blared and her face became a rosy red, but Keith smiled at Margie. "I hope you're right."

"Margie, I love you, but you have no idea what you're talking about. I was married for over twenty years to your son and I loved him," blurted Hannah as though she had been accused.

Margie who had finished eating got to her feet. "I know you did, Hannah. I'm only kidding, but I did think that was unusual."

"It was just a coincidence because we both love you and didn't want you to be hurt." Hannah arose from her seat and, picking up her plate, turned toward the sink.

Keith sent Margie a pleading look as if to say, "Please don't rock the boat." Margie nodded and picked up her plate as well.

The men headed for the living room and Margie helped Hannah clear the table. "I'll wash and you dry, Hannah, or would you rather wash?" Margie was a little fearful since she felt that she had upset Hannah.

Hannah turned. "Margie, please don't think there is anything going on between me and Keith. I appreciate him and like him as a friend, but I don't think I can ever trust another man again."

Margie turned on the taps and started filling the sink. "Hannah, I'm sorry. I was out of line, but really I was just kidding. No, that isn't quite true. I think Keith likes you and he trusts you, but I see you don't feel the same way."

Hannah shook her head in puzzlement. "I'm like someone who's been shell-shocked. I don't feel like everything is real . . . kind of like this is all a dream."

"I know all about that. I've been there and it takes time to break through the clouds, but remember the sun is just on the other side. This will pass and I don't think there is a finer man than Keith McCauley."

Hannah picked up the first plate and began wiping it. "You may be right, but I'm not seeing anything but clouds right now."

"Well, it's like the doctor told me. One morning you'll wake up and realize that life needs to be lived and the past can't be changed. Once you accept that and stop blaming yourself it won't be long until the world will seem to be a much better place."

"Oh I do hope you're right, Margie. I just can't believe that Bill could have been seeing that woman for the last two years and I never knew it. I must be stupid." Hannah stated in an angry voice.

"I know you want to believe that Sabrina Draper enticed Bill, but a man can't be enticed unless he wants to be, can he?"

Margie had never even cared for another man after Bill's father was killed and had no idea how to answer so she laughed. "Lord, don't ask me a question like that, Hannah, I'm more inexperienced than you are when it comes to men."

CHAPTER 15

THAT WEEKEND HANNAH FOUND THAT MARGIE'S words were very true. Margie really didn't have any experience with men, which was made evident when Steve arrived.

Keith was off-duty that weekend, but he still met with Steve and they were diligently investigating all the people who had worked for both Sam Henson and Chief Donaldson. David Shortt's father, Henry, was now acting police chief. City Council had met and since Henry Shortt had been a dedicated police officer all his life and was already a captain he was selected for chief of police for the City of Beckley.

"He'll do a good job. They should make the position permanent," said Keith when he learned of the appointment.

Back at Keith's house, the two women and Freddie cleaned, cooked, and played endless card games, even with the drapes closed in the living-room. The kitchen windows were high enough that people could not see in from the outside. They covered them at night just in case some light from the other rooms filtered through.

On Sunday morning, Freddie kept prowling around in the darkened house. He finally stopped in front of his mother. "Mom, I'm going to sneak out and get us some ice cream. I can't stand being cooped up like this."

"Freddie, try to be patient. Keith has worked so hard to keep us safe that it would be a shame to do something foolish. Besides, I don't really want any ice cream. All of us could use more clothes and I'd love to be in my own home. Keith will know when it is safe, though."

Hannah looked at him so solemnly that Freddie sighed reluctantly and picked up the deck of cards on the nearby table and idly began shuffling them.

Margie came in from the bedroom and yawned widely. "I'm like Freddie . . . bored to death. Let's plan a good supper for Keith. Mom used to say that doing something for others kept one from getting bored and depressed."

Just then the phone rang. Everybody froze. It was the first time the phone had rung since they had been there. When it pealed again Freddie started toward it.

"No, Freddie, don't answer it," warned Margie, grasping at his sleeve, but she wasn't quick enough.

"Hello," said Freddie and then Margie's warning registered and he dropped the phone and jumped back startled, leaving the phone dangling.

Hannah hadn't moved, but now she picked up the phone and listened. Hearing no sound she placed it back in its cradle. "Well, somebody knows now that Keith's house is occupied, that's for sure."

"I'm sorry. I reacted before I thought. Keith will be upset. Since I'm the one who goofed, I guess I should be the one to call him," said Freddie.

Both Hannah and Margie were worried. "Regardless of who calls him, he needs to know. Don't get upset, Freddie. I might have done the same thing had I been nearer to the phone," said Hannah.

"I think I'm the person they'd want since I recognized Chief Donaldson's voice, so you two would be better off away from me," said Margie.

"Margie, this may not be one of Donaldson's cronies. Remember I found Bill's file folder, which proved that Sam Henson wanted rid of him." Hannah looked at Margie solemnly.

Freddie grabbed his cell phone and punched in Keith's cell phone number. As they waited, Margie said, "We'll have to find another place to hide that's for sure."

"It could have been someone who mistakenly dialed the wrong number. I do that myself sometimes, don't you?" asked Hannah just as Freddie said, "Keith, it's me."

He quickly told Keith what had happened. "I'm sorry. I reacted before I thought." Freddie listened for a few minutes and then shut his phone down.

"He's coming home and he isn't upset with me, but he says something will have to be done."

When they heard a car pull into the driveway they all stood transfixed watching the kitchen door, which led into the garage. They listened for the sound of the garage door opening, but heard nothing. Then the front door knob turned. They knew the door was dead-bolted, but they still stood frozen in place, listening to stealthy footsteps moving around the outside of the house. In a row they tiptoed to the first bedroom and heard scraping and muffled mumblings at the windows just as another car sped into the driveway. It was then real curses were heard as well as loud thuds and feet running away from the house. Soon they heard more feet running in the same direction.

"I'd love to know what's going on, but I'm not making another move. I've caused enough trouble today," said Freddie, plopping down on the bed.

Nothing else was heard for some time and both Hannah and Margie went back into the kitchen. They both slumped into the chairs at the table. "This stress is getting to me, Hannah. I like to know what is going on. Don't you?"

"I certainly do. I'm used to thinking about how to manage a situation, not just sitting and waiting for the next shoe to fall." Hannah got up and ran some water into a glass and stood in front of the kitchen window. She drank her water and then turned back to Margie.

"We may as well cook dinner. When Keith gets in he'll probably be hungry." Hannah opened the freezer section of the refrigerator.

"What about baked chicken breasts? Keith may not like baked chicken, though."

Margie grinned. "If you cook it, Keith will eat it, my dear, and he'll like it also."

"Stop it, Margie. You're going to make me uncomfortable around Keith. He's just a kind man. If he had wanted a woman he's had ten years to find one."

"We'll see, but someday I'll bet you'll say I'm right, but I'll not mention it again."

Just then they heard the garage door opening and stood with eyes widened in fear. When Keith opened the kitchen door, both women sighed with relief. Steve Hammer was right behind him.

"Did you catch whoever was trying to break in?" Freddie asked as soon as he saw Keith.

"No. They got away, but we'll get them. We already have their car."

"Those men must have been pretty close when they called here, or did Freddie wait before he called Keith?" asked Steve.

"Maybe two minutes, but certainly no more than three," replied Margie, whose eyes had widened when Steve stepped in.

"Where have you been hiding? We've been here nearly a week."

Steve grinned. "You've been missing me, I take it. Since you've missed me so much I'll tell you. I've been out arresting all the people who may want to harm you." Suddenly the smile left his face and he turned to Keith.

"I thought you said this house had a security alarm." He looked at Margie.

"Did an alarm go off when they were turning the door knob or shaking the windows?"

"No alarm went off. Are you sure it was turned on?" asked Freddie.

"I checked it before I left when I called you and Hannah to come out here. The wires have probably been cut," said Keith. Both women nodded in agreement.

"So did you miss whoever was in the car?" asked Margie and at Keith's nod she continued. "That means I'm still not safe, doesn't it?"

Keith turned to leave the room. "I'll go check on the wires. They probably got to the one running along the edge of the eaves in the garage. Freddie followed him into the garage.

Steve kidded with Margie, trying to take her mind off her fears, until she said, "I guess I'm going to have to hide the rest of my life."

"Well, I suppose all of you will need another hiding place and right now I don't know where. Those men may not know you were here, but they were trying to make sure for the alarm was disabled," Keith said as he showed the snipped wires.

"I suppose the neighbors told them that all the windows were covered and they didn't know why." Keith looked so discouraged that Hannah patted his arm.

"Don't worry, Keith. We'll find some place." Suddenly her eyes lit up.

"Why can't we go to my farm?"

"We can't take Margie out of town until her trial, or I don't think we can. I'll check with the judge. He may agree if I'll take the responsibility and of course I will." Steve said, looking at Keith for confirmation.

"Why can't we go back to our house, Steve? We can go back after dark and not turn any lights on. Nobody will know we are there," suggested Freddie.

Both Keith and Steve who had taken a seat at the table sat thinking this over. "That might work for tonight and perhaps tomorrow, which will give us time to think of somewhere safer. What do you think, Keith?" asked Steve.

"I'd like to do that. We're out of clothes. I've worn this dress so long that it will probably fall apart when I wash it," Hannah said and laughed as they all looked at her.

"I don't smell any bad odors, so you could probably wear it another few days," Keith said and they all laughed as Hannah pulled at her bodice and sniffed.

CHAPTER 16

THERE WAS NO MOON AND THE stars only gave a faint light when everyone piled into Keith's patrol car. "I'm sorry but you people in the back should scrunch down as low as you can just in case someone should be watching the house," said Steve as they exited the garage.

Freddie had gotten in first, then Margie, and last was Hannah and they stayed that way until Steve said, "We're on Robert C. Byrd Drive and if anyone sees passengers in a patrol car they will only think we've made an arrest, so you can get up off the floor."

Keith dimmed his lights and pulled to a spot behind Hannah's house and killed the engine. "Wait! Let me check to see how many people have noticed us." He soon returned and gave an "all clear" sign.

They quietly exited the car and Hannah hit the garage door opener she had retrieved from her car that was left in Keith's garage. They were soon inside the house.

Margie shivered. "Gosh, it's cold in here. Didn't you close everything up before you left, Hannah?

"Yes, I did. Didn't I, Freddie," asked Hannah, shivering as well.

"You sure did and I doubled checked it so I guess it's just damp from being closed up."

Hannah shivered. "I feel a draft coming from somewhere."

Keith looked around suspiciously. "What are you looking for, Hannah?" Keith had been right behind her and stood watching her cautious movements.

"I think that so much has happened and I've learned about so many dishonest people that I am wary of everything. I don't see how policemen cope with being daily bombarded with evil."

"Not all people are evil, Hannah. Once in a while we run into really good people and that makes it all worthwhile," said Keith as he followed her from room to room.

They reached the back bedroom and Hannah thrust open the door to be hit with a blast of air. The wind had risen that evening and now the curtains were billowing out in long streams from a broken window.

"Oh my God! Look at that. Just like I thought, somebody has been in my house." said Hannah, stepping back against Keith who started to put his arm around her, but stopped when he thought of what her reaction might be.

"Steve, come see what we've found," yelled Keith and soon not only Steve but Margie and Freddie as well came trooping into the room.

Steve put his hand on the bed. "Sopping wet and it hasn't rained today so this must have happened earlier in the week."

"Well, the mattress on that bed is totally ruined and look at the mirror on the dresser . . . cracked all the way from top to bottom. This looks like senseless vandalism," said Margie moving into the room to investigate.

Hannah went hurriedly to the chest and pulled out the top drawer. She looked inside and gasped. "It's gone. They've taken the silver dollars Dad left for me. I also had Mom's knitting needles and some patterns in a metal box."

Hannah looked ready to cry and Keith couldn't stand it. "We'll try to recover them, Hannah, but since the rain and wind have been blasting the room for several days we may not be able to find any fingerprints."

"You know they'll spend the silver dollars, but if you know the years they were minted some bank may have issued paper money for them," said Steve.

"Dad had a silver dollar for every year from 1939 through 1960 and he left them for me," said Hannah.

"Is there anything else missing? We'll have to report this, but I don't think we can do anything tonight except cover up this gaping hole and sweep up the glass," said Keith.

"Well, I'm going to take all these bed coverings to the laundry room. We can at least save them, can't we, Hannah?" Margie began yanking at the soggy quilts.

"That's one of Mom's hand sewn quilts and I certainly don't want to part with it," said Hannah, reaching to strip the pillows.

"They must not have been too smart or they would have taken the quilt. One made like this is worth about $500.00 or maybe more," said Margie, taking a closer look.

"I saw one in Tamarack last week and it was priced at $800.00 and this one looks as good as it did," said Steve, giving the quilt a closer look.

Freddie had gone to get a broom and dust pan and when he returned he and Keith soon had all the glass and shattered wood swept into a neat pile. Steve had followed Margie and Hannah back to the kitchen, but now returned with a hammer and a square of oil cloth. "We'll have to use this tonight if we can find any tacks. We don't want to do too much hammering. It might wake the neighbors."

The three men worked steadily cleaning and covering the window and Keith lifted the mattress from the bed and stood it on end against the wall. "Steve, this looks like an ordinary break-in to me. What's your take on it?"

"That what I thought, too. It looks as if they were satisfied as soon as they found some money." Steve started opening drawers, and seeing that nothing had been moved in any of the chest drawers, he turned to the dresser.

Keith was looking too, and he found nothing else disturbed. "It looks as if they opened the top drawer and found the metal box and since it had money in it, that was all they wanted, or maybe they got scared someone would catch them."

Freddie had gone to get a large waste can and now returned. "Did they ransack all the drawers?"

"No, Freddie. The money was in the top drawer and it seems that is all they wanted. It may have been somebody living on this street who knew about this back window," said Steve.

Freddie's eyes opened wide. "I know two boys who are into drugs and they like to shoot pool, but I don't know if they've ever been out this way or not. This seems like something they might do, though."

"Well, don't you try to be Sherlock Holmes, Steve and I will check it out. We don't want anybody to know all of you are back here."

"I don't think they can stay here very long anyway, Keith. I'd say that this house is being watched." Steve gave Keith a knowing look. They both knew that Margie Meadows was a target for both Chief Harry Donaldson and Sam Henson.

Keith nodded as he turned to the bathroom in the hallway. He knew that he and Steve were off duty, but didn't know if Hannah would want him to stay there. He decided he would try to stay since he hated the thought of leaving Hannah unprotected.

CHAPTER 17

AN HOUR LATER, STEVE HAMMER WAS on his way back to his own apartment and Keith bedded down on the living-room sofa in Hannah's house. None of the people in that house saw the black car move slowly up and down the street in front of Hannah's house three or four times before a police cruiser came down the street. Then the car sped away and didn't return.

Keith was up at the break of dawn and went into the kitchen hoping to find a coffee maker. He was startled when Hannah spoke just behind him.

"What are you looking for, Keith?"

"I wanted to make some coffee, but instead I woke you. I'm sorry."

"I was already awake." Hannah looked up at him and smiled. Keith almost gasped aloud. Hannah looked just like she did the morning he had found her lying across the body of her dead husband. She wasn't as pale as she had been that morning, but her glorious dark-auburn hair lay in waves down her back. From that first vision, Keith McCauley had been entranced and held that picture in his mind. He didn't think his enchantment showed, but Hannah noticed something.

"Don't look shocked, Keith. I don't mind you making coffee nor looking in the cabinets either," said Hannah as she went around him and stretched up to get the coffee from the second shelf in the cabinet.

Keith reached above her head and lifted the coffee down before she could reach it. "Gosh, you sure are a tiny little thing, aren't you?"

Hannah lifted her arm up and flexed her muscle. "Tough though. Mama used to say I was wiry and tough, whatever that means."

Keith grinned. "You don't look tough, Hannah. You look as if a little puff of wind would blow you away."

Hannah spooned coffee into the filter, filled the carafe with water, and turned on the coffee-maker before answering. "Well, I'm still here, but it does seem like I've been facing one storm after another for the last little while. This will pass though, for life always has valleys and hills and sometimes mountains."

Keith stood looking out the window. "That's true, but I've done the most of my learning in the valleys. I guess when one gets down and has to climb out alone the lessons learned do the most good."

Hannah stood arrested by that remark. "I think you're right. I'd lived all my life trusting everybody and everything, but that isn't real. You trust who you want to, I guess, but they always let you down. I learned that in the lowest valley I've been in since Dad and Mom died."

"I think it is good to trust, but sometimes we do get disappointed. We all usually, or rather I usually did, let things happening to others sort of slide by, but when it happens to us then we let it make us stronger or we let it destroy us." Keith had turned and stood looking at Hannah thoughtfully.

"Well, I don't know, but I've sure learned a lot in a very short time. I now know that just because we care for someone it does not mean they care for us. I thought caring was reciprocal, but it isn't. Perhaps in relationships one always cares more than the other, but I don't know. I do know that it will be hard for me to ever let myself care for anyone again," said Hannah and turned to gets cups from the mug holder on the countertop.

"That isn't fair" . . . began Keith, but stopped at Margie's voice from the hallway.

"I smell coffee so I know somebody is up." She came through the door, tying the sash on her robe. "Ah ha, two people are up and making coffee. Has something happened to wake you two or are you both early risers?"

"I don't know about Keith," said Hannah, "but I am definitely an early riser. I love to watch the sun come up over the horizon."

Keith grinned. "Me too, I was usually the first one up when I was really young. Mom used to grumble that I got up with the roosters."

Margie walked on in and sat down in the chair Keith had pulled out for her. "Not me. I like to stay up late and sleep late in the mornings. Of course, I never was able to do that. I've been a working girl all my life."

"I guess you think running a house isn't work. It is though if you want to do it right," said Hannah going to get another cup. Keith was ahead of her again. He turned laughing.

"Where do you have the step stool hidden, Hannah? I know you can't reach that shelf without one."

"I don't use the cups on that shelf when I don't have company." She turned to a mug holder in the corner and pointed, smiling broadly. "Those are my coffee cups."

"Well, I wish I had known. Those are man-sized cups." Keith plucked a brown mug from its holder and felt its weight. "This is just right. May I claim it?"

Hannah laughed. "You sound like my brother Cam when he was little. Glasses came in the oatmeal boxes with the oats and Cam wanted to see them first and if it had a bird or some animal on it, that glass was his."

Just then Keith's phone rang and he was instantly alert. "Yes, I'm up. What's happening? You did! Well, hang on I'll be right over." He turned to the eager audience.

"Steve has apprehended a man trying to steal the car that was left at my house the night those men tried to break in. Steve changed his mind and went to my house instead of going to his apartment and it's good he did. He nabbed the man at three o'clock this morning trying to get into the garage."

"You haven't had any breakfast. Can you wait until I fix something? I'll be quick," offered Hannah.

"No, I'm sorry, he needs me now, but I'll take a rain check on that offer if that's all right with you."

Keith looked reluctant to leave, but finally said. "I don't really like to leave you all here, but I need to help Steve. Keep a close watch out the windows from all sides and if you see anyone acting suspicious, call me or Steve."

He started out the door to the garage, but stopped and looked back. "Don't answer the phone. If Steve or I need you we will call your cell phone, Margie."

He hurried away and left Margie and Hannah sitting with their coffee, mulling over their plight.

"He doesn't think it is safe for us to be here. What would somebody want from us now? Bill is dead and Sam Henson and Chief Donaldson are both in jail so I can't see how we could help or hurt anyone now, do you?" asked Hannah.

"I think it's payback to me. I think Donaldson's angry at me for recognizing his voice, even though it probably won't make any difference in his sentencing. I think Donaldson just hates women and particularly me." Margie looked solemn.

When Freddie finally awoke and came into the kitchen, Margie was there alone. "Isn't Mom up yet? She's usually up before anybody."

Margie grinned. "I think she was this morning as well. She's gone to take a shower. When I woke I smelled coffee and came in to see who was up and both she and Keith were in the kitchen."

Freddie picked a mug from the corner rack and poured himself a cup of coffee. Bringing it back to the table he sat down across from Margie and looked at her intently.

"I believe Keith's in love with Mom don't you?" he asked, but before she could answer that question, he asked another.

"Mar . . . uh, What do you want me to call you? I know you're my grandmother, but somehow you just don't seem old enough."

Margie grinned. "Thanks. That's a nice compliment. So, why not just call me Margie. We both know I'm your grandmother and very proud to be called that, but as you say, 'If it doesn't feel right then maybe it isn't right.'"

Freddie took a drink of coffee and put down his cup. "Good, that's settled. Well, then, Margie, do you think Keith's in love with Mom?"

"I don't know, but I feel he likes her a lot. I don't think Hannah feels that way about him, though. It's probably too soon. Bill hasn't been dead that long."

"He may as well have been dead for two years since he stayed here very little and he treated Mom pretty badly."

Seeing Margie's doubting look he said, "Oh, I know Dad was your son and you loved him. I did too, Margie. It almost destroyed me when I found out what he was doing, but more than that, he accused me of doing what he was doing himself."

"When did you find out, Freddie? I mean about him seeing Sabrina Draper." Margie was hearing things she didn't know and she had always tried to find out as much as she could about Bill's daily life.

"It was over two years ago when I dated Nicole Henson. She told me that every man that worked for CEE went out with women even if they were married. I told her that my dad didn't do that and she thought I was stupid." Freddie still recalled her look and now grimaced.

"She said, 'Oh, Freddie, grow up. He's been seeing Sabrina Draper ever since she went to work for him.'"

"I didn't believe her at first, but I started checking and found it was true." Freddie lapsed into a moody silence.

Margie got up and came around the table and put her arms around Freddie. "I'm sorry, Freddie. I know that must have been hard for you. It's hard for me now. I thought Bill was almost a God. He was so different from my Dad. I guess I thought he just didn't have any faults."

"I hate to think this, but Dad or somebody was poisoning Mom also. I didn't know that until after he died, though. I almost lost my mom and I did lose my dad due to Sabrina Draper and Sam Henson."

Margie had settled into the chair beside him, but was turned toward the window and now leaned forward with an intent look.

"Freddie, there's a man getting out of a car. Let's get out of this room."

CHAPTER 18

WHEN THE DOORBELL RANG THEY WERE both in the hallway that had no windows. Hearing the doorbell, Hannah came out of the bathroom and saw them. "What . . ." Margie put up her hand and shook her head.

The doorbell pealed again and again. Then the door knob turned. As it began to open they all stood petrified with fear and dread. They could hear someone in the living-room, but feared to try peeping around the corner. Whoever had entered was very soft-footed. They waited with bated breath and about three minutes later the front door swished as it closed. They didn't know if someone was still inside and had pretended to leave in an effort to get them to come out of hiding, or if that someone had actually left.

Finally Margie crept to the end of the hall and through the window saw the man enter his car, noting that it was a black Toyota sedan.

Margie stepped back into the hall. "He's gone."

"What's going on?" Seeing Hannah's frightened and puzzled look, Margie tried to explain.

"Hannah we saw a car stop and a man get out. We got out of sight and soon the door bell rang. That's why I warned you not to speak."

"How did he get in? Was the door unlocked?" Hannah looked at Freddie.

"Don't look at me, Mom. I haven't been in or out that door in over a week. Are you sure you locked it when we left?"

Hannah sighed. "I don't know, Freddie, but I'll make sure from here on." She dashed across the living room and turned the dead bolt.

"I didn't know we were going to have to run and hide the rest of our lives. I'm so tired of it all. Let's go to the farm." Hannah turned to the others with a questioning look.

"How, Mom? Your car is at Keith's. I think we should call Keith and see what he tells us." They had all reentered the living room and stood discussing the situation.

"I guess you're right, but I'm sick to death of having to depend on some man to protect me. That's what I depended on for over twenty years and it almost killed me," said Hannah.

Freddie picked up the phone, but Margie said, "Wait, Freddie. This line may be tapped. Let me call on my cell phone."

Margie soon had Keith on the line. "Keith, someone came and rang the doorbell, but we hid. He rang several times and then opened the door and came in. We knew he came in since we could feel a draft. He must have left the door open. We stayed hidden and finally he went back to his car and drove away. The car was a black Toyota sedan."

She stood listening for a moment. "I don't know if he went into the kitchen or not, but we did fry bacon and our coffee cups were on the table, or at least mine was. Oh Lord! You're right. Now they know for certain that someone is here." Margie ended the call and turned to Hannah.

"Keith's going to bring your car home, Hannah, but he's going to create some scheme to fool that man and whoever else is trying to get to us. He said it may take some time to work it out, so not to expect him for a while."

Hannah sighed. "Let's just pack our clothes and get him to take us to the farm. We'll have to rough it for several days since we won't have any electricity, but that's better than having to live like this."

Margie nodded. "I agree, but Freddie you keep watch until we get packed and then we'll let you pack. We don't want somebody trying to do us harm while we are packing."

Hannah had three suitcases packed and started out of the room to check on Margie when she heard the garage door opening. She froze in her tracks. Suddenly seeing Freddie's baseball bat that she had kept in a tall vase in a corner she grabbed it up and stepped into the hall. She stopped and listened. Hearing a noise behind her, she turned to see Margie with the bathroom plunger and Freddie with a long curtain rod right behind her. They inched along to the kitchen door and positioned themselves behind it, ready to do battle.

They didn't have long to wait as the kitchen door was thrust open and a tall form stepped inside to be instantly bombarded with three weapons. The only one that seemed to make contact was the baseball bat. The man stumbled, but quickly regained his balance.

"What the hell . . ." Then he saw Hannah with her loose robe flapping as she prepared to hit him again.

"Wait, Hannah! It's me," said Keith, grabbing the bat and wresting it from her hands only to have small fists flailing away in all directions." He grabbed her fists and pulled her against his chest to subdue her arms. Her heart was beating a rapid tattoo against his chest and he held her tighter, breathing in the fragrance of her newly shampooed hair.

When Hannah realized that it wasn't an intruder, she gasped and began to tremble. She looked up at Keith with still frightened but angry eyes.

"You could get killed with tricks like that. Did you think we were going to let someone break in on us and just stand and wait like we did earlier? That was unexpected."

Keith still held her against his chest, reluctant to release her. "I'm sorry I frightened you, but I thought all of you would hear the garage door opening. You're right though. A direct hit with that ball bat could leave a knot on my head."

Hannah wriggled to be free and Keith released his clasp. "Did you bring my car?"

Keith stood rubbing his head and wincing, but also trying to grin. "Didn't you people hear the siren? Steve pretended that someone had stolen the car and he was chasing them. They went right past the house."

"I was so scared that I could only hear my own heart beat," said Margie.

"Let me look at your head, Keith. It may be cut," ordered Hannah sternly as she pulled out a kitchen chair.

"Yes ma'am," said Keith plopping into the chair and bowing his head.

"Where were you hit?" Hannah began parting his hair in her effort to find the injury. When he didn't reply, she stopped.

Keith put his finger on a spot. "It's right here, but you can go all over my head if you want to. I believe that would help a lot."

Hannah turned red. "You're silly. I don't care if I did hurt you."

Hannah leaned over and parted the hair where he indicated and sure enough there was a swollen knot on his head. She straightened up. "I'd get some ice, but there isn't any. It isn't a very large bump though. I must have only hit a glancing blow."

"I think ice is the remedy for bumps on the head," said Keith, but maybe it's a hot pack. I don't think so, though."

Margie stood grinning. "Do you mean I didn't hit you at all? I don't guess I did since you're only complaining about a knot on your head."

Keith looked up. "A plunger hit me, but I can't show you where. Thank God, though, that Freddie didn't hit me with that long pole he was wielding."

"It wouldn't have hurt. He just had a curtain rod," said Hannah.

"Mom, I had that heavy drapery rod that we took down when the window got smashed. So, it's a good thing I didn't get to hit him. I was trying to hit him, but you were like a whirling dervish and I couldn't hit him without hitting you," said Freddie.

"I think I'll survive, so I think I'd better tell you that you won't get to leave here until after dark. We can all go over to the farm when Steve brings his car. He had to go back to the station after I whipped into the back driveway. Our ploy may not be of any benefit now since that man who came here knows that some people are here. I'm sure he didn't miss all the coffee cups and the smell of bacon. It seems our only options are to either stake out this place or all of you need to leave. Since we have two officers off sick I think you'll have to leave."

Keith asked if they'd had dinner. "If you haven't we won't be able to get anything until Steve gets here. It may be nine o'clock or later before he can make it."

"We've not had dinner. That bacon, the intruder may have smelled, was what we had for breakfast and I'm hungry," said Freddie.

"That's right, we haven't eaten. We can cook, can't we, Hannah?" asked Margie.

"Let me check the freezer. I've been gone so long and so much has happened that I can't remember what I have." Hannah opened the freezer section of the refrigerator.

"Aha! Here are some hamburger patties, but I don't know about buns. Yippee! Buns too! We're in luck. How about hamburgers for everyone? Will that be all right?"

"Good. I like hamburgers, don't you, Keith?" Freddie looked at Keith who was looking at Hannah with such intensity that Freddie just stared. When Keith didn't answer, Freddie asked again. "Keith, do you like hamburgers?"

Keith jerked around. "What? Oh, hamburgers. Sure, I like hamburgers."

"You men scatter and Hannah and I will have our dinner made before Freddie gets his things packed." Margie opened the freezer section again and got out the buns.

Keith stood looking out the window. "Hannah, has your friend, Sarah, already returned from Florida?"

"I don't think so, but she could have returned while I was away," replied Hannah, coming to look out the window. As she and Keith stood watching, a man came around Sarah's house and down the walkway to the gate and let himself out.

"I don't know that man. What would he be doing at Sarah's house? I'd better go over there and find out who he is and what he's doing around her house."

Hannah started drying her hands on a paper towel preparing to go, but Keith grabbed her shoulders.

"No you're not. You can't let anyone see you. I'll call Steve and have him check it out. In fact that may be a good idea. We could kill two birds with one stone. Steve can come out in his patrol car and get David Shortt to bring your car out after dark. We can't all ride to the farm in your car and take your luggage too, so this will work out perfect." Keith stood grinning down at Hannah.

"You would have gone over there, wouldn't you, and without one thought about your own safety?"

"Sarah is my dearest friend. I can't let somebody destroy her house and just stand watching,' said Hannah, trying to lean closer to the slit in the drapes that covered the window.

"You can't see anything else unless you get closer, which you shouldn't do. You might be seen. The man is gone anyway, but what would you have done had you gone over there?" Keith looked at her in a questioning matter.

"I would have asked what his business was," retorted Hannah.

"Hannah, surely you aren't that naïve. Do you think that man would stand and play nice so you could get a good look at him?" Keith laughed.

Hannah wheeled around and stalked toward the living room. "Freddie, are you almost finished packing?" She called loudly. "I need your help."

"Let Freddie finish and I'll do whatever you need," said Keith, turning back from the window and crossing the living-room.

"Why sure you can help, since I'm too stupid and naïve to do things right," replied Hannah sarcastically.

"I'm sorry, Hannah. I said that wrong, but it makes me uneasy to know you are so quick to jump into danger just because someone is your friend," said Keith.

"So you are a 'fair-weather' friend are you? I don't call that a friend at all." Hannah snapped and left the room, passing Margie on the way.

"What did you do to ruffle her feathers?" Margie asked.

"Just the usual 'foot-in-mouth' goofs that I make around Hannah Larkin," said Keith with a grimace." I'm getting nowhere fast with that woman."

"Why don't you slow down a bit and be just a friend. From what Freddie tells me, Bill had been treating her pretty badly for over two years. So, I think she is disillusioned and wary of any man," said Margie.

Keith shrugged his shoulders. "I guess you're right, but it is hard. I've been badly bitten with the love bug or had you already noticed?"

Margie grinned as Freddie came through the door. "Freddie noticed, didn't you, Freddie?"

"Noticed what? Don't tell me I missed another clue in this tangled mess." Freddie dropped the two suitcases he was carrying and plopped down on the sofa.

Margie laughed. "No, you didn't miss any clues nor did you miss that Keith loves your mother. Remember, you asked me what I thought this morning."

Freddie quickly looked at Keith. "I was right then. You are smitten, aren't you?"

"I'm afraid so, Freddie. Does that upset you?"

"No. Well, I don't know. I like you, Keith, and I feel you would be good to Mom, but this has all happened so suddenly. Around two years ago I thought Dad, Mom, and I were an exceptional family. Oh Dad had his dark spells sometimes and Mom and I had to tip-toe around him, but other than that we got along good."

"Then it was just like I thought, Bill and Hannah never had arguments and disagreements." Margie smiled with satisfaction.

CHAPTER 19

FREDDIE TURNED TO MARGIE WITH A sad expression. "I wish I could say they were the ideal couple, but that's not true. They had major disagreements, but Mom always gave in and went along with Dad, except for selling the farm. Dad always got really mad and would throw one of his tantrums. Then he'd go into one of his dark spells that lasted for a week or more. Both Mom and I dreaded those spells, but Mom never gave in when it was about the farm."

Freddie sat looking off into space as he shook his head. "One time Dad huffed around for about two weeks. He was so angry that time that I feared he would hit Mom and I wondered what I'd do if he did. He didn't go that far, though. Mom just kept refusing and he finally stopped harping about it."

Keith had been listening intently. "Were these dark spells more frequent lately, or worse, before he met Sabrina Draper?"

"I was in grade school the first time I remember him really going into a dark mood. It was about the farm that time and he went on and on about it. I thought he'd make Mom sell the farm and I remember crying and begging him not to sell it," said Freddie.

"From then on he hinted at wanting to sell the farm on a fairly regular basis. Neither Mom nor I would ever agree to sell it, however, and Dad would drop it for a while. He'd still bring it up about once a year or sometimes more often."

Freddie pressed his lips together in a straight seam. "Mom and I had gotten so used to it, that we mostly ignored it unless he was worse than usual. We often discussed his actions and we both felt that he wanted something to start an argument over so he could 'blow off steam' or something. Anyway, the last time he brought it up was about a year ago."

Freddie stopped and sat in a deep study and then said, "It was right after I graduated from high school when he threw the worst tantrum and he used the sale of the farm as a starting point that time. That was about the time he took on that Blennoc Project and later Mom said he was probably worried about taking on a big project like that."

Freddie looked at Margie. "I think, knowing what we know now, that he probably wanted to buy something to impress that Draper woman." This last came out in a snarl of disgust.

"Was that also when he started staying away from home so much?" asked Margie.

"I'm not sure, but I do know it was soon after I'd left home. For several months I don't really know what was happening here, but I do remember coming and asking Mom for money. I didn't think about it then, but now when I think about that night, I remember Mom looking terrible. She was thin and pale. Mom was always small, but she looked ill and now I know she was."

Freddie looked at Margie with such sad eyes that she wanted to hold him in her arms, but she didn't.

"I didn't want to leave, Margie, and probably wouldn't have, but he knocked me down and Mom came to intervene and he either knocked or shoved her down. I wanted to kill him, but Mom pushed me out the door. That's when I left since I thought it was because of me," said Freddie in a sad voice.

Margie looked at Keith and shook her head. "I would never have believed that my son could have been that kind of person. He must have inherited that violent streak from my Dad, who was too mean to live."

Both Freddie and Keith looked at Margie, hoping she would tell them more, but instead she jumped to her feet and left the room. She didn't return until Hannah went to check on her and she and Hannah came through to the kitchen together.

Dinner had been eaten and the dishes cleared away when Keith looked out the window and saw a patrol car parked in front of Sarah Preston's house. He turned toward his coat hanging on the hall tree and taking his belt, gun, and holster from beneath it began buckling it around his waist.

Coming in from the kitchen, Hannah stopped. "What is it Keith? Did you hear something?"

Keith pointed across the street. "That's Steve and I'm going to sneak around the back and get in place just in case he needs me."

An unexpected wave of fear washed over Hannah and she impulsively grasped his arm and blurted, "Keith, please be careful."

Then as if suddenly realizing what she was doing she dropped her hand and turned toward the kitchen again.

Keith looked at Margie with raised eyebrows and smiled a slow, happy smile as he started for the kitchen door.

Hannah got busy wrapping the two left-over hamburger patties and buns. She suddenly stopped and turned to Margie.

"Peep out the window, Margie. This suspense is driving me crazy. Steve doesn't know Keith is on his way and might accidently shoot him."

Margie didn't have to peep out the window. Freddie was standing with his eye trained across the street through the slight gap in the living-room draperies.

"Two men are coming around the house. The one in the front looks like he has his hands up, but it's too dark to see for sure. Oh, there's another man. That must be Keith," said Freddie and Hannah felt so relieved but wondered why.

Of course, I don't want anybody to get hurt, so it made me uneasy, she thought and finished wrapping the last hamburger.

Freddie stood watching and reporting the action. "They've put one man in the patrol car. It's leaving and somebody and . . . well, I guess Keith went with them for I don't see anybody at all, now."

"Huh! If he goes off without telling anybody he'll get told off when he comes back, if he gets back at all. We have no idea what he wants us to do and he already has a knot on his head. He strapped that gun on as if he thought he'd have to use it. What if he gets hurt?" Hannah dropped her head and started to leave the room, but stopped when Margie spoke up.

"Hannah, I don't think it would be safe for Steve to take the man in by himself. That's probably the reason Keith went with him and he couldn't come to tell us. We aren't supposed to be here," said Margie.

Her idea was seconded by Freddie. "Steve could be driving and that man could grab him from behind and choke him or cause him to wreck. I'm glad he went."

Hannah shook her head and pasted a smile on her face. "You both are so smart. I didn't think about that, but you are both probably right. I guess I'm a 'worry wart,' as Mom used to say."

Margie's phone rang. She looked at it suspiciously, but finally answered it. "Mr. Judson. Thank God it's you. We've been having some problems and have been afraid to answer our phones. Now, though, I'm afraid to hear what you have to tell me." She sat listening and there was complete silence from Hannah and Freddie.

"Tomorrow! When was that decided?" Margie had turned pale and her voice had a slight wobble.

"Will I have to go to jail?" The very air seemed to be holding its breath. Margie let out a long sigh.

"Oh, thank God. Mr. Judson, I do hope you're right. I think I would die if I had to be locked up."

Mr. Judson asked about her fear of answering her phone and where she was. "Well, I've been with Hannah Larkin and her son. We were first in Sergeant Keith McCauley's house with all the shades drawn, but we forgot and answered the phone. Then we had someone trying to break in and so we are now in Hannah Larkin's house, but we'll have to go somewhere else. We didn't know it, but this house has been watched the entire time."

Margie finally said good-bye and shut her phone down. "Well, the wait is over. My hearing is scheduled for tomorrow."

"What did Mr. Judson say? He doesn't think you'll have to go to jail, does he?" asked Hannah with fear in her voice.

Margie sighed. "Mr. Judson doesn't think so and I sure hope he is right, but I guess I won't sleep any tonight."

Freddie nodded. "We don't know where we'll be tonight, so none of us will get any sleep." He rose from his chair and came over to Margie. He stood for a moment and then impulsively threw his arms around her.

"Margie, I'll sneak out with you and we'll make a run for it, if you want to. We could go away and change our names and dye our hair. We could be grandmother and grandson and nobody would suspect a thing."

Hannah had sat watching this with mixed emotions. She was glad Freddie loved Margie, but was hurt that he'd go away and leave her all alone. That all changed when she saw Margie's face drenched with tears.

"Oh Freddie! You've made me the happiest woman on earth. You really love me, don't you?"

"Of course I love you. You're my grandmother." Then as if struck by a bolt from the blue, Freddie turned to Hannah.

"We'd have to take Mom, though. There is no way on earth I could go off and leave my Mom after all she's been through."

Margie grabbed a table napkin and swiped at her tears. "I guess we're both loved, Hannah. This precious young man has nobody to love but older women."

Hannah leaned towards them and both women hugged Freddie at the same time. "This is a group hug," said Hannah, laughing aloud, to cut it off abruptly as lights flashed against the window.

Each person looked around for a weapon. Freddie picked up the cast iron skillet, Margie grabbed a butcher knife, and Hannah snatched up a salt shaker just as a knock came on the kitchen door that led into the garage. There was total silence until Keith's voice asked, "May I come in?"

Letting out a held breath with relief, Hannah answered, "No, no, no, not by the hair of my chinny, chin, chin. You can't come in." She looked at Freddie and giggled mischievously.

All three of the armed residents gaped in surprise when they heard Keith say, "Then I'll huff and I'll puff, and I'll blow the door in."

He slowly cracked open the door to three people laughing until tears ran down their cheeks, but he was also laughing.

"You thought I was too old to remember The Three Little Pigs story, didn't you?"

"Hannah grinned. "No, but I didn't think a police officer would act silly like I was being. I just acted on a nervous impulse when I realized we weren't in danger."

Keith had such a desire to swing her up into his arms that he sounded harsh when he said, "Circumstance makes us all silly, I guess."

"Did you go to city hall with Steve," Freddie asked as he put down the skillet he had been brandishing.

"I was peeping through the window, but it was too dark to really see anything. I thought I saw two men come from behind the house and then another man came up, which I thought was you since you didn't come back in."

"It was me. I went with Steve to take Mrs. Preston's uninvited house-sitter to the clink. That worked out really well . . ." Just then there was a knock on the kitchen door. Keith walked to the door and opened it to reveal Steve and David Shortt.

"I'm glad you're here. Now we can pack up and get these folks to a place of safety." Keith looked at Hannah. "Are you ready?"

Hannah gave him a reproachful look. "We've been ready for hours and also scared out of our wits that you had gotten hurt."

Keith realized Hannah was scolding him, but she was also saying she had been afraid for his safety. This really pleased him, but he didn't know how to reply. He gave what he hoped was an apologetic smile.

Margie saw his dilemma and quickly turned to Steve. "I hope you guys have eaten. We had two meat patties and two buns left, though. "Do you want them?"

"David and I ate at Shoney's and they had fried catfish." He rubbed his stomach in a gesture of appreciation.

CHAPTER 20

KEITH PICKED UP A SUITCASE AND headed for the door and the others followed suit. Soon the three cars were packed and the two women again hunkered down in the back of the patrol car driven by Keith to prevent being seen as they passed under the street lights. David Shortt, drove away in the other patrol car and a half-hour later Freddie and Steve drove down the backstreet behind the Larkin residence in Hannah's old Ford Escort. Freddie held a flashlight and Steve drove without using his headlights since this street was more or less hidden and seldom used. As soon as he reached a main street, however, he switched on his lights and drove several miles until they came to a road that would take them back on Route 16 leading to Sophia and Mullens.

When Margie and Hannah could sit up, they sighed in relief. Hannah, however, was troubled. "Margie, I fear they will come back and destroy everything in my house."

"Do you think they will, Keith? Hannah is worried and I understand why. That's all she has of the life she and Bill had together and I'm sure she has keepsakes that can't be replaced."

I don't want her to have anything she and Bill had together, thought Keith, feeling shame as he thought it.

"I don't know, Margie. I think the break-in was probably just to get money since they didn't take anything else." Keith didn't continue since he felt his suspicions would give Margie and Hannah something else to worry about.

"I'd like to take a U-haul in there and get everything I have and move it to the farm. I'd do it tomorrow, but I want to go to Margie's hearing," said Hannah in a troubled voice.

"I think we need to all go back when it's daylight and pack everything up in a U-haul, but we need to take it someplace besides the farm for a few days. If anyone is still watching the house they would follow the U-haul and that would make the move useless."

Keith was now near the turn off to Route 54 leading to Mullens and turned toward Hannah.

"Is this where we turn off to reach the farm, Hannah? I haven't been over this way in years."

Hannah sat forward in her seat. "Turn left at that signpost. Is the sign still there? Do you see Honeysuckle Lane?"

"Yes. Is that the name of your road? Does it have honeysuckle growing along it?" Keith turned his headlights on high beam and sure enough some kind of shrub, which he supposed was honeysuckle, grew along the edge of the road.

"Somebody had to plant those if they are all honeysuckle shrubs. Did you do that, Hannah?" asked Keith.

"They're all honeysuckles, but Dad planted them the spring that we went west. Uncle Jess had to replant some of them, but now they'll probably need to be trimmed up," said Hannah.

"See, Margie. Didn't I tell you that there's no other place on earth like my farm," said Hannah with reverence. "It's like God planted a new Garden of Eden and allowed me to live in it. That's why it almost killed me to leave it."

After two more miles the house came into view and Keith stopped the car, but didn't turn his engine and headlights off.

"Hannah, it's perfect! I can see why you love it so much. If I had dreamed of a house it would look like this one. I only dreamed of land to farm and animals, but now I see that the house makes it so much better."

Keith shifted into gear and pulled up before the gate and Hannah jumped out. "We didn't have a garage. Daddy always parked his truck below the house beneath that tall Silver Maple." Hannah pointed to a tall tree outlined in the dark.

Margie, Keith, and Hannah were all standing before the gate gazing around at the beautiful scene before them. Even though shadowed by the dusky darkness it was almost breath-taking in its breadth and symmetry. Caught up in the moment they were all startled when another car came down the road and stopped behind the patrol car. With relieved sighs they welcomed Freddie and Steve as they got out and came to the gate also.

"What's the matter, Mom? Did you lose the key?" asked Freddie.

Margie turned and put her arm around Freddie's shoulder. "Keith and I were so struck by the beauty of this place. I can see why you didn't want your dad to sell it."

Hannah felt tears sliding down her face. "This isn't the kind of place that one sells. This is the home place and I'll never sell it."

Keith heard the emotion in her voice and turned to see her swipe her hand across her eyes. He looked at her and smiled.

"I can't wait until daylight. I'm sure this darkness isn't doing it justice."

"No, it isn't, but I don't know what kind of shape it's in. I haven't been over here in almost a year, but Henry Boyd, our neighbor, promised he'd look after it for me," said Hannah, stepping forward to open the gate that enclosed the front lawn.

Hannah stepped onto the board walk that led from the gate to the porch and stopped. She stood still, looking around and remembering how she had begged the Lord to let her see the farm one more time when she was hovering between life and death in the hospital. Everyone had stopped behind her and stood waiting. She turned and Keith was right behind her.

"When I was in the hospital and they thought I didn't know anything, I lay begging to see my home again and this is the sight that filled my eyes. I thought I had died and the Lord had transported me back to the place I love," Hannah said in a whispery voice, looking up at Keith.

Involuntarily Keith put his arm around her. "Oh Hannah, I didn't know your illness was that bad. I wish I could have been there."

Hannah, who had known for days that she felt more for Keith McCauley than she wanted to admit, felt so warm and protected that she didn't move for a moment. She couldn't remember ever having this feeling of being protected, even during the good years in her marriage to Bill. Momentarily she luxuriated in the warmth she felt, but suddenly realized where she was and jerked away. She looked around Keith to where the others stood waiting in front of the gate.

"I'm sorry. Come on in, but you'll have to forgive me. I've missed being able to come home again so much that, for a moment, it just got to me, I guess."

"That's all right, Hannah. We all want to stand out here in the dark, don't we, Freddie?" Steve laughed, but Margie elbowed him in the ribs and he stopped.

"I'm not quite as bad as Mom, but I'm not as old as she is," said Freddie cheekily.

Margie slapped him on the shoulder. "You better hope you look as good as your mom when you get her age."

"The women like my looks now, Margie, and look at the years I have to improve in." They all laughed and started up the steps

Soon they were all on the porch and when Hannah fumbled with the key, Keith reached for it. "Let me get that for you, Hannah. You're too excited."

The door creaked when he opened it and since there was no electricity, Steve turned on his flashlight. "There's a sofa, so I'm taking first dibs on it for my bed tonight."

"There are five bedrooms in this house, but unless the women want to share a room, you'll still have to use the sofa. You may have some mice for bed-buddies, but they may not like your taste," kidded Freddie.

"Let me borrow your light, Steve. We used to keep candles in the kitchen cabinet," said Hannah.

Keith took the light and went with her to the kitchen and soon he yelled back. "We're in luck, but I don't have a match."

Steve joined them with a cigarette lighter flickering. Soon four candles were lit and they each turned all around to survey their surroundings.

"Oh, what a beautiful cabinet! I wonder how old it is. Do you know, Hannah?" asked Margie, rubbing her hand along the ledge that supported the marble shelf in front.

Hannah looked pleased. "Daddy said that Granny Sarie bought it in an estate auction. The auctioneer told her that it originally came from England."

"I'll bet it's three or four hundred years old, don't you, Steve?" asked Keith, also examining it.

"I don't know a thing about antiques. I am interested in how much food is inside it, though," replied Steve.

Margie frowned. "Is food all you ever think about?"

Steve raised his eyebrows. "Oh no. I can assure you that food isn't the top priority in my life, but don't ask me about that, or at least not right now."

Margie felt heat rush to her face and was glad there were no lights. She quickly turned away and began examining the cabinet on another wall even though she could only see its outline.

"Keith, give me the flashlight and Margie and I will go upstairs to inspect the bedrooms so we can all get some sleep. Margie, and I suppose, you and Steve as well, will have to be in town by nine o'clock," said Hannah.

Keith handed over the flashlight and the women left the room. As soon as they were out of hearing Steve said, "I'm going back to town and take a swing by Hannah's house. For some reason, I'm uneasy about it or something. It's just a feeling, I guess, but I still want to check."

"Do you want me to go back with you? I could check on my house and at least get a shower and shave." Though the candle light didn't give a clear view, Keith was still gazing around the house and stood thinking *I'd love to get a chance to restore this beautiful place.*

Before the women came back downstairs it was decided that Keith would stay the night here on the farm and Steve would go back to town. Keith didn't like the idea of leaving Hannah way out in the country with no electricity. Both men were unsure as to whether they had been watched when they left the house in town.

"That Arnetta man had been camping out in Hannah's friend's house for a good while when we caught him. I'm thinking somebody is really interested in something in either that house or Hannah's. What do you think?" asked Steve.

"I think they were just waiting to see if Margie was there, but I could be wrong. They may be interested in both Hannah and Margie." Keith replied.

CHAPTER 21

WHEN STEVE GOT BACK TO HIS apartment he showered, but had such an uneasy feeling that he couldn't relax. Finally he went back to his car and drove to Hannah's house on Pike Lane. He lay down on the sofa and drifted into a troubled sleep. A noise penetrated his sleep and he was suddenly sitting up and very alert. He listened intently and knew the noise was coming from the garage.

Checking his gun, he crept to the door and quietly eased it open just as the silhouette of a man came through the garage door from the outside. Steve cocked his pistol and stood waiting until the man was completely inside.

He hit the light switch and the man gave a startled gasp. He turned, but at Steve's yell he stopped and thrust his hands into the air. Steve was within two feet of him with a gun pointed at his head.

"Okay officer, you got me. I was just getting my car back. It does belong to me," said the man who started to lower his arms.

"I wouldn't do that. This gun is loaded and the trigger only needs a wee bit of pressure," warned Steve, stepping forward and grabbing the man's arm and twisting it behind his back. Soon Steve had the man hand-cuffed and walking in front of him up the two steps and into the kitchen.

Steve knew he'd seen the man before, but didn't know his name. He remembered connecting his name with the nurse who had brought Margie the tainted medicine in the hospital, but the name still eluded him even though he was sure he knew the man. As he stood trying to remember, he, for some reason raked his arm across his forehead, and . . . *Ah ha! this is one of the men who had vandalized Margie Meadows' apartment and set fire to it,* he thought as his arm felt the rough edges of his stubby hair that was singed that night. Now he roughly shoved the man into a chair.

"You're Chad Rutherford, aren't you? What were you and your partner going to do when you tried to break into this house the other night, burn it to the ground like you attempted to do to the Meadows place?"

"Yeah I'm Chad Rutherford, but I didn't start that fire and it wouldn't me who you had that fight with either. That was Millard Arnetta, but he ain't such a bad guy. He's was just carrying out orders like I was."

Steve stood looking at him and then suddenly asked. "Do you know a Naomi Rutherford?" When Rutherford didn't answer, Steve said, "Nah, I don't guess you and your wife are both criminals . . . well, she's a murderess and so far I don't think you've gone that low, have you?"

Rutherford paled and shivered. "Naomi didn't intend to do that. She's a really good person who just got caught up in something she had no control over. She was forced to go to that hospital, but she was planning on pulling the wrong drip loose. I don't know what happened, but if she can get some way of doing it, Naomi will kill herself."

Steve almost felt sorry for him and silently wondered. *How did Sam Henson or Chief Donaldson get so many people scared or indebted to them?*

"How do you know Naomi? Is she your sister or what?"

"Naomi is my wife and I'd do anything to protect her." Steve knew that Naomi was the nurse who had been sent to Raleigh General Hospital to unplug the oxygen supporting Sabrina Draper.

"You wanted to know why I'm doing all this. I'm doing it for Naomi and our two girls. I've been willing to do almost anything to keep Naomi from being charged with murder. Stealing a car ain't near as bad as murder is it?" Rutherford said in defense of himself.

"You're in pretty deep, Rutherford, but we'll wait until the trial and see what else comes out," said Steve. On the night of the fire when they'd captured Rutherford they hadn't thought he was as bad as the Arnetta guy, but what neither Steve nor Keith knew was who else Henson or Donaldson had working for them.

Now Steve knew for certain that they were out to get Margie and if they had a suspicion that Margie was hidden anywhere, that's where they would be sent by somebody to murder if the need arose. Steve angrily jerked Rutherford to his feet and pushed him through the garage to the outside.

Back at the farm, Keith hadn't gotten much sleep, but at least, he knew that Hannah Larkin was safe. Of course he wanted Margie and Freddie to be safe as well, but his focus had been on Hannah. *I really love her and I don't think she cares a thing about me, except maybe as a friend*, he thought sadly.

He was relieved when daylight peeped through the living-room window and quickly rose from his bed on the sofa. He looked around briefly and saw that the room looked okay, but he couldn't wait to get outside.

From the porch he could see the distant mountains that enclosed this wide valley and smiled with pleasure when he heard a distant train whistle. *Oh this is absolutely perfect*, he thought, taking in deep gulps of the fresh, clean air.

The train whistle must have wakened Hannah also. She came almost running through the door.

"The train whistle! I heard the train whistle that always sounded as it came out of the tunnel. Did it wake you, too?"

Keith turned in surprise. "You like it too, do you? I was already awake and had just stepped out on the porch when I heard it. It is like a signal for a new day, isn't it?"

"That's the way I always felt about it, too. Can you imagine how sad it made me not to hear that sound? I've only heard it about ten times in the last twenty-five years. I lived back here, but not on the farm," said Hannah.

"If you don't mind I want to look over the place while you and Margie prepare to go to town. This place is so beautiful. I can understand you longing for it."

Keith not only loved the vista before him, but now his eyes became riveted on the picture Hannah made with that bright hair fanning out around her pretty animated face.

Hannah looked up at Keith. "It makes me happy that you like my farm and you can certainly look your fill. Margie and I will fix breakfast and call you so don't wander too far."

An hour later a breakfast of biscuits, gravy, bacon, and eggs was on the table and Freddie was sent to call Keith in. They heard Freddie yelling and sat down to wait.

"Margie, I think I'd be the happiest I've been in almost three years if you were free. I can't go back to that house on Pike Lane, not after spending the night in the place I love."

Hannah turned to Margie, who said, "I don't want to mar your happiness, Hannah. I got myself into this mess and I'll have to suffer the consequences. I still can't believe I would stoop that low; to know that Mylanta was doctored and still give it to Sabrina and not mention it. That's so opposite to everything I've believed in all my life. I thought last night that I may have inherited some of my dad's sadistic traits. Oh God, I pray that I haven't."

Hannah rushed to take Margie in her arms. "Don't cry, Margie. When this is over I would like to hear your story, but don't dwell on it this morning. You have enough to face today without reliving the past."

Margie swiped her sleeve across her eyes. "You're right. How did you get so smart at your age?" Margie gave her a cheeky grin. "I'm going to eat if those men don't get here soon."

"Let's get our coffee so it can cool a little while we wait," said Hannah, just as Freddie came through the door with Keith behind him.

"I had to climb to the top of that field that you always called 'the witching field,' before I could get him to answer. I think the field must have cast a spell on him," said Freddie as he walked into the kitchen.

Keith had such a broad grin on his face as he stepped through the door that neither woman noticed Freddie's drollery, but Keith got their attention.

"Freddie said you called it 'the witching field' because you always went there sad and came away happy. If that's so then I guess it is the witching field. I've never seen such a beautiful spot in my entire life. Why didn't your dad build his house there?"

"Dad didn't build it. My grandfather, Newton Horne, bought the land and built the house. As to why Granddad built here I don't know, except that Dad always told about carrying clothes down to the river to wash and I have thought he built here to be closer to the river." Hannah had a dreamy look on her face when she mentioned her dad.

Margie looked at the apple-shaped clock on the wall above the stove and gasped. "You people better hurry and eat. I have to be in court in a couple of hours and nobody is dressed for town."

This ended all talk of the farm as the two men wolfed down their food and the women left the kitchen in a hurry. They were soon dressed and came back into the kitchen to find it empty.

They hurriedly scraped the scraps into one plate and Hannah ran onto the back porch and tossed it all to the birds squawking in the lilac bushes beside the fence. There was no electricity to heat water, but they could have used the butane cooker to heat water as they had done to cook breakfast if they'd had more time.

Margie looked at Hannah as she put the last dish in the sink. "You'll have to do them again when you get back. That water came out of the rain barrel by the barn so wash your hands in soapy water and put some lotion on them."

"The water is good for the cattle and the garden, but it certainly isn't clean," said Hannah, liberally soaping her hands and then greasing them with the lotion.

When Keith appeared in the door, Margie said, "I'm ready except for my purse. If they put me in jail I'll send it back with Hannah.

Freddie came through the door just then, and going to Margie, put his arms around her. "Don't think negative, Margie. I can't have my grandmother in jail. I think we should all go to a higher power and ask for His help."

Margie hugged Freddie close. "You're right, Freddie. When I've thought there was no way out, God has always come to the rescue."

As they started out the door, Hannah stopped. "Keith, don't you think we should take my car? If we go in your patrol car you may be accused of abetting a criminal or something like that."

Keith stopped arrested in thought. "I have a better idea, Hannah. I'll call a friend of mine to come to that wide curve just as you turn on Route 54 and pick up you and Freddie."

Everybody rode with Keith until they were almost at the intersection with Route 16 since Keith had gotten the response he wanted from his call. "I'll take Margie on in since the news media already reported that she is out on bail."

"Yeah, that will throw anyone watching off. They'll think Margie has been hidden somewhere by you and hasn't been with me and Mom," said Freddie.

"Yes, let's do whatever we can to keep them from hurting Hannah or Freddie. I've been worried that I was putting them in danger already." Margie was on the verge of tears and hated herself for it, but until she became close to Hannah and Freddie she had nobody to care for except her secret son, Bill.

When they arrived at the curve on Rt. 54, there was a shiny new Lincoln Continental parked on the side of the road. "Oh, there's someone else here. What are we going to do?" asked Hannah.

"No, that's my friend, Nick Hart. He has another car, but only two people can ride in it. I guess you have the honor of being the first people, other than Nick, to ride in his new car."

Nick got out and walked jauntily around the car, but stopped dead in his tracks when Hannah came into view. *Wow! Keith has found an angel. No wonder he is bowled over,* he thought. He smiled and stepped toward Hannah with his hand extended.

"I finally get to meet the beauty that Keith keeps telling me about. It's nice to meet you, Mrs. Larkin, or may I call you Hannah?"

Hannah turned red, but kept her composure since he seemed so nice and he was really handsome. "I suppose it's all right since we'll be riding in your car."

Nick smiled and Keith looked like a thunder cloud as he saw the interest in Hannah mirrored in Nick's eyes. *Oh Lord, why did I forget what a flirt he is,* he thought as he turned toward Hannah. He was somewhat relieved to see that she had no such look on her face.

CHAPTER 22

HANNAH WAITED AS NICK AND KEITH walked around the car and stood talking, but her thoughts were troubled. She had never liked to ride with someone she didn't know well, but she had no choice and Freddie was with her. When Keith opened the front passenger door for her she quickly opened the back door and got in without speaking.

Keith looked at her in pleased surprise since his first thought had been, *Does she think I'd put her in the car with a criminal?* After seeing Nick's look, however, he was pleased that his friend's good looks seemed to have gone unnoticed by Hannah. He smiled as Freddie slipped into the front seat.

Keith closed the door and said, "Drive carefully Nick. One of your passengers seems nervous."

Nick looked across at Freddie who was grinning. "Well it isn't this cheeky fella beside me, that's for sure. It must be that beautiful little lady in the back." He turned to look at Hannah who was a rosy red.

"You don't need to worry. I don't want to damage my new car, so I'll not be speeding. " He threw up his hand to Keith and pulled onto the highway.

I guess both men think I'm crazy, but I have enough trouble talking to the men I know and I certainly can't do much talking to a total stranger. We could have driven my car anyway. These thoughts ran through her head as they rode along, but she soon began to relax and listen to the banter going on between Freddie and Keith's friend.

"I wouldn't have done this on the spur of the moment for anyone else but Keith McCauley. He's one of a kind and has had a lot of trauma in his life. I've known him for thirty years and I'd trust him with my life," stated Nick.

"Does he have any children?" asked Freddie.

"No. He would have been a great father, but Ursula would have died sooner if she'd had to have children," said Nick with a grimace.

Hannah wanted to hear more, but they were in the outskirts of Beckley now and the traffic was heavy. Suddenly Nick slammed on the brakes and Hannah was thrown forward so hard that hitting the back of the front seat kept her from going through the windshield. Still she blacked-out for a moment.

Freddie had on his seatbelt and the airbag came out as did Nick's. There was complete silence in the car until a police siren sounded. Nick used his free arm to open his door, causing an approaching the policeman to step back.

"Are you injured, sir?"

Nick shook his head and the policeman deflated the airbag. He helped Nick from the car just as another policeman appeared on the scene and opened the passenger's side.

That airbag was deflated also to reveal a white-faced Freddie with a bleeding nose. Before the policeman could inquire about his injuries he turned toward the back seat and asked, "Mom, are you all right?"

The policeman looked back to see Hannah gasping for breath. He jerked the back door open and peered at her. "Are you all right, ma'am?"

Hannah nodded and motioned that she wanted to get out. She was helped to the sidewalk and immediately sank to the ground before taking in the much needed air. She coughed and clutched her chest each time. She sat looking around with a wide-eyed vacant look and the policeman stooped to speak to her, but she shook her head.

"Can't you stand, ma'am?" The policeman had already called for an ambulance and now watched Hannah fearfully. The air, however, seemed to help her and she began breathing easier.

"Are my legs broken? I don't think I can stand." Hannah talked as if she was speaking of someone else. The policeman wanted to put her in the car where he thought she'd be more comfortable, but fearing she may have injuries he waited at her side.

"Freddie? Where's Freddie?" she gasped as she turned frightened eyes toward the passenger seat of the car. Freddie, with the help of the policeman, had untangled himself and put pressure on his bleeding nose and now turned toward Hannah.

"Are you hurt, Mom? I'm surprised you weren't thrown through the windshield."

Hannah tried to smile. "I just had the breath knocked out of me, but I think I'm all right unless my legs are broken. I'll probably be too sore to move tomorrow, though."

Suddenly realizing that Freddie was covering his nose and mouth she reached toward him.

"I'm all right, Mom. It's just a nose-bleed and a few scrapes. I think I was hurt more by the airbag than I would have been without it," explained Freddie, who then turned to the policeman. "Are her legs broken? She says she can't stand".

Just then Nick and the other policeman came around the car. "The airbag saved this man's life. He hit the brakes so hard that I'm surprised the steering-wheel didn't go right through him."

"I'll bet it would have if the airbag hadn't inflated," said Freddie.

A crowd had gathered and a woman came up to the policeman.

"I saw it all. A light blue Dodge Sprint ran a red light right in front of this fellow. I'm surprised it escaped being hit. It didn't stop, though. There was a young man driving and some other people were in the car."

"How do you know it was a Dodge Sprint, ma'am?" The policeman had a notepad out and was busy writing.

"Because I have one myself, except mine is light green."

The policeman turned to his partner. "I think these people need to be checked out at the hospital and I'll get the information from this witness." He walked around the car.

"The car isn't hurt, so if they don't mind, you can drive them to the hospital."

The policeman looked at Nick. "I'll have to drive. You're certainly not in any condition to drive right now." Nick nodded in a bemused manner.

Soon Nick, Freddie, and Hannah were back in Nick's new car again, but this time Freddie and Hannah were in the back seat. Before they pulled out the policeman drew a hand-held recorder from his pocket.

"Do you people mind if I ask you about the accident and record it? I can't drive and write and this will just save time."

Still in a shocked daze, Hannah's thoughts were of being late for Margie's hearing. Turning to look at Freddie, she said, "I'm fine with that if you guys are. Is it okay for him to record our information?"

So, by the time they arrived at the ER at Raleigh General Hospital most of what had happened had been repeated in three similar versions and they were ushered into the treatment areas. The three of them were sitting on a row of benches against the wall with Hannah in the middle. She turned to Nick.

"Mr. Hart, can you call Keith and tell him what's happened. We wanted to be at the courthouse for a hearing for our friend Margie Meadows."

Nick fished his phone from his pocket and soon had Keith on the line. When he said accident, they all heard Keith's loud, "Is Hannah hurt?"

Nick grinned and looked sideways at Hannah. "She says she isn't, but she got the breath knocked out of her and can't stand on her feet so they want to check us all out. Freddie has a nose bleed and a few scrapes."

Nick listened for a few minutes. "Well since you are so concerned, I'm bruised, but I don't think I'm hurt too badly. I don't know about bringing Hannah on to the courthouse. I know I can't if she has a broken leg even if we are allowed to leave the hospital in time." Nick listened a moment longer and then ended the call.

"That's the first time in ten years I've known Keith McCauley to be that concerned about a woman. You've got a fine man interested in you, ma'am. I hope you appreciate it."

Hannah grimaced. "I didn't ask him to be concerned about me, Mr. Hart. In case you don't know it, my husband was the man murdered in this court case and they still haven't discovered who actually did it. I'm not interested in Keith McCauley or any other man."

Nick jerked back. "Whoa! I'm sorry, ma'am. I can see why Keith is concerned. I guess I got the wrong impression."

"Mom appreciates Keith and so do I, but she has been through a lot in the last few years, which has made her hyper-sensitive, I think. She didn't mean to cut-up at you, Nick," said Freddie apologetically.

Hannah realized that she had been rash in her statement and turned to Nick. "Forgive me, Mr. Hart. I shouldn't have said all that. Keith has been a really good friend through all this and I really do appreciate it."

Nick nodded and smiled. "Prove it by dropping that Mr. Hart business. I'm Nick and like I said, Keith McCauley can't be beat for a friend and I'm honored that he is mine."

"I'm sure you're right about Keith, Mr . . .Nick. It's just that several people have made comments about me and Keith and it makes me feel like . . . well, like I'm being unfaithful to my husband."

Nick turned to look at her. "Oh, sorry, I didn't know. I understand and I was probably a bit premature."

"A decent woman doesn't stay married for twenty some years to one man and then as soon as he is buried begin another relationship, or at least I can't," said Hannah. Nick turned an appraising look in her direction. Again she thought he was really nice looking. *Bill was nice looking also but men can't be trusted whether nice looking or not.*

CHAPTER 23

THEY WERE STILL WAITING TO BE seen when Nick's phone rang again. Nick said hello and then mouthed, 'It's Keith."

"We're still here. No, we haven't been seen. I will if they want to come. Wait, I'll ask." Nick looked at Hannah and then Freddie.

"Do you two still want to go to the hearing after we've seen the doctor if we're allowed? Keith says they haven't started yet?"

"I would like too, but . . ." just then a nurse came and took Nick away. As he left he told Keith he'd have to call him back and ended the call.

"Do you want to go on to the hearing, Freddie? I do, but I wish we had brought our car," said Hannah, wincing as she turned toward him.

"Mom, you have a blue place right above your eye. Does it hurt?" asked Freddie, peering closely at Hannah's face.

Hannah grinned. "Well, your nose is swollen and turning blue so you don't look too good either. It may not be a good idea for us to go show Margie our battered faces. She has enough on her plate right now."

Before Freddie could reply, Hannah was called away or rather wheeled away since she still had trouble getting to her feet. She looked back at Freddie and smiled. "I guess we'll meet back here unless they decide to operate."

Freddie nodded, but as soon as Hannah was out of sight he put his hand to his nose and moaned. *I'm glad I don't have a mirror*, he thought. *If I look as bad as I feel it would probably scare me to death.*

Freddie was soon led away as well and they did not see each other again until an hour later. Freddie had a bandage over his nose, Nick had one arm in a sling and was bandaged around his chest, and Hannah was brought back in a wheelchair.

When the nurse had parked the wheelchair, Hannah looked at Nick and Freddie as she shook her head in amazement. "I don't think this motley crew should go to the courthouse today. We look awful . . . Well you and Mr. Hart look awful, but I don't have a mirror."

"Please drop that Mr. Hart bit will you? When two people wreck together and survive I think that leads to first name basis, don't you, Freddie?" Nick was trying to smile, but Hannah could tell it was painful.

"Are both your ribs and arm broken?" asked Hannah.

"I feel like every bone in my body is broken, but I'm told that I'm just all bruised and my arm has a muscle pulled. The doctor acted like I'd won a prize since I didn't have more injuries, I guess. He slapped me on the back so hard I yelled, 'hit me a little harder so I'll pass out.'"

Nick had a wonderful white-toothed smile and Hannah was glad none of his teeth were knocked out.

Hannah smiled at the droll description of his treatment. "I was treated better than that. I was lifted and placed tenderly in this wheelchair. See it's padded and everything. The only drawback is that the doctor thinks it will be my home for a few days. It seems that I did something to some ligaments and some other things that I can't remember their description. I know that right now I can't get on my feet without screaming."

Nick raised his eyebrows. "Well, for God's sake don't do that. I can't help you, and Freddie won't be able to see you, not much longer anyway." He touched Freddie's shoulder.

"That airbag did a job on your nose. I'll cut those things up just as soon as I'm able. That'll teach them not to go around breaking noses and things like that."

Freddie tried to laugh, but grabbed his nose and moaned. Hannah rolled to his side. "Your nose is broken, isn't it?"

Freddie nodded and shook his head. "I guess it could have been worse. It could have been my neck."

Seeing Hannah's alarmed look, he said, "That's what the doctor said, Mom. He said, depending on the impact, that people often sustained broken necks and collar bones."

Nick's phone rang again. It was in his right pocket. He tried to reach around with his left hand, but it was too painful. He turned to Freddie. "Reach in my pocket and get the phone. I certainly can't do it."

Freddie tried but couldn't move his neck and couldn't see very well for the swelling. "Mom, you'll have to do it. Nick. I'm sorry."

Nick went around to Hannah who had turned scarlet in the face. "I can't put my hand in a strange man's pocket."

"I'll hide my eyes and stand in front of you so nobody can see you. Besides we're drawing a lot of attention with the phone blaring," said Nick, backing up close to her.

Hannah hesitantly put her hand into his pocket, grasped the phone and yanked it out as if it was molten metal. She handed it to Nick, but wouldn't look up.

"We couldn't get to my phone. No, man, we're invalids. Freddie's nose is broken, my arm is in a sling and my ribs are bandaged, and Hannah is in a wheelchair. No, Keith, I haven't talked to her doctor. She said something about ligaments and not being able to get up and down for a while." Nick sat listening.

"No, none of us will be able to drive. A policeman drove us to the hospital. You'll need to send somebody to drive us home. Yeah, I suppose. The waiting room isn't very comfortable, but we've been here for hours already, so just take your time. No wait, not to worry. I'll call Dad and Mom. They can come out here, then Mom can drive their car and Dad can drive us in mine."

He ended the call and turned to Freddie and Hannah. "How would you two like to visit my Mom and Dad?"

He registered the shocked look on their faces. "Keith says the accident and the picture of the car is in the paper and on television and it wouldn't be safe for you two to be taken back to the farm. So, Keith thinks you and Freddie should go to Mom and Dad's place."

With eyes widened in shock, Hannah gasped. "We don't even know your parents."

Nick grinned. "Well, you didn't know me three hours ago and, you've just searched my pockets." Nick laughed when Hannah's face lit up like a flame.

"I . . . I had no choice, you ..." stuttered Hannah.

"Oh, Hannah, you are adorable. I don't think I've ever met a woman who looks so beautiful when she's embarrassed." He turned to Freddie.

"Has your mother always been this beautiful?"

Freddie mumbled. "I can't see her too good right now, but I've always thought she was beautiful."

"For goodness sakes, stop this foolishness and tell me why we can't go back to the farm," said Hannah in exasperation.

"Mom, we are crippled, maimed, done in and we can't stay out there with no electricity, no water, and . . . do you see what I mean?"

Hannah dropped her head. "Okay, carry on, Jeeves. Call the parents."

In a short while, a tall white-haired gentleman and a small silver-haired lady came through the door. They stopped when they saw Nick.

"You're rather stove-up, aren't you?" Albert Hart, Nick's father, said in an awe-stricken voice.

"We saw the news and started to come down town, but then you got out of the car and I saw you were all right," said his mother, looking at Hannah and Freddie.

"He looks like he got the worst of the deal. Is your nose broken, son?"

Freddie nodded and she could tell he was too miserable to talk. She turned to Hannah. "Do you have any broken bones, young lady?"

"No, ma'am, I only have pulled ligaments and something else. I think I was in shock or too groggy while I was being examined for I can't remember what else was said."

"Albert, let's get these people home so they can lie down and rest," she said.

"We have to wait on the doctor, Mom. He said he'd be out here in about thirty minutes, but that's been almost an hour ago," said Nick.

Albert Hart went back to the nurse's station and soon a doctor came out. "Hello, Mr. Hart. I expected you to be here before now. What kept you?"

Mr. Hart laughed. "Minnie saw Nick get out of his car on TV, so we knew he was alive. That was his new car and he cares more for it than anything else on this earth. I thought he'd have taken off down the street trying to find that kid or whoever it was that caused him to crash."

Seeing the martial gleam in Nick's eyes, his mother said, "What do we have to do to get these people home? They are in need of a long soak in a warm tub and a good sleep."

"What about the Larkins? Who is coming to get them?" asked the doctor.

"We'll take care of them also. So, just release them in our care. She looked at Hannah and Freddie who were both sagging in their chairs.

"Poor things, this isn't where they expected to be when they started out this morning, I'm sure."

CHAPTER 24

EVEN THOUGH MOVING WAS VERY PAINFUL, the three invalids were soon in two different cars ready to pull away from the hospital. Before Albert pulled out, however, he drove alongside his wife's car and let down his window.

"Minnie, wait a second. I want to pull down that sunscreen on the passenger side so your passengers can't be seen. Also, it will be safer if you take the back roads just in case someone is on the lookout."

Minnie looked at her husband as if he'd lost his mind. "What are you talking about? Am I hauling criminals? If not, why do I need to be so secretive?"

Albert shrugged his shoulders. "Nick insists that you do what I asked. He said he'd explain later, so let's get them home. He assured me that they are not criminals." Without any other comment, Albert came and put the screens down and returned to his own car.

Hannah was seated across from Minnie in the passenger seat and winced with every breath from her pain. Still she tried to explain. "Mrs. Hart, we . . . my husband, Bill Larkin, was murdered and . . . somebody thinks we know something, but . . ."

Minnie leaned over and patted Hannah's hand. "Stop dear, I can see it is very painful. I can wait." From there on to the Hart mansion there was complete silence except when Hannah tried to turn to check on Freddie, and found it to be too painful, so instead she asked, "Freddie, are you all right?"

"Sure, Mom, I feel like dancing." Freddie gritted his teeth to stop the scream that was on the verge of erupting, but hoped his joking manner would ease his mother's worry.

After an eternity, or so it seemed for Hannah, they pulled to a stop beside a stone edifice and Minnie Hart slid a card through an aperture on the stone's wall and then drove on to the driveway of a house, the likes of which Hannah had only seen in movies or when driving through the better residential sections of big cities. Her eyes widened in amazement.

"Why did you bring us here? I don't even know where I am," said Hannah.

Minnie turned to look at her as she opened the door. You're in Beckley, but on the outskirts. This is Glade Springs Village. It's a gated community and probably the safest place you can be until all this is settled.

"Well, if we have to be kept hidden, this is the place I want to be hidden," said Freddie, making a grotesque smirk when he tried to smile.

Soon, Albert, who hadn't taken the back roads, was at the passenger side to help Hannah out. "I'll get her wheelchair, Minnie, while you help her son out. I think Nick can make it by himself.

It wasn't easy, but soon both Freddie and Hannah were inside the house and seated, Hannah still in her wheelchair, facing a beautiful mantle above a fireplace surrounded by marble.

"I think a shot of brandy will do all three of you good, how about it, Nick?" Albert was standing beside a bar on which glasses, decanters, and all the necessities for a cocktail party were in place.

"I certainly want one, but I don't know about Hannah." Nick looked at Hannah who was sagging in her chair, but roused to shake her head.

"I don't think I should. I've never tasted alcohol in my life and I hope Freddie hasn't, but I don't know."

"I won't give you enough to make you drunk, Mrs. Larkin. Brandy makes you sleepy and you all look as if sleep is what you need right now.

"Fix me one, Mr. Hart. I've had a few drinks before and I know brandy is good when people have had something traumatic happen to them," said Freddie, whose voice came out as a nasal twang.

"Good boy," cheered Nick. "You'll feel much better in the morning and so will your mother." He sat looking at Hannah and suddenly continued. "It just doesn't seem right. I mean, Hannah being your mother. You look as old as she does, but she's much prettier."

Albert looked at his son and groaned. "Nick, Nick, do you think this is the time or the place for that?"

"That? What? I'm only stating a fact that I'm sure Hannah has heard many times before now," said Nick.

"Albert, your son is a fake. He isn't hurt. If he was very bad he wouldn't be trying to chat up the ladies," said Minnie, smiling at Hannah. Hannah was so sore and ached so badly that none of their comments registered.

Albert nodded his head in Hannah's direction. "I'll get Mildred to help Hannah to bed. What about you, young man, would you like to lie down as well?"

"Call Mildred, Albert, but tell her to send Jane upstairs to get the beds ready first."

"Someone will have to carry her," said Minnie as she rose to her feet.

"I'd be glad to do that, Mother, but I think I'll wait a few days," said Nick and grinned at his mother's glare.

"If you think you're sore now just wait until the morning. That's when the pain and soreness will be its worst," said Albert as he turned to leave the room.

Soon two men came through a door to the right and with one on each side of her chair, carried Hannah up the stairs. Nick and Freddie followed and soon they were all in their rooms. Mildred, the maid, stayed to help Hannah undress and get into the bed.

The Harts had just started to relax when their doorbell rang. Terrence, the butler, opened the door and Sergeant Keith McCauley stepped into the room.

"I'm sorry to intrude without calling, but I couldn't get an answer from Nick. I went by the hospital and was told that Hannah, uh . . . Mrs. Larkin, was released in your care. Is that correct?"

Mrs. Hart looked at her son's friend since kindergarten and smiled. "Well, come on in and sit down, Keith. You don't need to be so formal with us."

She waited for Keith to get seated and then said, "She's upstairs in bed, Keith. We thought this would be the safest place for her and her son since it is a gated community and nobody would make a connection between the Larkins and us."

Keith seemed to instantly relax. "I think you're right, Aunt Minnie. I didn't know where she had been taken and her son, too, of course. I knew she couldn't stay at the farm until the utilities are hooked up and I didn't know how badly she was injured. Do you think she's all right?"

"The doctor said bruises and pulled muscles or ligaments, but not broken bones. She's supposed to use the wheelchair for a few days due to something in her back, but after that she will presumably be all right."

Minnie offered this information in order to note Keith's reaction. She saw what she hoped she'd see. She knew that Keith and Nick were friends from childhood and if Hannah had caught Keith's attention she felt Nick would look another way, or at least she hoped he would.

Keith seemed to relax. "Thanks so much. I've been worried about where to take them since Nick called me about the wreck. I think this is a safe place for her.

Albert looked at Keith. "Would you like a drink? I know you like gin and tonic."

"No thanks, Uncle Albert. I think I'll quit alcohol altogether. Lots of people relax without it and I'm going to test that out," said Keith and Minnie Hart stored that bit of information away as well. Hannah Larkin had said she had never tasted alcohol and now Keith had decided he didn't want it either.

"Do you think the car that caused the accident was a planned set-up or just a group of kids out joy riding?" Albert had taken a seat across from Keith.

"I'm not sure," said Keith, thoughtfully. "This case has taken so many unexpected turns that I sometimes wonder if we'll ever untangle it all. We thought with the chief and Sam Henson in jail that the case was sewed up, but it isn't."

"You were at the Grand Jury hearing on Margie Meadows, weren't you?" asked Albert.

"Yes and I hoped that today would be the last day that we would have to keep a watch over Margie, but Judge Wilson became ill with a virus or something and the hearing was halted until Monday." Keith was tired and he'd been worried about Hannah all day and now it showed in his face.

"Keith, have you had dinner? We've eaten, but I'm sure Peggy has left something in the refrigerator that's fit to eat," said Minnie.

"No thanks. I've not eaten, but I need to check in with my partner, Steve Hammer, and we'll probably grab a bite somewhere. If you all don't mind, I'll call in the morning to see how Hannah is."

Albert saw him out and on the steps in front of the house they both stopped. "Keith, are you interested in Hannah Larkin?" asked Albert with a very intent look.

Without hesitation, Keith said, "Yes, sir, I am. I, at first, thought I loved Ursula, but I think I was too young to know what love was all about. With Hannah there is a connectedness that I've never felt before in my life. I don't know whether she feels that way or not, but if she doesn't, I'll still care for her."

CHAPTER 25

WHEN ALBERT RETURNED TO THE LIVING room, his wife gave him a questioning look. Keith McCauley was like another son to them and had been from the time he and Nick were in kindergarten together. To Keith they were Aunt Minnie and Uncle Albert, but they were not really related.

Keith's dad had been at West Virginia University with Albert Hart. Keith's mom had been Minnie Draper Hart's best friend from kindergarten until the day she died in a fatal plane crash.

"I knew you were worried, Minnie, so I just asked him and there was no hesitation at all. He is truly interested in Hannah, but he doesn't think she feels anything for him except friendship."

"Men! How is the poor girl expected to feel anything for another man with her husband being buried such a short time ago?"

Albert looked at his wife. "I may not know much, but I do know that he'd better make it clear to Nick. Did you notice that Hannah's every movement or word was noted by our son?"

Minnie sighed. "Yes, I did. That's what has me worried. I'd love to have him home for a while, but don't you have a deal you need settled in China or Australia?"

"Not right now, but I don't think he'd take it on, even if I did. He was already tired and wanting to stay home for a while and meeting Hannah seems to provide the extra reason he needed."

Albert returned to the seat he had vacated when he saw Keith to the door. He looked at his wife with a furrowed brow.

"I know Nick is a notorious flirt, but I've not seen him act so taken by a woman in years, well, not since Beth left him at the altar. I thought, at the time, it was the extreme embarrassment he felt, but it must have been much more than that. Since then he hasn't seemed to trust women at all and I was beginning to think he never would." They both sat pondering the 'what ifs' of the situation and not coming up with satisfactory answers.

"Well, let's go to bed, maybe our dreams will yield a solution," said Minnie, rising to her feet. Albert followed her and soon there was silence in the Hart Mansion, but Nick wasn't asleep. He was thinking about his reaction to Hannah Larkin.

She is certainly a beautiful woman and I love her glorious hair, but women know they can use men and that's what they do. I'll bet she's just like all the others once you get to really know her. Nick's thoughts went around and around, but stopped when he thought of Keith.

If Keith's interested in her then I'd better get these thoughts out of my head right now. Life dealt him a rougher deal than it did me, thought Nick worriedly. Nick tried to turn over but his chest hurt too badly so he lay there trying to sort out the reason for his attraction to Hannah Larkin.

Hannah, lying down the hall from Nick, had no such problem. The brandy, coupled with whatever she had been given at the hospital, plus the trauma, was a strong sleeping potion and she was taking full advantage of its benefits.

Meanwhile, Keith McCauley had also taken note of Nick's interest in Hannah when he met them on Route 54, and now he was worrying away at what might be the consequences.

Nick is a wealthy man, nice looking, and a really good friend, but if he develops an interest in Hannah I don't know if we'll still be friends or not, thought Keith as he drove to meet Steve Hammer.

Keith pulled into Shoney's parking lot, where Steve had said they'd meet, with Hannah Larkin still on his mind. The outside lighting wasn't very bright and Keith stood for a few seconds searching for Steve's car. He sighed in relief when he saw it parked not far from his on the end row.

Now his thoughts had turned to the death of Hannah's husband which was yet another piece of the puzzle he had been trying to piece together all day. He felt that if he could tie all the different pieces of evidence, that had been uncovered, together he would know who had actually put the poison in the Mylanta that Bill Larkin had drunk.

If he hadn't been so worried about Hannah, after he learned about the accident, it might have been easier to study the ins and outs of this case, but right now he was as much in the dark as the first day it had happened. Now, he had other worries . . . He didn't really know how badly Hannah had been hurt, but another worry was Nick's reaction to her.

God, *I wish I hadn't asked him to drive her to the courthouse*, he thought morosely. He shook his head as if to clear the cobwebs from his brain.

He knew that having Margie's hearing over with would take some of the worry from Hannah's mind and also the mind of Inspector Steve Hammer. Today would have settled it, but nobody had expected the judge to get a virus which caused another delay.

Keith turned to lock the patrol car, intending to enter the restaurant when his attention was caught by a man acting in a peculiar manner. The man was sneaking along the row of cars where Steve's was parked. Keith unsnapped the holster flap on his gun belt and in a hunched over manner slid silently behind his own car and inched along behind the row of cars leading to Steve's car. About three feet from Steve's car he raised back to his natural height just as a swishing sound came from that direction. His eyes swiveled from left to right and saw the same suspicious-acting man walking away from Steve's car. He jumped to the front of the row of cars and yelled, "Halt."

The man's head jerked around and seeing Keith with a gun in his hand, he instantly put his arms in the air. Keith heard a clink of metal hitting the asphalt as he walked forward.

"Pick up whatever it was you just dropped and don't try any funny stuff," ordered Keith. Before the man could do anything, a crowd of people came out of the restaurant. Keith feared that the man would make a dash for it and someone might get hurt. He quickly reached the man's side and putting the gun to his back ordered him to move forward, intending to get him to the side of the restaurant and out of sight.

"Hold on there, officer. What'd he do? You can't arrest a man for nothing. I saw him walking toward the restaurant when you popped up and started yelling with that gun pointed at him," said a tall, burly, dark-skinned man.

"Look what I found! A switchblade knife! Did he drop this, officer?" This came from a petite older lady holding out the blade toward him by the handle.

God, please help me, thought Keith as he saw the dark-skinned man moving toward him. Then a voice spoke up from the doorway of the restaurant.

"Okay folks, go on about your business or you could be charged with obstruction of justice." Steve Hammer took in the situation at one glance and soon stood facing the tall, dark-skinned interceder.

Steve looked at the man and asked. "Is the man my partner has detained a friend of yours?"

The man with Keith's gun prodding his back blurted, "Tell him. Raymond. You know I didn't want to do it, but . . . He didn't get any farther. The tall man lunged at him with fists flying, knocking him backwards into Keith who lost his footing as they both toppled to the ground. Keith's gun went off with a loud bang.

The tall man turned to take on Steve who stood ready. His right fist shot out, stretching the man full length on the asphalt and knocking the lady with the switchblade down as well. She let out an ear-splitting scream that centered the crowd's attention on her. This gave Steve time to step over the man Keith had arrested and help Keith to his feet.

"Are you hurt?"

Keith shook his head. "No, but if you hadn't arrived just as you did I think I would have soon been hurting."

The elderly lady had been helped to her feet and she again offered the switchblade. Steve took it from her and thanked her before again ordering the crowd to disburse. Soon the parking lot was much emptier than it had been twenty minutes before.

Keith had pulled the man on the ground to his feet and handcuffed him before helping Steve do the same for his assailant, who shook his head like a wild bull and started hurling all kinds of obscenities at the man who had blurted his name. With guns at the ready, Steve and Keith moved the two men toward the side of the building where the light was dimmer. Hoping their guns wouldn't be so obvious, but their captives would still be under control, they moved as close to the building as possible. Once there, Steve put in a call to the station for a patrol car.

"What did this man do, Keith?" asked Steve, pointing to the man in front of Keith.

"I'm not sure, but I think he slashed your tires." Keith gave the man a threatening glare.

"Why were you slashing his tires?"

The man looked away from him toward the man he had called Raymond, and said, "I don't know."

"Are you telling me that Raymond told you to do it, but didn't tell you why?" Keith put his gun barrel closer to the man's chest.

"Don't shoot me. I really don't know why. He . . . I was just told to do it." He looked at Raymond and turned whiter than he already was. Even though dim, the outside entrance light for the restaurant shone directly on his face.

"Shut up, you stupid idiot. Running your lip will get you killed and you know I'm telling the truth. The boys have a way of finding people."

The man called Raymond started to step forward but stopped when he felt the bore of Steve's gun against his neck.

"Unless you want your jugular vein full of holes, you'd better not move again, Raymond."

"I'm not moving now, but I know some people that will be moving in a few minutes," he threatened, looking up the street where two cars had signaled to pull off.

Steve glanced to the side and saw the cars as did Keith. They instantly grabbed their prisoners and getting behind them with their guns against their backs they stood waiting. Suddenly shots rang out and the man Keith held screamed.

"Don't shoot! Don't shoot! I done what Raymond told me to. I swear I did." He didn't get to finish as other shots rang out.

Steve's man had been shot as well, but only winged. He yelled. "You damn fools, I'm Raymond. Don't you know what you're doing?"

This produced another volley of shots and Raymond slumped to the ground and Steve fell to the ground as well and lay still behind Raymond's body. More shots would have been fired, but the police siren was heard and the cars careened out of the parking lot with tires squealing.

Sergeant David Shortt jumped from the first patrol car and ran to Keith who he saw on the ground.

CHAPTER 26

"KEITH! KEITH! ARE YOU ALL RIGHT?" Sergeant David Shortt asked as he bent over Keith. When there was no answer or movement, David fell to his knees and pressed his ear against Keith's chest. Hearing a faint but steady beat, he raised his head and hit the emergency button on his phone. The light was so poor that he feared moving Keith and decided to check on the man in front of him. He got no response and heard no heart beat. Still he felt his pulse and it too was absent.

Another patrol car sped into the parking lot and it was the trooper in that car that discovered Steve. The heavy dark-skinned man was lying almost on top of Steve, but when the patrolman rolled the man off him the trooper was stunned to hear a murmured, "Thanks."

"Are you injured?" asked the patrolman, bending down to look at Steve.

"I feel like my skull is cracked, but I don't think I'm hurt anywhere else," mumbled Steve as he tried to sit up. The patrolman helped him to sit up and Steve slowly moved his head.

"No wonder I cracked my skull with this big bruiser falling on me. At least he took the shot instead of me." Suddenly he remembered that Keith was there and tried to get up.

The patrolman put his hands on his shoulders and eased him back down. "I don't think you should get on your feet until the medics get here. Our dispatch said there was a lot of gun fire," said the patrolman.

"Where's Keith . . . Sergeant McCauley? I came out to help him. Where is he?" asked Steve in a panicky voice.

"He's over here, Steve," yelled David Shortt. "I think he's been shot, but he's still alive. The light's too dim for me to tell much about him, but I can hear a heartbeat and he has a pulse."

By this time Steve was on his feet, but was very dizzy and had a terrific headache. *Thank God, Keith's alive, but he may have serious injuries*, thought Steve, swaying on his feet.

About that moment he began sliding toward the ground again, but the siren of the ambulances was heard. The patrolman caught Steve before he fell full length on the concrete pavement and gently eased him down to the ground.

They loaded Steve in the first ambulance along with the man they recognized as a Pakistani man who worked in a Club right off I-77. The second one moved in nearer to Keith's position.

With the brighter light of the powerful torch carried by the ambulance, they could see that the man lying in front of Keith was riddled with bullet holes and so they stepped over him to get to Keith.

When they examined Keith, they saw that he had been shot in the left side just below the heart. "I sure hope the bullet angled down to the right. He's lost a lot of blood so get that drip going as quick as you can," ordered the EMT as he tied a tourniquet firmly in place. Soon Keith was loaded and on his way to Raleigh General Hospital.

David Shortt was really upset. "I'd like to get my hands on whoever did this. Keith McCauley is one of the finest men I've ever met in my entire life."

A voice spoke from the shrubbery under the windows of Shoney's Restaurant.

"There was a carload of them. They drove in and opened fire on everybody. I jumped behind these bushes, but was still scared I'd get hit." The voice came from a teenage boy who was still white and shaky.

David turned to him. "What's your name and did you see it all?"

"I'm Willie Drake and I did see it all. I started to leave the restaurant when I saw a man acting sneaky so I hid to watch him." The boy was shaken up and paused to get control.

"He was sneaking along that row of cars." The boy pointed with a shaky arm to where Steve's car was parked.

"He was nearing that patrol car and I thought I'd crouch low and sneak around behind some cars in that row. Then I saw a policeman and stayed where I was. The cop was slipping along behind the cars as well, but was coming this way. He was almost to the patrol car when he suddenly straightened up. There was a loud swishing sound, like air coming out fast, and then that same man that I'd been watching started to run away from the patrol car, and it was then I recognized Sergeant McCauley who yelled, 'Halt.'"

Now the boy was trembling all over and David realized he was in a bad shape himself. He patted the boy's shoulder.

"Come on, Willie, let's go inside where it is warmer and I'll get you a drink."

Soon they were seated in an isolated booth and both had coffee. "I don't usually drink coffee, but I need something warm," said Willie.

"Are you alone or is someone with you?" asked Sergeant Shortt, looking around the restaurant.

"I'm by myself. I just got off from work at Walmart and thought I'd splurge and come to Shoney's for supper," answered Willie.

"Do you think Keith will be all right? He's a really good man and I like him better than anybody I know. He helped me get my job at Walmart."

"I don't know, Willie, but I certainly agree with you. Keith is a really good man," said David soberly. "He still had a heartbeat so that's some hope."

"Will you let me know? I've never had anyone else to be nice and try to help me until him. I've seen that dark-skinned man that they said was from Pakistan in Walmart several times. I hope they find out who he was working for," said Willie as he rose to leave.

"Where are you going, Willie? If you're going home I'll give you a ride. Where do you live?"

Willie looked at David warily. He'd heard that some police officers in town liked young boys too much. He didn't want to take a chance, so he said, "That's all right, Sergeant. It isn't far to my place."

"Okay, Willie. Keep safe and I'll find you at Walmart when I find out about Keith," said David absentmindedly. His thoughts were on Keith.

He hurried to the patrol car and turned toward Raleigh General Hospital. Once there he went to admitting and asked if Keith McCauley had been admitted. The nurse looked down the list. "No, we don't have a Keith . . . oh, I guess you mean the policeman. He's in surgery, or that's what the EMT said when he was leaving."

"What about the other officer, Steve Hammer? Was he admitted?" asked David.

Again she looked down the roster. "Yes, he's in room 206 in the east wing."

"Is it too late for me to see him?" asked David.

"No, I don't think so. They didn't send down any special instructions," replied the receptionist. David hurried away to the elevators and was soon on the second floor. He asked for Steve Hammer at the nurse's station and was directed down the hall.

"The third door on the left, but you can't stay very long. He needs to rest."

When David tapped on the door and went in, Steve turned to look and then grinned.

"I was hoping you were someone bringing news of Keith, but I'm glad you're here. I don't really think I needed to stay, but the doctor insisted and here I am."

David pulled up the only chair in the room and sat down beside the bed. "Do you know how many shots were fired and who they were aiming at? This was the craziest thing I've ever seen."

Steve grimaced. "The only thing we know for sure is that one of the men slashed the tires on my patrol car and we don't know why he did that. That man was scared to death and would have spilled the beans if Raymond hadn't smashed in his face with a fist."

"There was a witness to the whole thing and I talked to him. His name is Willie Drake and he works at Walmart. According to him, he watched Keith sneak behind cars to apprehend the tire slasher, but before he got there the man started away and Keith yelled halt. The man stopped and put his hands up. Keith was getting ready to cuff him when his buddy, Raymond, came out of the restaurant and intervened and you know the rest of it."

David sat waiting for Steve to tell him more, but instead Steve put his hands over his eyes and said, "God, I have a headache. Go get the nurse, will you, David."

The nurse was in the room in minutes. "Your headache has come back, hasn't it?" Steve nodded and groaned. She turned to David and asked him to tell the nurse at the desk to page the doctor.

"This happens with a concussion, but I want the doctor to check you before I give you any medication," she said as she put a cold washcloth on Steve's forehead.

"You'll need to leave, officer, but visiting hours are over anyway. He may have these headaches for a few days but the CT Scan didn't show any abnormalities associated with a concussion. You can visit him again tomorrow if you like," said the nurse. David left, after stopping by the nurse's desk to ask if Keith McCauley had returned from surgery, to be told that he had not.

CHAPTER 27

ALTHOUGH KEITH MCCAULEY CAME THROUGH THE surgery, he had lost a lot of blood and was still in a coma. The bullet he took barely missed the aorta and in its path caused lesions in the tissue in the lung and side areas. One blessing was that the bullet hadn't actually penetrated any of the vital organs.

"He's a blessed man except for the coma. We think he fell and was knocked unconscious from the fall, and the other man falling on him kept him from regaining consciousness," explained Dr. Vector, the surgeon.

Sergeant David Shortt stood looking at the comatose body of his dearly loved friend and mentor.

"How long do you think he'll be unconscious? I mean, in cases like this, how long does it usually take for a patient to be back to normal?" David found it hard to look at the vulnerability of this strong, virile man who had gone into harm's way many times in order to save him.

The doctor sighed. "I wish I could give you a definite answer, but they are never alike. If it isn't severe he could come out of it at any time, but we have him sedated right now to keep him under. We don't want him to become restless and cause more damage than has already been done."

The doctor checked the drips and wrote on the bedside clipboard. Turning to David he said, "Are you just a co-worker or are you related?"

"He feels like an uncle or an older brother, but he is just the best friend I've ever had," said David.

"Is he married and does he have children?" The nurse was the one asking questions now.

"No to both questions. He was married but his wife has been dead for ten years or more." While he stood watching, such a grimace crossed Keith's face and David cringed with pain himself.

"Did you see that? He must be suffering terribly. Can't something be done?" Tears crept into David's eyes as he saw Keith's body give a slight jerk.

"Do something for him, dammit."

The nurse came to David's side and touched his arm. "Please let me take you to the waiting room. I believe in his mind he is trying to defend himself and even though it looks terrible it is probably a good sign."

This relieved David a little, but he knew he had to get away. He rushed from the room and sped down the stairs. Too many people rode elevators and right now he needed to get away from people. His car was parked away from other cars and when he was inside he dropped his head on the steering wheel and sobbed aloud.

After several minutes, he pulled out and drove back to the scene of the crime where he methodically combed the entire side of the parking lot with a plastic bag opened and ready.

Frequently he stooped to the ground and picked up something, using his handkerchief in order to not disturb any finger prints. He even picked up some half-finished cigarettes and a soda can that could have been tossed from the car. He started back to the car when he noticed a space where the asphalt was broken leaving a muddy spot. He walked closer and saw a very good tire tread imprinted in the mud.

David put in a call to a fellow policeman who worked in the investigative department. "Reed, are you busy on something? If you aren't, I need you to help me lift a tire tread that I feel sure will match the tread on the car from which the shots came that got both Keith and Steve."

"It's three o'clock in the morning and you want me to lift a tire tread! How can you see anything? I just stepped out a few minutes ago and it is as black as pitch out tonight," said Reed Summer.

"I'm in the Shoney's parking lot and I have a really powerful flashlight. I almost missed it and would have if I hadn't decided to check around to see if I had missed anything discarded during this massacre," said David.

"I guess I can come since Little Jim just came in to mind the store," replied Reed.

An hour later, if anyone had been watching they would have seen two policemen playing in the mud, or so it seemed, but the work they did that night would prove to be very valuable with a little more investigation.

On the outskirts of town, everyone in Glade Springs Village was still asleep except for Albert Hart. He was always the first to arise, or so Minnie said.

"Albert, you are retired. You don't have to get up at the break of dawn. You don't have a job waiting for you," she often scolded, but to no avail.

"I've been getting up at the same time since I was a boy and awoke when the roosters crowed. You and I don't have roosters, but they certainly trained me," was one of his excuses.

The morning after the wreck Albert was the first person to awake. He quietly eased out of bed not wanting to wake his wife and, donning a robe, he used the bathroom and opening the bedroom door stepped into the hall. Not hearing any noises on that floor he silently made his way down the stairs to the kitchen. He knew Mildred would have coffee ready and pushed open the door in anticipation.

Mildred was standing in front of the wall-mounted television, with the carafe of the coffeemaker in her hand.

Albert didn't speak, but also stood riveted at the television. "The two policemen are in the hospital and their two prisoners are dead," said the reporter, "but no names are being given out at this time."

"What's that about, Mildred?" asked Albert. Mildred whirled around with blaring eyes and gaping mouth.

"Oh, Mr. Hart, you startled me."

Albert reached out and took the carafe from her. "I think I did more than startle you, Mildred. You looked like someone who was about to be attacked."

She pointed to the television. "Well, that happened right here in Beckley and close to us too. Shoney's restaurant is just five miles from here. It ain't safe nowhere anymore," said Mildred as she slowly turned and made her way to the sink.

"You say something happened at Shoney's Restaurant? I heard the reporter say that two policemen were in the hospital, but he didn't give any names did he?"

The first thought that went through Mr. Hart's mind was Keith McCauley saying he would meet Steve Hammer last night and then eat. They could have met there. *I don't know Steve Hammer, but Keith McCauley is almost as dear to me as Nick,* he thought and pulled out a stool from under the bar and seated himself. He knew that with this kind of news there would soon be an update.

He was right, for twenty minutes later Chief Shortt, who had taken Harry Donaldson's place, held a news conference. As soon as the reporters were ready he began. "Last night at approximately eleven o'clock a policeman entered the parking lot at Shoney's restaurant and when he exited his car he saw a man acting in a suspicious manner. The officer apprehended the man as he was leaving a vehicle after slashing the tires. The vehicle was a police patrol car."

"Was the man armed?" interrupted a reporter.

The police chief shook his head. "Not at the time, he wasn't. He had just thrown his switchblade knife away. The officer shouted 'Halt' and the man obeyed, but then a friend of the arrested man came out of the restaurant and began questioning the officer in a threatening manner.

A federal investigator, who had been waiting for the officer, stepped out of the restaurant and saw that an assault was about to happen and intervened. Both men were then arrested and taken to the side of the building where there would be less danger of bystanders being hurt while they waited for assistance. .

"We heard that both officers were shot and the other two men were killed. Did they shoot each other?" Another reporter had interrupted since each one wanted his paper or media to get the first information.

The chief grimaced. "While my men were waiting with their prisoners, a car pulled into the parking lot and opened fire. Both of the arrested men were killed on the spot and one officer was injured but not seriously. The other officer is in a coma and I don't have the doctor's report this morning."

"Can you give us any names?" called out a reporter in back.

"Not until the families have been notified." The police chief turned to walk away when a reporter yelled. "A source told me that Sergeant Keith McCauley is dead."

Albert heard a gasp and turned. Minnie was standing in the doorway looking like she was ready to faint.

"Albert, is that true? Did someone kill Keith?"

CHAPTER 28

"I DON'T KNOW, MINNIE. I HAD just come into the kitchen when I heard the news that two officers had been shot," said Albert, to be interrupted by Mildred.

"They said one of the officers was in a coma and then a reporter or somebody said that he'd heard that Keith McCauley was dead." Mildred was now standing like a statue except for her hands, which she had put under her arms in an attempt to hold them still.

When Albert had first walked into the kitchen he had seen Mildred's condition and had taken the carafe from her trembling hands and put it on the cabinet beside the sink.

Knowing that both Mr. and Mrs. Hart would want coffee, Mildred grabbed the carafe again only to have it slip from her grasp.

When it hit the tile floor the carafe shattered into pieces that went flying in all directions. Mildred screamed and covered her face.

Minnie covered her face as well just as Nick asked from behind her, "What in the world is going on in here?"

Albert had jerked to the side as parts of the carafe sailed in his direction, but now that the danger was past he took command of the situation.

"Wait, don't anybody move until I get a dustpan and sweep up the glass."

Everyone was stunned into silence until he came back with the dustpan and began the clean-up.

"Okay, now what caused all this . . . ruckus?" Nick eased himself on through the door as his dad cleared a path and pulled out a chair.

Before sitting he glanced down and said, "Damn! I almost sat on a big piece of glass. Give me that pan."

"I'll get it. I'm afraid to turn Mildred loose with this broom. She's still shaking so badly she may knock something else down," said Albert.

"Well, in case you don't know it, Keith McCauley saved my marriage as well as little Bo's life. When I heard he was dead it tore me all up," said Mildred.

"Keith's dead! Keith McCauley! Where did you hear that? It can't be. He's the same as a brother. Turn the channel, Dad. I just don't believe it's true."

Nick was so agitated that he lurched from his chair and hobbled to the television, but before he reached it the news came on again.

"In a late night shoot out in the parking lot of Shoney's Restaurant, two men were killed and two policemen injured, but one is not thought to be serious. The other one is not expected to live, but is being cared for at Raleigh General Hospital. The names are being withheld until further notice." The reporter went on to tell more of the incident but nobody in the Hart residence was listening.

"I'm going to call the hospital. Maybe I can get some reliable information. We may be making assumptions that are not accurate," said Albert, reaching for the telephone.

When his call was answered he was told that the only information that they could give out was that one of the officers was in critical condition in intensive care.

"I'm sorry, sir, but until given permission I cannot reveal any names," said the receptionist and ended the call.

"Well, he isn't dead and that's a bit of good news," said Albert, looking at Mildred.

"Do we have another coffee pot? I need some strong coffee." This ordinary speech seemed to break the spell that held Mildred immobile.

"I'll get it, Mr. Hart. I'm sorry, but that was enough to upset anybody," said Mildred as she hurried into another room to return with another coffee-maker.

"You'll be busy for hours just making coffee with that thing. I could drink that empty by myself," said Nick.

"Albert, don't you know someone on the police force that could give you more information?" Minnie didn't try to get up after she had sat down so quickly when she first heard the news.

"We all know Keith, but we can't ask him. He was always my contact if I needed something from the police," said Albert.

They heard some kind of noise in the house and Albert quickly left the room to stop dead in his tracks when he entered the hall.

"Hannah, you aren't supposed to be on your feet. How did you get down those stairs?"

Hannah grinned. "With a lot of pain, but I made it. I can't stand to be dependent on others."

Hannah was so weak and in so much pain that she sank to the bottom step, but still looked up at Albert and smiled.

"Well, since you're already down, let me help you into the kitchen. We all gather in there for coffee every morning," said Albert as he helped her to her feet.

When they arrived in the kitchen, Nick looked startled. "Hannah, you aren't supposed to be on your feet. How did you get down the stairs?"

"Very carefully," she said with a wide smile as Albert helped her toward a chair that was beside the table.

"I'll bet she heard all the noise and came down to investigate, didn't you, Miss . . .?" Mildred stopped since she couldn't remember Hannah's last name.

"The doctor told you to use that wheelchair for several days. What if you've damaged yourself and become paralyzed?" asked Nick in a chiding voice.

Hannah didn't answer Nick, but turned to Mildred. "I did hear something that sounded like glass breaking, but I was coming down anyway. Did something break?"

"Mildred broke the coffee carafe and now we have to wait for our coffee," said Minnie, looking at Hannah who she realized was a really beautiful woman.

"Are you sure you did the right thing by not following the doctor's orders?" Minnie asked.

"Well, he didn't say that I couldn't walk. He just said it would be very painful if I did and that I should use the wheelchair for several days," replied Hannah and winced as she moved to what she hoped would be a more comfortable position.

Hannah looked at Nick. "Have you heard from Keith? He'll know what happened in Margie's hearing and I'd love to know."

Nick looked at his father and then his mother. "No, Hannah. None of us have heard from Keith, except that we know he's in the hospital."

"Hospital, Oh no.What's wrong with him?" Hannah asked, turning pale with shock.

"There was a shoot-out last night and both Steve Hammer and Keith were shot and both are in the hospital," said Albert.

"How bad is it? I mean . . . is Keith hurt . . . badly?" Hannah asked in a near whisper from trembling lips that she was trying to control.

"We don't know, dear," said Minnie, getting to her feet and coming to Hannah's side. She turned her eyes to her husband and then Nick and slightly shook her head.

"We are waiting until we have our breakfast and then my husband and Nick, if he's able, will go down to the hospital and see if they can find out and maybe get a chance to talk to him." She looked at Mildred who was busy pouring coffee.

"Bring one of those cups of coffee to Hannah. I think she needs it more than anyone right now." She stood waiting beside Hannah until the coffee arrived,

"Do you want cream and sugar, Hannah? It might be better for you with sugar in it until you stop shaking."

Hannah shook her head. "No, I don't like sugar in my coffee, but I do like cream. I need to go up and wake Freddie." Minnie shook her head and started to protest, but Hannah interrupted her.

"If Freddie is able he needs to go see if he can get in to see Keith." Hannah had a very troubled look. "Keith has been so good to Freddie even though he is the officer that arrested him when B . . . my husband was found dead." She looked at Minnie Hart.

"You may not know it, but Chief Harry Donaldson sent Keith to arrest my son for the death of his father. Freddie found him dead in the floor when he got in from work at two o'clock in the morning. Of course, the grand jury found Freddie innocent, but all during the time Freddie was in jail Keith acted like a father or an older brother to my son."

"We knew about the trial, Hannah, but we didn't watch it closely. Actually we had gone to New York to meet Nick's plane. He was returning from a trip the company sent him on to Guam in the Mariana Islands. So, we were away during most of it," explained Minnie.

Hannah looked at Nick in surprise. "I apologize, Nick. I thought you were one of those rich playboys."

CHAPTER 29

"**Oh, I'm both of those, but** I like the playboy bit the best," he said with a wicked grin.

Hannah ignored him. Minnie Hart dropped her head and grinned to see the disconcerted look on her son's face. Hannah looked at Albert.

"Do you not know anyone who can tell us something? Keith is . . . such a good friend." Just at that moment Freddie came slowly into the kitchen. His face looked terrible.

"Oh Freddie, your eye is swollen terribly. You need an icepack," said Hannah. She started to pull herself up, but clamped her lips together to stifle the groan that partially escaped and sank back into her seat. She looked up at Mildred.

"I hate to be such a bother, but do you have something to make an icepack for his eye? I'd do it myself, but I don't know where things are kept in this house."

"I sure will, Miss Hannah. I have the very thing," said Mildred as she turned to the freezer section of the refrigerator. Soon a flat icepack wrapped in a tea towel was being held in place over Freddie's eye by a makeshift bandage.

"Thanks. That feels much better," mumbled Freddie, sitting very still in the chair Albert had pulled out for him.

Seeing Nick across from him, Freddie said, "Where's your battle scars? Mom can't walk and I can't see, but you got off scot-free, it seems."

"It wouldn't be decent to show you what a wreck I am. That airbag broke a rib and I'm bruised all over, but at least I can walk around," said Nick, wincing as he moved to a better position.

"You all better be glad you ain't in the shape Keith is in," said Mildred as she pulled some bacon from the refrigerator.

"What are you talking about? Was Keith in a wreck too?" asked Freddie in alarm.

Nick looked at Hannah as if asking for approval. Hannah shook her head and turned to Freddie. "There was a shoot-out or something last night and both Steve and Keith were shot, but Keith is the only one really serious."

Freddie's eye was in such shape that nobody would have thought he could shed tears, but he did. "Oh my God! Keith is the best man I've ever met. How bad is he, Mom?"

"Freddie, we only know what's been on the news and we can't find out anything. Mr. Hart called the hospital, but they wouldn't even give a name. We don't have a contact and we don't know where Margie is or . . . Freddie, what about Steve?"

Freddie rose from his chair. "I have his cell number in my phone. I'll call Steve. If anybody will know it will be him." Freddie went as fast as he could without screaming from pain and soon was back with his phone. He handed it to Hannah.

"Here Mom, look down through the favorites and hit Steve's number. I can't see well enough to do it," said Freddie before easing himself back into his seat.

Hannah quickly found the number and soon Steve answered. "Hannah, where in the world are you? Margie has been worried sick."

"Didn't Keith tell you? Oh, no, he didn't know. No, Keith got his friend Nick Hart to meet us just before we came to the intersection of Route 16 and Route 54. Freddie and I were to ride on to the hearing with Nick so that it would be thought that Margie had never been with us," explained Hannah.

"But you never came to the hearing. What happened?" asked Steve.

"We were in a wreck and Nick's father, Mr. Albert Hart, suggested that we come home with him since he lives in a gated community. I assumed that Sergeant Shortt had told you and Keith."

"I was out of town and didn't know about this. Keith and I were to meet at Shoney's last night to fill each other in and we did meet, but we got ambushed. I'm in the hospital with a concussion, but Keith is in a much worse shape. He's still alive, but only by a thread. I'm going to go see him as soon as they let me out of this room. In the meantime, please pray for him." said Steve.

"Where's Margie?" asked Hannah from a white, tear-washed face.

"I have her hidden away in a very safe place, so don't start worrying about her, right now. I'm glad you called so that when I get to see Keith I can tell him that you and Freddie are safe. I know that you have been on his mind, if he's still alive," said Steve.

"No, don't say that," said Hannah harshly. "Keith can't die. Oh God! Keith is such a good man." Hannah handed the phone to Freddie and dropped her head into her hands.

"Mom's all torn up and can't talk right now. Will we be allowed in to see Keith if we come to the hospital?" asked Freddie.

"I don't know, Freddie, but I'll try to find out today and let you know. I'm glad Hannah called. Margie has been worried sick. Did either of you get hurt in the wreck?" asked Steve.

"They sent Mom home in a wheelchair, but she came down the stairs without it this morning. The airbag did a bad job on my eye and my nose is broken, but I think we got off lightly compared to you and Keith," said Freddie and then suddenly handed the phone to Albert.

"Steve wants to talk to you."

They talked only a few minutes and Albert handed the phone back to Freddie.

"Mom's crying. This has really shaken her up and me too. Try to get us in to see him, if you can," said Freddie and ended the call.

Steve sat twirling the phone as it lay on the bedside table. *Hannah is crying. Hmm-mm. I wonder if that means she does care about him,* thought Steve slipping his feet into his shoes that he'd found in his table drawer.

The doctor came through the door and Steve was instantly alert. "How is my friend Keith McCauley this morning?" Steve's question caused the doctor to look at him directly.

"So, you're the other patrolman. I knew there were two, but I wasn't on duty last night. You seem to be in pretty good shape. How do you feel?" asked the doctor, picking up Steve's wrist to check his pulse.

"Your pulse rate is up. What are you excited about?"

Steve shook his head. "I'm not excited, but I am concerned about my friend." The doctor made no comment but began checking his heart, temperature, nose and eyes.

"How's the headache? Concussions usually produce headaches, but with no lasting consequences," said the doctor, stepping back from the bed. "Have you been up and walking around?"

"I haven't been allowed out of this room or I would have been to see Keith McCauley," grumbled Steve.

As if suddenly making a decision the doctor said, "There's no time like the present. Get your shirt on and I'll walk you to his room."

CHAPTER 30

Although Steve had known that Keith was in serious condition, he was not prepared for the apparition that appeared when he entered the ICU unit right behind the doctor. One of the nurses saw the color leave Steve's face and quickly produced a chair.

"Here, I think you'd better sit down. We don't have another bed," she said as she gently pushed Steve into the only chair present.

Steve shook his head. "I'm all right. I just didn't realize how bad he was."

"You're weak yourself, officer, and Mr. McCauley is doing much better today," she said as she looked at Steve and put her finger in front of her lips.

Steve nodded in understanding and rose to his feet. He stepped to the side of the bed and put his hand on the only free spot on Keith's arm. "Good morning, Sergeant. Did you think I'd forgotten you?"

Keith's eyes opened at Steve's voice. The nurse quickly moved in. "Mr. McCauley, can you hear me?" When there was no response, she moved in closer.

"Sergeant McCauley, look at me, please," she said again, but Keith's gaze remained on Steve. The nurse motioned for Steve to try.

"Keith, can you hear me?" Steve watched closely and smiled at the nurse when Keith's eyelids quivered.

"I'm going to call the doctor. He wants to know of any change." When she walked out, Keith was still staring at Steve. Then he became agitated as if he was trying to say something. The doctor came through the door and also saw this first evidence of awareness.

"I think the Sergeant is trying to tell you something," said the doctor, but Keith closed his eyes.

"Maybe he wants to ask me something," said Steve and turned back to Keith.

"Is that it, Keith? Do you want to ask me about something?" Both Steve and the doctor waited as Keith finally blinked his eyes.

"Well, I'm glad you're back with us, Sergeant," said the doctor, but Keith never took his eyes from Steve. The doctor checked his vital signs and started to leave. He stopped at the door and turned to Steve.

"Keep asking him questions to see if you get any other reaction." He looked at the nurse.

"You pay close attention and make a note of what reaction he gets, if any."

Steve stood looking down at Keith whose steady gaze had never left his face. "Do you want to know what happened?" Steve watched Keith's eyes and saw no movement or anything except that stare.

"Do you want to know where Margie is?" asked Steve, but this too got the same stoic stare. Steve stood trying to think what Keith wanted to ask, but his mind was blank.

When Steve didn't say anything the nurse noticed that Keith's blood pressure was going up, an indication of frustration, and he seemed agitated. "I think he must be getting tired. Let's let him rest, okay?" asked the nurse, stepping to the bedside.

Steve patted the bare spot on his arm. "Go easy, my friend. I'll be back later and we'll try again to figure out what you want to know."

He made his way slowly from the room very disturbed to leave Keith, still not knowing what was bothering him. *Maybe he wanted to know if we caught the people that shot us*, he thought as he arrived back at his room.

Around nine o'clock his phone rang. "Steve, this is Freddie. Have you gotten to see Keith yet?"

Steve told him about his experience with Keith and Freddie said, "He knew about our accident. I'll bet he wanted to know if we were all right."

When Steve hung up he felt better. *That's what he wanted to know. Why didn't I think of that? I know he likes Hannah, but I must have been so concerned about Margie's future that I didn't realize how much he did care.* His thoughts settled and soon he was watching a rerun of Jeopardy on the television anchored to the wall.

Meanwhile in the Hart residence, Freddie reported on Keith's condition after hanging up the phone with Steve.

"Did you ask if we could get in to see him?" asked Nick.

"No, I forgot, but I can call him again if you want me to. We're in no shape to pay a visit today anyway," said Freddie.

"Freddie, did you tell Steve that Keith came out here last night?" asked Hannah.

"I didn't know he did. When did he come? It must have been after ten o'clock. That's the time I believe I finally went to sleep," said Freddie.

"It was late, Freddie. You, Nick, and your mother were already in bed when he came. He said he wanted to know how badly all of you were hurt, but I think he was really only concerned about Hannah," said Minnie Hart, smiling broadly.

Hannah blushed and shook her head. "He did tell Nick to drive carefully before we left. Did he know you were a bad driver, Nick?"

Nick grinned. "Is that why you didn't want to ride with me? I wondered why you got in the back seat."

Minnie sat watching and listening. She knew her son was adept at flirtation, but she didn't know how Hannah would react to it. She hoped that Hannah would ignore it since Nick had a record of flirting and walking away.

She smiled to herself as Hannah said, "I'd just met you and I'm uncomfortable with strangers, especially men."

"Why is that, Hannah? Has some man tried to 'chat you up'? Nick had an amused smile on his face.

"No, men don't 'chat me up,' Nick. I don't give them any reason to and to me that isn't funny," said Hannah, giving him a stony look. She turned to Freddie.

"If Steve says it's all right, you ask him if you and I can come to the hospital to see Keith and please ask him about Margie."

"Yeah, I'd like to know where my grandmother is, myself," said Freddie worriedly.

"She's probably with some family Steve knows in the Flat Top Lake Community. That's the only other secured community in this area," said Albert.

"You're right, Dad. Steve did say he had her in a safe place, didn't he? He had probably taken her there before the shoot-out occurred."

Hannah sat still in her seat thinking, *I don't want to be rude to these nice people and I allowed myself to get upset at Nick. I guess I should apologize.* She turned toward Nick and smiled.

"Nick, I hope you'll accept my apology. I was rude. I think I misunderstood your intent to make a joke."

Nick smiled. "No, I think I was out of line. I don't think I've ever met a woman like you before. You intrigue me."

Hannah looked bewildered. "I don't know what there is about me to intrigue anyone. I'm just a recently made widow of a man I'd been married to for more than twenty years."

"Did you have a good marriage, Hannah?" asked Nick and his mother gasped as did Hannah.

"Nick, you . . . ."

She didn't get to finish. Hannah's eyes blazed as she said, "That's none of your business, Mr. Hart." She arose from her chair and looked at Minnie.

"I'm sorry, Mrs. Hart, Freddie and I will go back home tomorrow. I think I don't belong here. Thanks for your kindness." She hobbled out of the room and nothing was said until they heard her climbing the stairs.

Freddie slowly rose to his feet. "I'll go help, Mom."

CHAPTER 31

"NICK, DON'T YOU THINK THAT WAS too personal? I mean didn't you just meet the woman yesterday?" scolded Minnie.

Nick looked at his mother with a speculative glint to his eyes. "If her marriage was happy wouldn't she have automatically said yes?"

Minnie had an arrested look. "Perhaps, but that isn't the point. I don't think you are well enough acquainted to ask that kind of question."

"I just don't believe that Hannah Larkin is the epitome of everything wise, good, and beautiful that Keith McCauley has pictured in his mind."

"Keith may see what he wants to see or Hannah may be a lot different than the women you are acquainted with," said Minnie.

Albert Hart, who usually remained silent in this kind of discussion, looked at Nick. "If Keith likes her then that shouldn't bother you, Son."

Nick arose from his chair and walked toward the coffee pot. "I know that, Dad, but I don't want Keith to get hurt again."

The look Minnie Hart gave her husband seemed to say, 'I hope that is all he's concerned about.'

"Well, you've upset her and she's apt to call a taxi and leave here for good, unless I miss my guess." Albert pulled his pipe from his pocket and tapped it against the trash can.

"I'm going to check on my garden. Do you think your carrots are up, Minnie?" he asked as he started toward the door.

"Nick, when Keith stopped by here last night after the wreck he was so concerned about Hannah staying out on the farm right now. You two have been friends since kindergarten. I'd hate for Keith to know you upset her enough to make her put herself in harm's way," said Minnie, rising to follow her husband.

Nick gasped. "That's right. Keith didn't want her to stay on the farm for some reason. Damn. I forgot about that. That's why he wanted me to meet him and drive her and Freddie to the court house." Nick sat looking down at the floor with a frown on his face.

"I'll have to think of something before she goes or Keith will never forgive me," said Nick, also wrenching himself to his feet.

Freddie had followed Hannah into her room and slumped into the chair by the lamp table. "Mom, I don't think you should have gotten so upset. Nick is just different from anyone you've met before. You know he's traveled all over the world and seen so much that he probably didn't think that question was rude."

Hannah sat down on the side of the bed. "The Harts have been good to us. I guess I shouldn't have been so quick to take offense, but he looks at me as though I'm a fake or something."

She shrugged. "Well, maybe not that, but he unsettles me and I don't need that until I know that Margie and Keith are all right. I still want to go home, but we don't have any electricity, or I don't think we do."

She sat silent for a moment. "Freddie, I don't want to do anything that will worry Keith. I know he doesn't want us to stay at the farm until this case is settled, but we need to do something."

Freddie put his hand up to his eye. "I wish this thing would hurry and get better. I can't even touch it without hurting it." He arose from the chair and sat beside Hannah on the bed.

"You're right, Mom, I know that Keith doesn't want us out on the farm by ourselves. Too many devious things are happening and he fears for our safety."

Hannah sighed and laid her head on Freddie's shoulder. "Oh, Freddie, will our lives ever get back to normal? I don't like this having to move from one place to another. I think I'd rather be home and take the chance of something happening to us."

Freddie put his arm around his mother. "Mom, I know you don't want to think it, but Keith does really like you. I also think you're wrong, in not giving him a chance. We both know that it had been almost three years since Dad had been a loving husband who came home every night. In fact he was seldom at home, especially this last year, so in effect you've been a widow for nearly three years, haven't you?"

Hannah dropped her head. "I know, Freddie, but I still find it hard to believe your dad was seeing another woman. I've certainly been stupid, haven't I?"

Freddie sighed tiredly. "No, just trusting, but these things happen all the time, Mom. You just happened to be the victim this time."

"Well, I'm not going to take that chance again, that's for sure," said Hannah firmly and rose to her feet.

"I want you to call Steve again and ask if we can go see Keith tomorrow. I don't know why, but I feel that I need to, for some reason. Anyway, Steve and Keith will have talked about the situation and Steve will know whether or not it is safe for us to go home."

Freddie agreed and also rose to leave, to be stopped by an exclamation from Hannah. "Let's ask Steve to take us wherever Margie is and then we can be safe together."

Freddie was in agreement with this and went to his room. As soon as he crossed the hall he saw Nick laboriously climbing the stairs.

"You're still sore, too, aren't you?"

"Yes, I'm sore as hell. I think I have bones in places they shouldn't be, but I have to keep up a good front when Mom is around so don't tell her I said anything," said Nick as he reached the landing.

Freddie started to turn but Nick stopped him. "I really upset your Mom, didn't I?"

Freddie hesitated. "Well . . . yes. She's pretty riled up, but she'll be all right. She wants to go somewhere else though. She's wary of you or something. Uncomfortable is the word I think she used."

"I'll have to mend my ways I guess. Do you think she is interested in Keith at all?" Nick stood waiting.

"I don't know for sure, but I think she is. She just isn't aware of it yet. She's got it in her head that to admit something like that she would be admitting unfaithfulness in her marriage. Mom is a very committed person and if she makes a vow she sticks with it, come hell or high water."

Nick walked along beside of Freddie since both their rooms were down the hall from Hannah's. "I'll bet Hannah had a lot of boyfriends in high school, didn't she?"

"No, she didn't. Dad always laughed and kidded her about latching onto the first boy that asked her out. He was the only boy she dated and they were married twenty-two years," said Freddie.

"I don't understand that. Your mom is a beautiful woman and I'm sure the boys noticed her," said Nick in a puzzled manner.

Freddie stopped since they were near his door. "Dad told me that lots of guys tried to get to know her, but she always just smiled and walked away."

Nick was more puzzled than ever. "Hm-m-m, that is strange. Did your dad ever say why she didn't date?"

"Dad always thought she didn't trust men. He said it was all because of Mom's sister, Betty. Aunt Betty had a lot of trouble, I guess."

"What sort of trouble?"

"I don't know much about it. This happened a long time ago." Nick could tell Freddie was uneasy so he slapped his shoulder lightly and said, "See you later, pal."

Nick hobbled on to his room thinking *how interesting . . . something so bad with the sister that it made a 'shrinking violet' of Hannah. I'd like to know what happened.*

CHAPTER 32

HANNAH HAD NO IDEA THAT NICK was trying to find out more about her, but she was trying to think of what she and Freddie should do. This was the second day after the wreck and she needed to do something. First, she felt she needed to apologize to Nick's parents and perhaps to Nick as well. *I don't feel easy around Nick. He stares so and looks like he is studying me or something.* She knew she would never feel comfortable around him, but also knew he had tried to take care of her and Freddie after the wreck.

Before she left her room she decided to get Steve to take her and Freddie to wherever Margie was. "If I can't go back to the house on Pike Lane and can't go to the farm I can at least be with Margie," she mumbled as she made her way clumsily down the stairs.

When she got to the bottom of the stairs, she listened to see where everyone was. When she heard laughter coming from the living room, she made her way there. Steve Hammer had arrived and was seated in a Queen Anne chair facing the hallway door.

As Hannah came in he rose from his seat. "Here she is, now. I thought I was going to have to send someone for you, Hannah. The hearing time has been changed."

"I want to know how Keith is. Have you seen him this morning?" was the first thing that popped into Hannah's mind and she said the thought aloud.

Steve seemed pleased at her concern for Keith. "He's some better, Hannah, but still not 'out of the woods.'"

Hannah nodded. "Well, that's some hope, isn't it?" She came on into the room and sat down beside of Steve.

"I'm glad you came. Freddie told me that you were coming to take us to Margie's hearing. I told Freddie to be ready by ten o'clock just in case, so, I guess I'd better go back upstairs and hurry him along." Hannah's face was wreathed in a broad smile as she rose to leave but met Freddie at the door.

"Good! I won't have to climb the stairs again," said Hannah. "Steve's here early and we have to leave."

Nick was standing in the doorway leading to his father's study watching Hannah closely.

"Hannah, can you spare the time to speak with me for a moment?"

Hannah didn't really want to and looked at Steve in hopes that he'd say there wasn't time. Instead he looked at his watch and said, "I think we have an extra ten minutes."

"I believe that will be sufficient," said Nick, and Hannah silently followed him into the study. Nick turned and closed the door and motioned to a chair beside the desk.

Hannah sat down, stoically waiting. Nick walked to a chair about two feet away and eased himself into it.

"Hannah, I'm not going to put on an act so I'll be blunt. I suppose that you felt I was impertinent with my question the other night, but I didn't think I was. You see, I can't believe that you are all the things Keith McCauley thinks you are. I thought I could get a better picture of who you really are if you had a good marriage and so I asked. I don't believe you had a good marriage or you would have automatically said yes, wouldn't you?"

Hannah sat silent for a moment, but anger was swirling inside ready to erupt. She arose from her seat. "As I said before, Mr. Hart, my marriage is none of your business, good or bad. I don't care what you or Keith McCauley thinks of me for I don't intend to get to know either of you any better than I do now. Thank you for the ride and the wreck for it certainly opened my eyes. I thought you were full of yourself when we first met and that opinion hasn't changed, so good-bye, Mr. Hart, and I'm not glad to know you."

Every head turned when Hannah burst through the door and said, "Let's go, Steve." They could all see she was on the verge of tears.

Minnie Hart jumped to her feet. "Hannah, what did Nick say to you? I'm so sorry, dear. We've loved having you. Please believe me."

Hannah dropped her head, but couldn't hide the tears dripping off her chin. "I'm sorry, Mrs. Hart. Thanks for your kindness."

She clutched her purse like a weapon and rushed toward the door. Freddie and Steve followed her. Albert and Minnie Hart stood still in shock wondering what Nick could have said to cause that kind of reaction.

Once they reached the car, Hannah quickly got into the rear seat and closed the door. Steve looked back. "Hannah, you could have ridden up here. Freddie wouldn't mind, would you?"

Freddie put his finger on his lips and said, "No. It doesn't matter to me where I sit. I think Mom likes the backseat better, don't you, Mom?"

Hannah nodded, but did not raise her head. Both men knew she was crying and wondered what Nick Hart had said to upset her so much, but didn't ask.

"I'm glad they are finally having Margie's hearing. I know she's been worried sick and has wanted to know the decision, whether it is good or bad," said Freddie, sighing sadly.

"Margie has lived a terrible life, Freddie. She hasn't told me much about it, but before I left the state of Washington I did a little nosing around and found out a few things. I plan to find out more, but I haven't told her yet," said Steve.

Then he looked over at Freddie and grinned. "How would you like to have me for a grandfather?"

"You . . . you mean that you're going to marry Margie?" Freddie cocked his head at an angle making his black eye look worse than usual and grinned. "I think that would be great, but how does Margie feel about it?"

Steve looked across at him and winked. "She doesn't know it yet." He glanced at his rear view mirror and saw Hannah sitting up.

"Ah ha! You heard me, didn't you, Hannah? How do you feel about it?" Steve couldn't look back right then since they had reached a busy intersection and he didn't see Hannah's happy smile. When he was able to look back, he asked again.

"Well, how do you feel about me marrying Margie?"

"You're asking the wrong woman. The answer will have to come from Margie, not me," replied Hannah and then grinned. "This reminds me of Miles Standish and John Alden. You'll have to speak for yourself, John. Do you remember that story from the settlement of the Plymouth colony?" She giggled and then sobered.

"I like you, Steve, and if Margie wants to marry you I think you'd be good to her."

"If he's not he'll have to answer to me. After all I'm the only kin she has," said Freddie. "Well, as far as I know I am, but as Steve says, she has a lot of history that none of us knows about."

"Steve, when can we get in to see Keith? I've been really worried. He probably thinks that none of us care about him," said Hannah.

"First things first Hannah, but I promise to check as soon as I'm able."

By this time they had reached the courthouse and Steve pulled into a parking space on the left-hand side of the building. Soon they were out and Steve led the way into the court room and found seats for them close to the front of the room.

A few minutes later a pale, sad, and somber Margie came in escorted by Jerome Judson, her lawyer. The first face she saw was Hannah's and her countenance immediately changed. Instead of sadness there was a radiant smile as she hurriedly walked to the seat indicated by Mr. Judson.

She had just gotten seated when the bailiff cried, "All rise. Judge Nathan Wilson presiding."

Margie was again sworn in and took the seat in front of the judge and in full view of the jury. Jerome Judson introduced the case and explained to the jury Margie's part in the poisoning of the Mylanta that killed Bill Larkin.

Judson then turned to Margie. "Ms. Meadows, during the trial of Sam Henson you stated that Bill Larkin was your son, but he did not know that, nor did anyone else. Do you still affirm that statement to be true?"

Margie was now pale, but seemed very calm. "Yes, that is true."

"Did you give him up for adoption at birth?"

"No, I didn't. My father did. I was in a coma and was not expected to live," said Margie as a forlorn look of loss crept over her face.

"Was the coma caused from complications in the delivery?" asked Mr. Judson with a penetrating gaze.

Margie stared at Judson in puzzlement as if wondering how he knew about her life. Then after a heavy sigh, she said, "No. It was caused by a beating."

"Who beat you, Ms. Meadows?"

Margie gripped the edge of her seat and pressed her lips firmly together before answering quietly. "My father."

'Poor thing' and 'My God, how awful' and 'What kind of father would do that?' was heard from around the room.

Judson saw that Margie was getting very emotional, but trying valiantly to keep control. Fearing that she would collapse he said, "Do you know how long you were in a coma, Ms. Meadows?

"A nurse told me I was out for three weeks, but I'm not sure. Sometime during that time I must have been semi-conscious. I remember my father being in my room. He was bending over me and saying that my baby was dead and that I was going to die as well. I heard him, but I didn't care. He had killed my mother and my baby was dead. I had nothing left. I didn't want to live, but I guess the Good Lord knew better than I did, for my baby was alive."

"How did you learn that your baby was alive and who had adopted him? Usually that is kept secret until the child is grown and asks," said Judson.

"A nurse told me after I promised to never try to contact him or interfere with his life in any way," said Margie.

"Did you keep your promise?"

Margie choked back the threatening tears, but nodded before she opened up and the grief and anguish came flowing out as a mighty river that had been held in until a tiny crack caused it to flood. The jurors saw the joy, the pride, and the anguish of a mother who couldn't be a mother displayed on Margie's face.

"I was always there. I knew what parks he played in, the kindergarten he went to, the bus he rode to school, the kinds of clothes he wore, the people who adopted him, and I attended every school function he was a part of all through high school. I also knew when he enrolled in college and met Hannah. I never got to see Hannah, but I knew Bill was dating a nice girl." Margie stopped, and took a drink of the water the bailiff provided.

At Judson's nod she picked up the story. "The company I worked for sent me to Hawaii for a year and Bill was married and ready to move before I returned to the states."

Margie convulsively grasped the tissues Judson handed her and wiped her eyes, now flooded with tears, and started again. "I was always in the background. Can you imagine what it's like to love somebody, but live as an observer in their lives?" Margie was sobbing now and suddenly she turned a wild-eyed stare toward the jury.

"My son never knew that I was alive. He only got to know me because I found work that would allow me to move to West Virginia, when I learned that he was moving there." Margie choked out as she attempted to control her nerve-shattering emotions.

"How did you get a job in the same company in which your son was hired?"

Margie wiped a hand across her mouth. "I prayed and prayed when I learned Bill was moving to West Virginia. I'd heard that Hannah was the cause of him moving there and I didn't like her. She was causing me to lose what little I had of my son."

She looked at Hannah with such sorrow-filled eyes that Hannah wanted to run to her, but knew she couldn't. She mouthed the words, 'I love you,' as Margie gazed at her. This seemed to have a rejuvenating effect on Margie. She wiped her eyes again and looked at Judson. "May I continue," she asked.

Judson nodded in the affirmative and Margie cleared her throat. "The Lord heard my prayers and allowed me to meet James Harrison. During a company dinner I was seated beside Mr. Harrison and we struck up a conversation. Upon learning that he was from West Virginia and was starting up a pilot company in the southern part of that state I became very interested. Before the dinner was over I had an appointment to talk with him about a possible job with his company. I was hired as Mr. Harrison's personal secretary and when Bill Larkin applied I asked Mr. Harrison to hire him."

Margie began crying again and couldn't seem to stop. Judson approached the bench and asked for a brief recess, but before the judge could grant it, Margie stood up. "I followed him all his life and then I sent the poison to him that killed him." Margie's face was the color of chalk and she was trembling like a leaf. "Oh God, forgive me. I didn't know it was poison."

Judson helped Margie from the witness chair, when the judge called for a recess. Steve stepped forward to escort her back to her seat in the courtroom, but she wanted to go to Hannah. Judson looked at the judge who nodded approval. Margie was soon seated beside Hannah and once there she gathered Hannah into her arms.

Steve and Freddie stepped back and patiently waited until the women had their emotions under control and then took seats on either side of them. Freddie looked at Margie. "I'm your grandson. Don't I get a hug?'

This helped Margie regain her composure and soon she was talking quietly to Freddie. Steve said he would go and find a cola, but she refused his offer saying that she didn't like colas. But, Hannah and Steve insisted that she drink it.

"Its sugar content will give you a boost in energy to get you through this ordeal, won't it, Hannah?" Steve looked at Hannah for support.

"I think Steve's right, Margie. I know that Daddy used to take what he called 'the weak trembles' when he had to deal with something strenuous and Mom would always take him an RC Cola," said Hannah.

Margie shook her head. "I don't like colas but you two would worry the fur off a bear, so get the darn thing."

Steve winked at Freddie and hurried to the outside hall where a soda machine was located.

CHAPTER 33

WITH SODA IN HAND, STEVE RETURNED to join the close huddle of the two women and Freddie. They sat engaged in a soft, whispered conversation for the ten minute recess and at its end Hannah and Freddie gave Margie an encouraging hug before Steve led her back to the stand.

After she was seated, Judson walked to the front of the jury box. "Ladies and Gentlemen, previously Margie Meadows admitted to knowing that the Mylanta she allowed Sabrina Draper to take from the conference was doctored, but she didn't know it had poison in it. However, until today we did not know the circumstances that led Margie Meadows to take that step." Mr. Judson stood looking seriously at the jurors before continuing.

"From her testimony today we are beginning to see the story of a young girl who was beaten so badly that she did not know she even had a baby. Neither did she know that her father sold her baby and received $300 in cash."

This caused angry murmurs to be heard around the room and Judson took advantage of it.

"Needless to say, Margie Meadows finally left the hospital a broken spirited girl who had lost everything she held dear. The nurse who was there when the baby was born and her family took Margie in and gradually she became emotionally and physically stronger. She and the nurse became good friends and one day the nurse told Margie about her baby and who had adopted it. From that day forward Margie Meadows became an "observing mother." She couldn't touch, hug, feed, hold, or speak to her baby, but she did all she could do. On a daily basis she gazed with aching arms and heart and watched her baby grow up."

Hannah looked at the jury and realized that almost all of them were crying and she understood for she was crying as well. Judson now knew that there was sympathy in the jury for Margie Meadows and he relaxed.

"We have already heard how Margie followed her son from the state of Washington to West Virginia. We also know she helped him get a well-paid position in the company in which she worked. When she accidentally heard a conversation about Mylanta being doctored to give to Bill Larkin to make him sick for awhile, she, with only the intention of protecting her son, sent that Mylanta to the man she suspected of doctoring it, or so she thought at the time."

Judson studied the jury and looked around the courtroom. He asked Margie if she was all right and asked if she wanted water. Margie nodded and the bailiff hurried from the room. Margie thanked him on his return, but, now she was paler than when she first came in, and looked so distraught that all eyes seeing her held compassion.

Judson then stepped back to stand to the side where Margie could be viewed easily. "We all know that Margie should have reported what she had heard and not accepted the Mylanta. She doesn't deny that her action was wrong, but I ask each of you if, under the same circumstances, you might not be tempted to take the same action. This woman has done more good for people than she's ever done bad and she had no idea that poison was anywhere near the Mylanta she took back to that conference room that day. It is my fervent hope that this group of jurors will look into their hearts and realize that this woman has not willfully committed a crime."

Judson looked at the judge and said, "I rest my case."

Margie was allowed to step down and the Judge turned the case over to the jury and declared the court in recess until the next morning at ten o'clock.

Steve met Margie before she had taken many steps away from the witness chair. "Don't get discouraged, Margie, about having to wait for the decision. I'll take Hannah and Freddie back with us and you'll have your family with you tonight."

Margie looked at him and put out her hand. He clasped it in his own and walked with her back to where Jerome Judson stood waiting. Judson motioned Margie to a seat beside him. The three sat talking for a few minutes until the judge remanded Margie back to the custody of Steve Hammer. Steve walked with Margie to join Freddie and Hannah who now stood waiting for her.

Hannah enfolded Margie in her arms and murmured, "I'm sorry, you have to wait, Margie, but the court wants to be sure they are fair to you. We always think the worst about everything and most of the time it turns out fine."

Steve who was still holding Margie's hand spoke up. "The jury may not want you to serve time, but will need to decide if they should convict you at all."

Margie widened her eyes in astonishment. "Steve, I'm guilty. I knew that Mylanta had been doctored, but I still gave it to Sabrina Draper. I wish to God I hadn't, but that doesn't change the fact that I did."

Freddie shook his head. "That's my grandmother. That woman won't let anybody cheer her up. She wants to be guilty so let's just get out of here and go get something to eat."

Hannah gave Freddie a glowering stare. "Don't talk like that to Margie. She's worried enough already."

Margie looked at Freddie and grinned sadly. "Well, he's right, you know. I am guilty and no matter what anyone says I still know I'm guilty."

Steve, put his arm around her shoulder. "Okay, you're guilty, but we lo . . . like you and don't want you to be in jail."

Margie looked up at him and smiled. "I know. Thanks, Steve, and you too, Hannah and Freddie. I feel like your love is encircling me so let's get out of here before I make a fool of myself and start bawling again."

They walked out of the courtroom together and Hannah noticed that Steve still kept his arm around Margie's shoulder. *Margie seems to not mind and I'm so glad,* thought Hannah.

Soon they were in Steve's patrol car on the road to Ghent toward the gated community of Flat Top Lake. Steve kept looking through his rearview mirror and Freddie noticed him. "Do we have company, Steve?"

"I hope not, Freddie, but that car is staying pretty close so if I dart up one of these side roads don't be alarmed."

Margie, who was in the front passenger seat, swiveled around and peered out the back glass as did Hannah and Freddie.

They went around a curve and suddenly Steve left the highway and sped downhill on a road running between trees that sheltered the road. He pulled the car into a wide space between some trees and shut off the engine and they waited in silence.

Finally, Steve said, "I'm going to walk back up to the main road so stay where you are until I get back."

Freddie climbed out of the car saying, "Steve I think it would be better if I went. Your uniform would be a dead giveaway."

Steve looked at Freddie. "You're probably right, but I don't want to put you at risk."

"They don't know who I am. They'll think I'm one of the locals who lives down this road."

"Okay. You try it. You might act like someone trying to hitch a ride. People still hitch rides, especially young men," said Steve.

Margie had now gotten out of the car and was looking down the road. "Steve, I believe this road leads down near the river and I'll bet it connects with another road that runs back to the highway. Let's try that first. I don't want to put Freddie into danger."

Steve agreed and twenty minutes later they came back to the highway and found that they were only five miles away from the Flat Top Lake community.

As they traveled that back road, Hannah's thoughts turned to Keith. "Steve, how can we find out more about Keith? I feel like we have let him down. He may be lying there thinking that there's nobody who cares about him."

"I was thinking about Keith too, Hannah, and I will call and check on him as soon as I get you women folks to safety."

CHAPTER 34

WHEN STEVE PULLED UP IN FRONT of a palatial mansion, Hannah and Freddie were very impressed. "Is this where you've been staying, Margie?" asked Freddie.

Steve stepped out of the patrol car and proceeded to open the door for Margie, who watched while Hannah and Freddie exited the back seat and stood looking around with wide excited eyes.

"Yes, it is. I thought I'd won the pools," said Margie with a wide grin.

"This place belongs to James and Cindy Tolliver, friends of Jerome Judson, but they are vacationing in Florida right now. Mr. Judson has their approval for Margie and now you and Freddie to stay here," Steve explained.

Margie smiled. "The servants are here and I've been treated like royalty. Now, you'll get to see what that is like."

Hannah finally turned her bemused gaze on Margie. "Nick Hart's parents have a grand place, but it isn't up to this standard. This looks like a palace."

"Let's go in. You've not seen anything yet. The inside is better than a museum. The art work is absolutely fantastic." Margie stepped up the shallow steps to the vast ornate door and rang the bell.

As they stepped through the door, Hannah gasped in amazement. "Oh my! This is like a picture in a glossy magazine. Don't touch anything, Freddie. We couldn't ever replace it if you broke something. These treasures are worth more than my farm."

Steve smiled and gave Hannah a speculative look. "Would you trade your farm for this, Hannah?

"Good gracious, no. This is not the kind of place I belong in. I'm a farm girl and I love it." Thoughts of the farm made her think of Keith and she looked at Steve.

"Can you check on Keith now? He loves the farm as well. I'd like to know how he's doing. In fact, I'd love to go see him,' said Hannah with a worried frown creasing her brow. She recalled the persistent thoughts of Keith that had been pestering her periodically through the day.

I wish Keith could talk or hear. I think he would love to know that Hannah is worried about him thought Steve and hit the hospital's numbers on his phone. He heard several rings and then a voice asking how to direct his call.

"Third floor east nurses station, please," said Steve and looked at Hannah who was eagerly waiting. When a nurse answered he asked about Keith McCauley.

"Is this his friend, Steve? Good. He's been restless ever since you were here. Can you come back out here? He's agitated and nothing seems to calm him down." The nurse sounded worried and Steve assured her that he was on his way.

Hannah grasped his arm. "Steve, I want to go with you. May I go, please?"

"I don't know if that's a good idea or not, Hannah. It may upset him more." Steve was concerned about Keith and hesitated about doing anything that would make matters worse.

Hannah stepped in front of him and Steve noticed how determined she was acting. "Steve, I need to go. I don't know how I know, but I do. I feel certain that my going won't upset Keith. Please let me go?"

Steve looked at Freddie and Margie and they nodded approval. "Okay, Hannah. Let's go and I hope you're right."

Hannah gave Steve a level look. "I don't think you believe me, but I'd never do anything to hurt Keith McCauley. This need to see him is something different though. I can't explain it, but I know that I need to see him."

Steve clasped her arm. "You sound like Nora Bonesteel in one of Sharyn McCrumb's novels. Do you 'have the sight' as it is called in her book"

Hannah looked puzzled. "I don't know what you're talking about. I just know how I feel." Steve looked at Margie and Freddie.

"You two keep the 'home fires burning' while we're away. I'm taking this woman to see Keith. She's gotten me believing she knows something I don't. We'll see you in an hour, I think."

Steve walked Hannah back through the door and they were soon in the patrol car on their way back to town. Hannah was sitting forward in her eagerness, or so it seemed to Steve.

"Are you comfortable, Hannah? You seem to be tense."

Hannah turned to look at him, "What? Did you ask me something?"

"I asked if you were comfortable?" repeated Steve.

"Oh, I suppose. I don't know how I feel right now. Are we nearly there?" Hannah kept her eyes straight ahead.

"We should be there in about ten more minutes unless we get tied up in traffic. Do we need to be there at a certain time?" Steve waited for her answer, but she paused so long that he thought she hadn't heard him.

"Can Keith talk and hear, Steve? I need to talk to him, but if he can't hear, what's the purpose?" She turned doubtful eyes his way.

"He hasn't been able to talk, but I believe he hears. I'm not sure, though. I guess we'll just have to wait and see. It seems to me that if you're as sure as you act then you shouldn't doubt. I mean if you were given the desire to see and talk to him then whatever you have to say won't fall on deaf ears. What would be the purpose of giving you that desire and then put a stumbling block in the way." Steve was pulling into a hospital parking space and turned to look at Hannah as he cut off the engine.

Hannah gasped and turned red. "Thanks, Steve. I'm ashamed. I had started to doubt, but you called my attention to my weakness. I'm all right, so let's hurry.

Soon they were on the second floor and walking toward Keith's room, but were stopped by a nurse who looked at Hannah. "Who's this? Someone else may disturb him."

Steve noted the determined look on Hannah's face and said, "She won't disturb him. You go in with us and if he gets agitated we can leave."

The nurse hesitated for a moment and then walked toward the door of Keith's room. She opened the door and stepped inside with Steve and Hannah behind her. "Sergeant McCauley, your friend Steve is here to see you. Can you open your eyes?"

Steve and Hannah stepped to the side of the bed and stood waiting. Keith's body twitched, but he didn't open his eyes.

Hannah stepped closer and reaching down picked up his hand and said, "Keith, I've come. Open your eyes."

Keith's whole body jerked and before the nurse could intervene he opened his eyes. His eyes suddenly filled with tears and Hannah's face was drenched in tears as well, but she grabbed a tissue from the box on the table and gently dabbed his eyes.

"You've been calling for me, haven't you?" Hannah whispered.

Hannah felt a slight squeeze on her hand and Keith blinked his eyes in answer.

Hannah smiled. "I heard you, but I didn't at first know what it was, but I did know that you wanted to see me. I begged Steve to bring me with him and now you're going to get better. We all need you and I want you to see the honeysuckles when they bloom on the farm."

Keith was crying again, but the nurse had rushed out to page the doctor and didn't see this. Hannah feared that seeing his tears might be a concern to the doctor, so when they both returned, Hannah had already blotted the tears from Keith's eyes again and he had a smile on his face.

"Well, well, Sergeant McCauley, it looks like a pretty woman should have been called in much earlier."

Keith twitched his head from side to side and the doctor said, "Oh, I see. It is only this woman that puts that kind of smile on your face isn't it?"

Keith blinked his eyes rapidly and everyone but Hannah laughed merrily. Hannah was ready to cry again. Now she knew that Keith loved her, but didn't know how she felt. She didn't want him to be sad so she patted his hand and smiled.

Keith began trying to move his lips and finally said, "l-lo-ve," but try as he might he couldn't get anything else out.

The doctor said, "Now, Sergeant, I want you to rest, but I don't think you will as long as she is here. What about asking her to come every day to see you for a while?"

Keith blinked his eyes again and smiled. The doctor looked at Hannah. "There's your answer. With this kind of results we may need to hire you, young woman."

Hannah looked at Steve. "I don't know if I can come every day. There are circumstances . . ."

"Oh yes, you can, Hannah. It may not be the same time, but I'll see that you get here every day," said Steve. "This is what he was asking about on my last visit, but I couldn't understand what he wanted. He was asking for you, Hannah, so I'll get you here. That's a promise."

"Did you hear that promise, Sergeant? This young lady is coming to see you every day. Is that what you want?"

Keith squeezed Hannah's hand again and this time the doctor noticed it, since Hannah looked to where their hands were clasped. The doctor smiled and patted her shoulder. "You're the medicine our good Sergeant needs. What made you decide to come?"

Hannah didn't know what to say, but Steve said, "This woman has 'the sight' like the character, Nora Bonesteel, in one of Sharyn McCrumb's books."

The doctor left Keith's room shaking his head after Steve related the events that led to Hannah's visit. *Does a person's spirit really communicate with another's spirit*, he thought as he walked back to his office.

Steve and Hannah left Keith McCauley a much more relaxed and happy man, or so it seemed to the nurses. Steve walked behind Hannah until they got to the elevator, but on the ride down, he said, "I guess you feel much better, Miss Hannah."

Hannah pursed her lips. "I did what I thought I was supposed to do. I just hope it helps Keith get better."

"Have you any doubt after the reaction you got? To me it was a miracle, but now you sound unsure." Steve was puzzled.

Hannah shook her head. "Well, one never knows, but right now I want to see Margie happy. Let's just forget this and go see about her."

This is the strangest woman I've ever met in my life, but I like her, he thought as they reached the car.

CHAPTER 35

MARGIE AND FREDDIE WERE ELATED WITH their report on Keith, but amazed as well.

"Hannah, how did you know that Keith wanted you to visit him?" Margie asked.

Hannah looked puzzled. "I really don't know, Margie. There was just a persistent awareness that Keith needed me or something. His face kept appearing before my eyes and I felt drawn or . . . aw, I don't know how to explain it. I just knew inside that I needed to go see him."

Freddie grinned. "She was always like that with me. I remember once at school I had a virus or something and wanted Mom. In a few minutes the principal came to my room and said that Mom had called. "She's on her way to pick you up. She says you are ill, are you?" he asked.

Steve looked at Margie and they both looked at Hannah. "Did this happen very often, Hannah?" Steve spoke up before Margie could ask.

"I'm a mother and of course it happened when Freddie needed me. Don't all mothers act the same way?" Hannah turned red and looked upset.

"No, Hannah, all mothers don't do that. In fact, I don't think I've ever talked to another mother that had that talent," said Margie in an awe-filled voice.

Steve raked his hand back through his crew-cut hair. "I haven't either. What about your husband? Did you know when he was in trouble?"

Both Hannah and Freddie had arrested looks on their faces. "You didn't, did you, Mom? I think Dad would have been alarmed if you had, since he was such an analytical thinker." Nobody said anything for a moment.

Hannah tilted her head to one side. "I don't remember ever feeling that way about Bill. Of course, he was an adult and able to care for himself. That's probably why."

"Perhaps so," said Steve and then laughed.

"Right now though, I wish you'd conjure up some food. I'm hungry."

"You sure did miss a good dinner. I don't know the name of it, but Della, the cook, fixed the best chicken I ever ate in my life," enthused Freddie, rubbing his stomach in appreciation.

"There's probably some left. I'll go ask her," said Margie, going toward the kitchen. This left Hannah still puzzling over Steve's comment about 'conjuring.' She didn't want anyone to start thinking she was a sorcerer . . . that *would be sinful,* or at least she'd always thought that's what the Bible meant. She'd read where King Saul had gone to the woman with a familiar spirit and asked that she call up Samuel. Hannah recalled that the woman was afraid to let Saul know she had this spirit. To have this kind of talent or spirit must have been against the laws at that time, so when she read that story Hannah had assumed that this spirit or whatever it was must have been wrong.

"Steve, I hope you don't have it in your head that I do black magic or things of that sort. I can't conjure up things," said Hannah, giving him a serious look.

"I don't think you're a voodoo doctor, but you'll have to admit that you seem to have something a wee bit different."

Freddie had been listening and now spoke up. "I once had a professor who talked about something like that. He called it ESP (extra sensory perception) and said not a large number of people have it. I told him of some of Mom's experiences and he wanted to meet her. That was about the time I left home and so I just forgot all about it."

"I wouldn't have met him. Your dad wouldn't have approved and I wouldn't have wanted to anyway. This isn't so unusual, or at least I never thought it was, for I always knew when my Dad wasn't feeling well. I was really close to my Dad," said Hannah reflectively.

Margie came back. "You're in luck. Della says she thought you two might be hungry so she kept some back. She has it on the table and is waiting for you."

While they ate, Margie and Freddie kept them company and they discussed what they hoped the outcome of Margie's case would be.

"I know I'm guilty of doing something that could make somebody sick, but I certainly didn't think that the Mylanta had poison in it. Still, you'd think a woman my age wouldn't try to get revenge for wrongdoing by hurting someone else." Margie shook her head in regret.

"Gosh, Margie, if I'd heard what you heard and knew it involved my son, I would have probably done worse," said Hannah with venom in her voice.

Steve drank the last of his coffee and stretched. "I think we'd all do well to make it an early night. Talking about what we don't know will create more stress than we're already feeling."

Soon the house was quiet since footfalls on the thick carpet could not be heard. Margie paced the floor trying to pray and Hannah as well. A big portion of Hannah's prayers, were centered on Keith.

Lord, I want Keith to get better, but I don't want to hurt him by letting him believe I care for him. I don't want to care about another man.

It hurts too much to be betrayed, so please, please help Keith and help me to understand how to handle this situation, she prayed silently.

Neither Margie nor Hannah slept very much and were groggy when their seven o'clock alarms went off. They both hurried to shower and dress and simultaneously opened their bedroom doors. Margie's room was across the landing from Hannah and they both stood gaping and then smiled at each other.

"Are you ready to leave, Hannah?" Margie had thought she would be the first one down that morning.

"Yes." Hannah replied. "We think alike, don't we? I thought I'd be the first one up, but you had the same idea."

They grinned as if sharing a bond as they met at the head of the stairs and descended them together.

"Hannah, have you heard anything else from the Harts since you left there? Steve said you were upset when you left. Were they not nice to you and Freddie?"

Margie had been curious when Steve first told her about the incident, but she hadn't thought of it again until that moment.

Hannah stopped halfway down the stairs. "Margie, I was so angry at Nick Hart that I suppose I acted awful. I still don't know what that man was all about."

"What do you mean, Hannah? Was he rude or out of line?" Margie had stopped on the step below Hannah and stood looking up at her.

Hannah swept her hair back in an exasperated action. "No . . . well. I don't really know. He asked me to speak with him privately. We went into his study or den and he started telling me that he didn't want Keith McCauley hurt."

"Why would he say that to you?"

"Margie, I'm sure I was staring at him like I was demented. He wasn't making any sense to me. I can't remember exactly what he said, but it was along the lines that Keith thought I was perfect and no woman was perfect. I took it to mean that he thought I was leading Keith on or something."

Hannah frowned at the memory. "I listened for a moment and then I just got so angry I couldn't help myself. I told him that I was not interested in Keith McCauley or any other man and that what I did was none of his business. I went marching out of that room and told Steve I wanted to go and we left."

The two women proceeded on down the stairs as Hannah explained. "Now, I'm sorry that I lost control. Mr. and Mrs. Hart were so nice and kind to both me and Freddie. I did have enough sense to thank her for her kindness before I left and I thank God I did."

"I thought Keith and this Nick were best friends. Steve said they grew up together," said Margie as they entered the dining room. They found Steve and Freddie finishing their breakfasts.

"I thought we were going to have to set off an alarm to get you two awake," Steve said with eyebrows arched in question.

"We thought we'd beat everybody down, even though neither of us slept very much, but you guys must have got up with the chickens," said Hannah.

"Chickens! You can certainly tell you are a farmer's daughter." Steve laughed as he rose from the table and pulled out Margie's chair and then Hannah's.

An hour later, the patrol car pulled out of the main gate of the Flat Top Lake village and sped away. Steve looked through the rearview mirror and saw an SUV slide into traffic behind him. He hit a button on his cell phone and then turned on his siren. In this way he knew he would draw attention and perhaps make his pursuer think twice about following him.

The ruse worked, especially after another patrol car sped by with its siren going full blast. They pulled into the courthouse parking area ten minutes before court was scheduled to begin.

As they got out, Margie took the arm Steve offered and whispered. "What was that all about?"

He squeezed her arm and replied. "We had someone on our tail and I thought that would be the best way to cause him to lose interest. It worked, didn't it?"

Margie dropped her head and moaned. "No matter what happens here today I'll still have to stay hidden. What do these people want?"

Steve stopped to let Hannah and Freddie precede them into the courtroom. "Margie, I think either Chief Harry Donaldson or Sam Henson thinks you know something that will send them to the electric chair. I think they are trying to make sure you never reveal what you know."

Margie looked up at Steve and shook her head. "I don't know anything else, but there's no way I can get that across to them."

Steve pushed her on through the door and closed it behind them. "Stop worrying. Let's just see what this day brings. You know that old adage, one step at a time?"

CHAPTER 36

MARGIE LOOKED AT STEVE AND SIGHED softly as she moved to the table where Jerome Judson was seated and quietly took the seat beside him.

Judson looked up and noted her weary look and the dark circles under her eyes. He smiled. "This has been really hard on you, hasn't it?"

Margie grimaced. "These last six months have been terrible, but not as bad as it was when I found out my baby had been given away."

Judson patted her shoulder just as the judge came through the door and the bailiff said, "All rise. Judge Nathan Wilson presiding."

When everyone was seated again and the courtroom was quiet, Judge Wilson asked the jury foreman if they had reached a verdict. The jury foreman, C. J. Looney, arose and stated that the jury would like to ask Miss Meadows two more questions. Judge Wilson looked at Jerome Judson, who silently nodded agreement, and the judge called Margie Meadows to the stand once again.

Margie looked at the jury with such a forlorn expression that some of the women on the jury smiled at her. She walked quietly and took her seat. Judge Wilson reminded her that she was still under oath and Margie nodded.

Looney rose from his seat and said, "We want to know how long Ms. Meadows worked for CEE? We also want to know if Ms. Meadows had any other knowledge about projects or chemicals in which Mr. Henson and Chief Harry Donaldson were involved. Our

FATAL CHOICES AND SECOND CHANCES

reason is to be assured that a similar event didn't occur in other incidents."

Judge Wilson looked at Margie. "Ms. Meadows, how many years did you work for Civic Enterprise Endeavors?"

"Twenty-three years, sir," replied Margie.

Judge Wilson waited for a moment and then asked, "Is that one incident relating to projects or chemicals the only one you were involved in during your tenure with CEE?"

Margie wet her lips nervously. "I was Mr. James Harrison's personal secretary and anything he was involved in for the corporation I knew about. However, Mr. Harrison did not keep up with the day-to-day business of each project, so I wasn't personally involved. He did have a team hired that periodically checked to make sure each project was operating efficiently and honestly and they reported to him. If those reports showed anything irregular Mr. Harrison immediately went to work on it. He did this privately and other than me and, perhaps Mr. Mitchell, no one knew of this team. Now, I suspect that he knew what Sam Henson was doing and that's why he visited him that evening."

Margie drank from the water the bailiff had brought and continued. "I saw all those reports, but only as to filing, typing, and responding to questions to which Mr. Harrison dictated replies."

Judge Wilson looked at the jury. "Does that answer your concerns?"

The foreman looked at the other jurors and they nodded. "We have one other question. We know that Ms. Meadows was escorted from the courtroom to the hospital and a policeman was constantly with her, but where has she been since leaving the hospital and has she been under the surveillance or protection of the police?"

Judson spoke up. "Your honor, if it is satisfactory with the court I can answer that question."

The Judge agreed and Judson explained. "Ms. Meadows, as you know, was under constant watch by the police while in the hospital. When she was released from the hospital she was in the custody of Inspector Steve Hammer who has kept her in a secret area for her own protection and also by order of the court. She has not been free to do and go as she pleased from the time the court first learned about the poisoned Mylanta."

Judge Wilson looked at Looney. "Are there any further questions?

Looney said there were none, so the jury was sent back to the jury room to resume deliberations, and Margie was allowed to step down.

Steve walked with her back to her seat beside Jerome Judson, "Ms. Meadows, that jury did you a big favor today. Do you realize that?" Judson asked.

"What do you mean, sir? I thought they only wanted to make sure I wasn't involved further," said Margie.

Judson smiled. "They were doing that, but in so doing they allowed you to swear under oath that you had no further incriminating evidence to reveal on anybody."

Margie's head jerked up. "They did, didn't they? Thank God they did, if it puts a stop to this 'hide-and-seek' existence I've been living."

Steve had also realized what had just occurred and he looked at Margie and made an a-okay sign. Margie put her hands together in a prayerful manner and nodded.

She jerked back to attention when the door in the back opened and the jury filed in and seated themselves.

"Mr. Looney has the jury reached a decision?" asked Judge Wilson.

Rising to his feet, Looney said, "We have, Your Honor. We have written it on this paper." He handed the paper to the bailiff who passed it to the judge.

Judge Wilson read the verdict and looked up. "Ms. Meadows, the jury has found you guilty . . . of a misdemeanor, but they recommend probation, which you have fulfilled already by the time you've spent under police surveillance."

Margie Meadows had first turned ghostly pale when she heard the word 'guilty' but when she heard the rest of the verdict her face became suffused in color and drenched with tears.

There were sighs and clapping coming from all areas of the courtroom and several men rose quickly and left. Steve made a mental note to himself to check those men out. After a few seconds, the judge tapped his gavel and called for the court to come to order.

Giving Margie a direct look, he said, "Ms. Margie Meadows you are free to go and resume your life as before. God Bless you. We all hope that your life is more pleasant from here on."

Margie rose to her feet and said in a trembling voice. "I wish to thank all of you and I deeply regret my involvement in this, but I intend to do something to return the kindness that has been shown to me. I don't know what just yet, but when I've made a decision, I'll be sure to make it public."

Judge Wilson tapped his gavel again. "This court is adjourned until ten o'clock tomorrow when we return to conduct the trial of Harry Donaldson."

As Steve, Hannah, and Freddie rose to leave they made it through the courtroom door to be blocked by cameras flashing and reporters thrusting microphones at Margie.

"What do you plan to do now, Ms. Meadows? Do you think you received a fair trial? Will you stay in this part of the country now that you're free?" These were only a few of the questions posed as Steve tried to part a pathway to get his party to the patrol car.

Margie looked out at the crowd and said, "I don't know how to answer any questions right now. I just need to find some place to rest." Three more patrolmen came up and cleared a path and in this way Margie Meadows, Hannah Larkin, and Freddie Larkin left a place they had learned to dread visiting. They all hoped they were seeing a courtroom for the last time for the rest of their lives.

Once they were in the car, Hannah and Margie were talking a "mile a minute" according to Freddie, when Hannah looked out the window and said, "Where are we going? Aren't we going back to Flat Top Lake Village?"

"You promised to visit Keith every day. Did you forget about that?" Steve looked through the rear view mirror at Hannah and seeing her startled gaze realized that she hadn't once thought of Keith.

CHAPTER 37

Hannah had forgotten her promise to visit Keith. She knew that being so relieved about Margie was one reason, but she also knew she wanted to put her feelings for Keith out of her mind. She wanted to help Keith recover, but Nick Hart's comments on the matter had really upset her.

I wonder what his reaction will be when he finds out I've been visiting Keith. He'll probably come out with another scathing remark about me leading Keith on, she thought as she recalled her parting barb at Nick that she wasn't interested in Keith McCauley or any other man.

Now, what am I going to do? she silently asked herself as she said to Steve, "Gosh, I got so excited about Margie that I did forget. Are we going to the hospital now?"

"We certainly are. Keith McCauley is one fine man and I want him better. You seem to be the catalyst that has begun the healing. I intended to take you to see him even if you didn't want to go, but you did promise," said Steve.

Hannah didn't have an answer, but felt she should say something. Finally, she said, "I want Keith well too, Steve, but I don't think I had anything to do with his improvement. I think the Lord wanted me to tell Keith that he needs to get better and I did. I did promise to visit him since the doctor asked me to, but I think he'll get better whether I visit him or not."

Steve pulled into a parking space at the hospital and killed the engine. "You may be right, Hannah, but just in case Keith wants to see you, I still plan to bring you out here every day."

Everyone crowded into the elevator and soon arrived on the third floor where they made their way to Keith's room. Steve tapped on the door and opened it to reveal Mr. and Mrs. Hart and Nick. Hannah's pulse quickened. She gasped in shock at her reaction to Nick's 'movie star' allure.

White-faced she turned to leave, but Margie grabbed her arm and whispered. "Don't you dare run and hide. You haven't done anything wrong." Hannah knew that Margie thought her change of color was totally due to the disagreement she'd had with Nick before leaving the Hart residence.

It wasn't though. *I'm drawn to his looks, just like I was to Bill's,* thought Hannah, not liking that feeling at all.

Nick flashed his fabulous smile at Margie and said to Steve, "Aren't you the lucky one, Inspector, getting to travel with two pretty women?"

Minnie Hart turned to Hannah and put out her hands. "Hannah, it is so good to see you." Relieved, Hannah took Minnie's hands in her own and smiled. This diversion gave her a chance to recover from her reaction to Nick.

What is wrong with me? Hannah asked herself silently, wondering why she would feel attracted to Nick. Bill, her husband, also a handsome man, had almost destroyed her. *I must be crazy. Handsome men seem to only care for themselves, but I'm still drawn to them,* she thought as she released Minnie's hands.

Keith had been lying with his eyes closed, but when Minnie said "Hannah" his eyes popped open.

Albert Hart, who stood on the other side of Keith's bed, looked amazed. "Well, look at this, Minnie. Our Keith is awake."

Minnie moved to her husband's side where they both were thrilled by the sudden change in Keith. He hadn't moved or opened his eyes since they had arrived twenty minutes before. Now, Keith's eyes began moving from one side to the other.

"Why's he doing that? Is he looking for something?" asked Minnie.

Steve pushed Hannah forward. "Yes, he is looking for Hannah, aren't you, Keith?"

Keith smiled and blinked his eyes.

Steve turned to the others. "He only reacts to pretty women. See how alert he is?" Steve pushed Hannah to the side of the bed. "Here she is Keith, just like I promised."

Keith looked at Hannah and moved his hand. Hannah put her hand in his and he breathed a blissful sigh. Nick and the other Harts were fascinated by this change.

"Is this the first time you've been here, Hannah?" asked Minnie.

"No, we visited him yesterday, didn't we, Steve?"

"We sure did and we got the same reaction then too. The doctor wants Hannah to visit every day," explained Steve.

"That must mean she has the magic touch, I guess," said Nick, moving to Hannah's side near the bed. Keith looked up and his face twitched in an agitated manner.

Hannah tried to move back to give Nick space, but Keith would not release her hand. She looked at Steve as if begging for help.

"I think our friend doesn't want you here, right now, Nick." Steve looked at Keith. "Am I right, Keith?"

Keith looked at Steve and blinked his eyes twice before looking at Nick and trying to smile.

At first Nick's face clouded, but when he saw Keith's valiant effort, he nodded and smiled also.

"You got your wish, Bro. I'm going, but I'll be back."

Nick didn't even glance at Hannah, but turned quickly and walked out the door where he turned to his mother.

"I'll be home around dinner time, Mom." Minnie gave him a thoughtful look.

"I'll tell Mildred. Otherwise, you won't have anything to eat."

Again, Hannah tried to pull her hand from Keith's, but he held it tighter. Staring fixedly at her, he said, "St . . . ay."

While Nick had stood by her side, Hannah felt his animosity toward her, but she hoped Keith hadn't noticed anything. However, now that Nick was gone Keith seemed more relaxed.

I don't want Keith to get the wrong idea about how I feel, she thought as she stood wondering what she should do. She turned to look at Minnie Hart who saw the turmoil in her expression.

"Keith didn't want Nick to be that close to you, Hannah," said Minnie, causing Albert to chuckle.

"That's the way they've always been. If Keith liked a girl Nick always tried to cut him out, but they still remained friends. No, they were more like brothers than friends, weren't they, Minnie?"

Minnie smiled. "Since they were four or five years old and Keith's family moved next door to us they practically stayed together until Keith married."

Hannah looked stricken. "I don't want to cause a rift in a friendship like that. I just promised to visit Keith because the doctor said he thought it would help."

A movement on her hand got Hannah's attention and she looked down. Keith was trying to move his thumb over her hand. Hannah could tell that he was agitated. As she stood looking down on his face his eyes looked so sad. Hannah felt tears welling in her eyes and she leaned down closer and whispered.

"It's all right, Keith. Don't get upset. I want to visit and I'll be here every day."

Keith's sad expression made her want to gather him in her arms to soothe the hurt.

"Keith, don't look so sad. I promise. I'll visit every day if I have to hire a taxi to bring me."

The situation was tense and awkward, especially for Hannah. Sensing her angst, Albert said, "Keith can't explain himself, but I think he just wants to visit with Hannah right now. We've already been here a good while anyway." He stepped to the bedside and touched Keith's arm.

"Do you want to just visit with Hannah, Keith?"

Keith blinked his eyes rapidly and tried to smile.

"See there, that's all he wants."

As he patted Keith's arm, Albert said, "We're going now, Keith, but we'll be back."

The older man moved away from the bed so his wife could move in closer. She bent and kissed Keith's hand, which still held Hannah's, and said, "I love you, Keith. We all want you better and back home."

Keith looked at Minnie and smiled and then his eyes roamed around and not finding Nick, he seemed to really relax.

"Nick's gone, Keith. He isn't upset at you, though, He'll be back," said Minnie as she also turned to the door.

CHAPTER 38

THE DOCTOR WAS IN THE HALLWAY as the Harts were leaving. "How did you find Mr. McCauley? Did he know you two?" The doctor was smiling as if expecting them to be very enthused.

"He knows us, but we were here over twenty minutes and he didn't even open his eyes. That changed though when Hannah Larkin came in. The minute he heard her name, he became a different man," said Albert with a smile.

The doctor smiled broadly. "Yes, I was hoping she'd come back today since she seems to have such a great effect on him."

Minnie was standing silent during this interchange, but now the doctor turned to her. "How do you account for this phenomenon, ma'am?"

"I think Keith's in love with her. He wants to talk to her so he tries harder."

"Ah-ha! You may have hit on the truth. How long have they known each other?"

Albert interrupted. "We don't really know. We only met Hannah this week, but I think Keith was working on her husband's murder case."

"I'd forgotten for a moment. Mr. McCauley is a police sergeant, isn't he?" asked the doctor.

"He certainly is and a very good one too," blurted Minnie. She was having trouble with her emotions and turned her head away.

Albert felt he should explain his wife's behavior. "He's been like a second son to us and I'm surprised my wife has held up so well." He took Minnie's arm.

"Come on dear let's get home before Mildred throws our dinner out." Minnie walked a few steps and turned.

"Make him well, doctor. If any man ever deserved happiness, Keith McCauley does."

The doctor nodded. "I'll do my best, Mrs. Hart." He turned toward the door to Keith's room, but looked back to see Mrs. Hart leaning heavily against her husband as he bore most of her weight to the elevators.

When he stepped into Keith's room it was like a *tableau vivant*, reminding him of the opening scene in My Fair Lady. Margie and Freddie were standing near the wash basin in the corner and Inspector Hammer was looking out the window, but nobody was moving or making a sound, except Keith McCauley.

"Han-nah, oh Han-nah . . . I . . . dream," were the only words the doctor could make out, but Keith McCauley was actually talking.

With a broad smile the doctor stepped to the foot of the bed and said, "Did I hear you talking, Sergeant?" Hannah answered for him.

""Yes, doctor, you heard him talking. He started that today. Isn't it wonderful?" This brought a smile to Keith's face.

The doctor moved to the other side of the bed and stood looking down at Keith. "If you keep this up, we'll remove some of these hoses and have you sitting up in a few days. How does that sound?"

Keith's face twisted into a smile. "Gu ... d."

The doctor laughed. "There's nothing wrong with your hearing is there?" He bent to check the catheter bag and then stood tall again.

"Let me check a few things and I'll let you enjoy your company. That seems to be more help than anything else right now."

Soon the doctor left and Steve suddenly turned from the window. "Margie, let's go out to the lounge and take Freddie with us. He can go find us a soda or something." He grinned and nodded toward Hannah and Keith.

Margie and Freddie quietly followed Steve out of the room, closing the door behind them. Hannah still stood with her hand in Keith's. He didn't want to let it go, but she was tired of standing in the same position.

"Keith, please let my hand go. I'm not going to leave, but I need to move into another position." Slowly his grasp relaxed and her hand was free. She stretched her arm over her head and pulled her shoulders from side to side in relief.

"I sor-ry." Keith struggled to talk and Hannah smiled.

"Don't worry about that. I want to know about you, Keith. Does it hurt to talk?"

"No, not hur-t. Hard."

"Is it hard to form words or does it hurt your throat?"

Keith looked as if he was thinking. "No hurt . . .slow."

Hannah thought for a moment. "Maybe that's because you were in a coma so long."

Keith's eyes widened. "Co-ma! How . . . lo-ng?"

Oh Lord, I probably shouldn't have said that, thought Hannah. She patted his arm.

"Keith, I think the doctor wanted you to sleep. I guess they thought it would help you heal faster."

Keith looked at her in a thoughtful manner. "Oh, . . I . . . see."

Hannah stood wondering what to say to him, but Keith supplied the answer. "You . . . see farm?"

Hannah smiled. "No, but I called my neighbor and he said the honeysuckles were in bloom as well as the early apples."

Keith's eyes lit up. "Good!"

Hannah made a mental note to tell the doctor that his speech was getting better with use. "I can smell them now, when I close my eyes.

I wish I could go back to the farm, but I don't think Steve will let us go." Suddenly Hannah remembered the verdict in Margie's hearing.

"Keith, my friend Margie is free. There are no more charges and she doesn't have to serve any time in jail. Isn't that wonderful?"

Keith smiled. "Good! Good! . . . I see you . . . are hap-py."

"Yes, I am. She will go to the farm with me, I hope. I'm so tired of feeling unsafe and not being allowed to go home. It's so . . ." Hannah stopped abruptly as she saw the sad look that had come into Keith's eyes.

"I'm sorry, Keith. I'm still in better shape than you are, right now. I guess we both need to concentrate on making things better, don't we?"

Keith put out his hand, and Hannah eagerly grasped it, saying, "Keith, you lifted your hand. Oh, thank God. You are getting better, fast."

Keith gripped her hand, not strongly of course, but noticeably stronger than he had before. He smiled. "I'm try-ing."

The door opened and a nurse came in bearing his lunch tray. "Are you ready to eat, sergeant?" Keith dropped Hannah's hand and gave the nurse a stern look.

"Leave it," said Keith and the nurse's eyes opened in surprise.

"You're talking. Does the doctor know about this?"

Hannah smiled. "Yes, he knows he said one word, but now he is making sentences."

The nurse moved his bedside table in place and put the tray down before looking at Hannah with a big smile. "Soon, he'll be able to feed himself, and I won't have to feed him"

"You don't have to now. I'll feed him when I'm here," said Hannah, lifting the cover. "Um, Keith, this smells good."

Keith slowly tried to move his head from side to side. Hannah recognized that he was saying no. "Don't you want me to feed you? I'd like to do that for you."

Keith looked upset, almost as if he wanted to cry. "I thought you liked me, Keith. Why don't you want me to help you?"

Keith's hand came out again. "No, Han-nah. I want you to help . . . but I feel bad . . . for you to feed me."

The nurse looked at Hannah. "I think he's embarrassed because he's so helpless."

Hannah's eyes widened. "Is that what it is, Keith? Are you embarrassed to have me feed you?"

Keith closed his eyes. "I'm a man."

"Men get hurt, Keith, and people that care for them try to help them. That's all I'm trying to do." Hannah was surprised to know that she truly wanted to not only feed him, but do anything she could to help him.

Keith saw her look and after a brief pause he said, "Okay. Get-the sp-oon. I'm hung-ry."

With the nurse's help, Hannah soon had the head of Keith's bed cranked up to a little better position for eating. He wasn't yet allowed to sit completely up. The nurse left with the advice to call her if she had any concerns.

Hannah placed a towel over Keith's chest and, one small bite at a time, she began feeding him. At first she felt awkward and uneasy, but gradually she relaxed. After several minutes he put his hand up. "No more."

"You've not eaten half the food yet, Keith. Are you tired or just don't want to eat?"

"Both." Keith looked at her and tried to smile.

"All right, but take one more bite of your chicken and potatoes," Hannah coaxed.

Keith grinned. "Bossy . . . " Before he could add to that the door opened and Steve, Margie, and Freddie came in.

"Whoa! Hannah has taken over and even Keith is fussing," said Steve as he watched Hannah shovel another bite in Keith's mouth.

CHAPTER 39

HANNAH TURNED WITH THE SPOON IN her hand. "He is trying to get out of eating and he can't get better if he doesn't eat."

Steve was now standing at the end of the bed. "Sounds like you're on the right track, Hannah." He looked at Keith.

"Why don't you want to eat?"

"I want to . . . talk." Keith looked so serious that not only Steve, but Margie and Freddie also came in close to his bed. They were surprised that Keith had said a complete sentence.

"Keith, when did you start talking so easily and what do you want to talk about?" Steve stood waiting and Keith looked at Hannah as if asking her to answer for him.

"He still talks slowly, but that's just because he went so long without talking, I think," said Hannah. "He's just gotten better with using his voice, haven't you, Keith?"

"Yes. It is easi-er if I talk more." Keith lay silent for a moment and then looked at Steve.

"Is it . . . safe for Han-nah to go to farm? She wants to go home, don't you, Hannah?" Keith looked at her with such gentleness that Hannah felt her heart flutter or something. She'd never felt that before and wondered what it was.

Steve shook his head and smiled at Keith. "I wish I could tell you, yes, but I can't. I think we need to wait until Donaldson's trial is over. I'm taking Hannah to the same place Margie has been staying. She'll be safe there."

Keith reached out his hand toward Hannah and she took his hand in hers. "I'm sorry, Han-nah. May-be I can take you . . . to the farm." Just saying this seemed to please Keith since he smiled widely.

Hannah squeezed his hand. "You want to be on the farm as much as I do, don't you, Keith?" He gripped her hand more snugly and had a sparkle in his eyes.

"Okay, I'll eat a few more bites. It will help . . . to get out sooner."

Again, Hannah picked up the spoon and Keith had eaten several more bites when the door opened and Nick Hart walked in again. Nobody spoke until Nick walked to the foot of the bed.

"Hello Keith, I said I'd be back and here I am. I see you have a new nurse." Keith gave Nick a mutinous look and swallowed the food that had just been spooned into his mouth.

"Hel-lo Nick, how are you?"

Nick gave him a speculative look. "Take that look off your face, Keith. I'm not going to kick you while you're down." Nick suddenly realized that Keith was talking.

"Keith, you're talking! Man that's wonderful. When did you start that?"

Seeing that Nick was really pleased, Hannah said, "Today. The doctor is very pleased and so are we."

"Well, so am I. So, what's the doctor saying? How soon before you can walk?" Nick was really excited.

"Mom and Dad will be elated. I think they love you more than me, Keith."

Hannah could tell that Keith was relieved or something. "I know they love me, Nick, but . . . not more than you."

"Do you want anything else to eat, Keith?" Hannah had stood waiting during the exchange between Nick and Keith.

"No, no more, Hannah . . . Thanks!" Hannah spread the napkin over the remaining food and moved the table away from the bed.

She looked at Steve. "I think we need to go, Steve. Margie needs to get some rest and these two friends can talk."

"I'm ready whenever you are, Hannah. Margie's been through a trying time today, and does need to rest."

Keith stretched out his hand. "Hannah, wait." Hannah quickly stepped to his bedside and put her hand on his arm.

"I'll come back tomorrow, if you want me to, but we do have to go now."

Keith nodded and said, "What time?"

Steve spoke up. "It will probably be later tomorrow. I need to sit in on the Donaldson trial and it won't be over until about four. Unless Hannah plans to attend the trial, I'll have to go back and get her after that, so I'd say about five-thirty."

Keith gasped. "Five-thirty! She won't get to stay. . . long."

"I could bring her, Keith . . ." began Nick to be stopped by Keith's emphatic "NO."

Margie interrupted. "Hannah, Freddie, and I will come out about one o'clock in a taxi. Does that sound better, Keith?"

Keith grinned. "Yes, much better. Steve could come out after the trial to take you home."

Steve shook his head. "Keith, I don't know if they're safe yet. I'll go get them at the lunch break and leave them here until evening. Is that all right, girls?"

"How do you know we'll be safe here? They got to me in the hospital or tried to," said Margie.

Steve grinned smugly. "My dear lady, do you think I'd leave my friend, Keith, in an unsecure room?"

Hannah gasped. "Do you mean the people that shot Keith may try to do it again?" She turned fear-filled eyes toward Keith.

"Don't be afraid, Hannah. I'm safe," said Keith, but still looked pleased that she was concerned.

Nick had stood silently watching this scene with mixed feelings. He noted the solicitude with which Hannah treated Keith and the pleasure that gave Keith, but he felt women could really put on an act. *I'm going to keep an eye on Miss Hannah*, he thought as Steve opened the door to leave.

Margie turned to wave at Keith and Freddie came over to the bedside. "A lot of work needs to be done at the farm and I could sure use some help, so hurry and get better."

Keith grinned. "Don't start without me, Freddie." He turned his eyes to Hannah.

"You promise to come tomorrow?"

Hannah smiled. "Yes, Keith, I'll be here. You visit with your friend and concentrate on getting better. Okay?"

"Okay, I promise. Bye, Hannah. See you tomorrow."

Hannah turned to go and then looked back. "Bye, Keith"

As soon as the door closed behind her, Keith swiveled his eyes toward Nick. "I want your promise, Nick. Don't go after Hannah. I'm not on my feet yet, but if you do, I'll . . . I need her, Nick."

Nick could see that Keith was getting agitated. He put out his hand and grasped Keith's. "I promise to stay hands off, Keith." *I will for as long as he's here in the hospital*, he thought to himself.

Keith seemed to relax. "How are you spending your time, back here in this little town of Beckley?"

Nick pulled a chair up to the side of the bed and straddled it. His face broke into his usual 'devil-may-care' smile. "Well, there's a new girl in that production of "Honey in the Rock" and I've been busy getting acquainted."

Keith grinned. "I might have known. Don't you ever want to settle down, Nick?"

"Nope, I'm just not the marrying kind. Besides Dad sends me all over the world and what woman wants a man that is gone all the time?"

"Take her with you, man," said Keith. "Lots of women want to travel the world."

Nick slanted his eyes at Keith. "Hm-m-m, that's a thought." *Perhaps Hannah would like to see the world*, but he kept that thought inside.

From there they talked about Nick's last trip to Guam and several other Pacific islands. "Women are the same all over, Keith. They all have dollar signs in their eyes."

Keith grimaced. "Nick, you are . . . ster-o-ty-ping all women and they aren't all like that."

"I know you have stars in your eyes about Hannah, but, Keith, you don't really know her. How do you know she won't act just like Ursula? I'd be really wary if I were you."

"Nick, I know Hannah isn't perfect, but she is an honest person and she has a kind heart. You think what you want to, but I trust Hannah." Keith had such assurance in his eyes that Nick halted the retort he started to make.

"Okay, brother, I'll take your word for it. I want whatever helps you to get well and if Hannah's visits do that, I'm all for it."

CHAPTER 40

BACK AT FLAT TOP LAKE VILLAGE, Hannah took a shower and settled down for the night. She couldn't go to sleep, though. She knew that for a moment, while there with Keith, she had felt so much caring and tenderness and yet her pulse quickened when Nick entered the room. *I don't trust him and don't really like him so why would I feel excited when I see him?* Her thoughts were so troubling that she arose from her bed and went down the stairs in search of something to read.

The house was quiet as she walked down the carpeted stairs, but when she opened the library door she gasped in surprise. Margie was being kissed by Steve Hammer.

When the door opened Margie pushed Steve away and stood staring from wide eyes and a red face. Steve saw how embarrassed she was and tried to ease the situation. "Hannah, you need to knock before walking in. I was just kissing the woman I love and now she's so embarrassed I may never get to again."

Hannah turned red. "I'm sorry. I didn't hear any noise."

"I'm not a sloppy kisser, Hannah, so I don't make noise." Steve laughed at Margie's outraged gasp.

Steve looked at her. "Well, I'm not, am I?"

"Oh Steve, be quiet. Both Hannah and I were surprised. We didn't expect anyone and she didn't think anyone was still out of bed."

"Margie, I've already told Hannah and Freddie that I want to be a part of their family so now Hannah knows I'm serious. Right, Hannah?"

Hannah smiled. "We did approve, Margie, but only if you were in agreement. I guess this means you are."

Margie looked at Steve and smiled. "Well, he has been taking very good care of me."

"I'm not a sloppy kisser, either. Tell her, Margie. I don't want that kind of word to get out about me." Steve gurgled with laughter at Margie's expression.

"I know, I know. I'm crude and all that other stuff you said, but you like me, don't you?" He suddenly pulled her back into his arms where she stayed.

Hannah shook her head and smiled, but was also surprised at Margie's look of contentment standing encircled in Steve's arms.

"I'll just get a book and then leave you two lovebirds alone."

Hannah went back up the stairs with her thoughts in a jumble. *Margie doesn't seem to have any trouble trusting Steve. Why can't I be like that? Of course, Margie wasn't married for over twenty years to someone who betrayed her trust.*

Hannah had reached the top of the stairs and turned to her room when she heard the library door close. *Did they think I was going to sneak back down to spy on them,* she thought. Quickly she opened the door to her room and stepped inside. She had been so embarrassed that she had grabbed the first book she saw without even looking at the title. Now she turned it over and looked.

"Pride and Prejudice! For heaven's sake, I've read this three times already. Well, I'm not going back down there for another one," she muttered aloud, flinging the book onto the bed.

She read the first chapter again after she had tried everything else to get her mind off the problem of Keith and her reaction to Nick. *I wish I had somebody I could trust to talk to, but I don't even think I can talk to Margie about this,* she thought as she turned over for the fourth time.

She heard a tap on her door and realized she must have gone to sleep, but didn't know what time. The last time she'd looked at the clock it was two a m. She pulled the cover up over her shoulders and called, "Come in."

Margie opened the door and came in. "You look like you haven't slept a wink."

"I don't think I slept much, but I was asleep when you knocked. Is it time to get up?

Margie grinned. "It is if you want breakfast before noon. What kept you awake? Surely you didn't allow the episode in the library last night to upset you, did you?"

Hannah swung her feet over the side of the bed and rose to her feet. "How late is it?" She turned to look at her clock on the nightstand. "Gosh, is it really nine o'clock? I was awake at two this morning, but if this clock is right I've still gotten in seven hours of sleep."

"Well, hurry and get showered and dressed. Steve's going to send David Shortt to get us at eleven-thirty. I want to have lunch with him," said Margie, giving Hannah a saucy smile.

Hannah looked at her narrowly. "What are you up to, Margie" You've got that 'I've got a secret look' that Freddie uses sometimes."

"Freddie! What kind of look is that? Do you mean that Freddie has a mannerism like me?" Margie acted almost excited.

Hannah had taken some clothes from the closet and headed for the bathroom, but now turned. "Sure he has mannerisms like you. You are his grandmother, remember."

When she left Margie walked to the window and stood looking out, but not seeing anything. *Hannah didn't say whether seeing me and Steve together had upset her or not, but I didn't answer her about a secret either. She and I need to have a long talk.*

When Hannah came back into the room she started to ask her again about the incident in the library. "Hannah, we need to talk . . ."

"Yes, but right now see if you can get this zipper to work. It's stuck." Hannah turned her back to Margie who went to work on the zipper.

"Margie, I need somebody to talk to, but right now I'm too mixed up and besides we don't have time."

Margie slid the zipper to the top and patted it. "There, I did it. That's a pretty dress. You look dressed to the nines and here I am in slacks."

"They look nice. You're not wearing jeans and a tee-shirt. That's the fashion today with high heels. I think heels look ridiculous with jeans, don't you?" Hannah picked up her purse and turned to the door.

"Of course, I don't have two men interested in me, Hannah, so I can see why you dressed up."

Hannah dropped her head. "Please don't say that, Margie. I don't want two men interested in me. Besides, you heard what Mrs. Hart said about Nick and Keith and I don't want to be a party to destroying a lifelong friendship."

"I heard Mrs. Hart, Hannah, but I thought she was amused by sibling rivalry. I didn't think she thought it was anything serious." Margie stopped on the bottom step and looked up at Hannah. "Did you think she was serious?"

Hannah looked thoughtful. "Well, yes I did, especially after the abrupt 'no' that Keith gave Nick's offer to come out and get me."

Margie shrugged. "You may be right, but even so, you're not doing anything to cause it."

Steve suddenly stepped through the door leading from the dining-room. "I thought I was going to have to help Margie wake you, Hannah. I thought you were a farm girl."

Hannah grinned. "I am, but I didn't hear the rooster crow and you know the saying that farmers get 'up with the roosters."

Steve chuckled. "Well, I'm glad Margie is more refined. I don't want to have to keep a rooster in my bedroom. We'll just use an alarm clock."

CHAPTER 41

STEVE LEFT AT NINE-THIRTY AFTER REMINDING them to be ready for David Shortt at eleven-thirty. He whispered to Margie on the way out.

"Did you tell her?" He nodded at Hannah and Margie shook her head. Steve shook his own head as if he just didn't understand her and went to his car.

"Tell her what?" asked Freddie who walked in just as Steve was leaving.

Margie walked over and gave him a hug. "He said, 'her' and you, young man, are not a 'her.'"

"Oh, I get it, secrets-talk." Freddie grinned. "That means, I don't need to know." Margie flapped her hand at him. "You're sharp, grandson."

Margie was thankful that she could allow Steve's slip-of-tongue earlier, to go unanswered. She didn't want to tell anyone her secret yet. *I'm afraid my chance of happiness will slip away, I guess. All my life people and things that I loved have been snatched away from me. This time I just want to wait to make sure*, thought Margie as she made her way to the dining room.

They sat around the table talking about how nice it would be to feel free to go shopping, go bowling, or just go out walking on the street without looking over their shoulders.

"I really think that I am the only one anybody wants right now. I hope Mr. Judson is right and my hearing took away any need they had to bother me."

"Margie, will you come to the farm with us, if we are no longer being followed?" asked Freddie. "I want you with us and so does Mom, don't you?" He turned to Hannah.

"You don't have to ask me, Freddie. Margie knows that she has a home there if she wants it." Hannah left her crumpled napkin on her plate as she rose from the table.

"Of course, Steve may have other ideas if he's serious about Margie. He is, isn't he, Margie?"

Margie turned red. "He says he is, or at least he's as serious as I allow him to be."

"Good men are hard to find, Margie, so you'd better snap Steve up while you can," said Freddie with a wicked grin.

"Good women are also hard to find and Margie needs to be sure, don't you, Margie?" Hannah gave Margie a questioning look.

Margie stopped just inside the dining room door. "I think I'm sure of Steve, but I'm afraid. It seems like something always happens when I care about somebody."

Hm-m-m, Margie is afraid too. I'm afraid to trust another man and Margie fears fate . . . Perhaps that's what I fear as well, thought Hannah as she followed Margie from the dining room.

Freddie followed behind Margie and Hannah. "It sounds to me like you fear the unknown, Margie."

"I do. I don't want to be hurt again. Loving someone is so painful. It was pure torment to know a little boy was my son and yet not be able to hug him, talk to him, or even let him know I was there." Margie shook her head vehemently.

"I've never talked about it and don't know why I am now. I guess I want to give a reason for my fear."

They went to the living room and sat down to wait for the arrival of David Shortt. "Freddie, you were afraid of being sent to prison and that was being afraid of the future, wasn't it?" Margie gave him an intent look.

Freddie looked at Margie with astonishment. "I had been arrested, though, and I knew I could be sent to the penitentiary."

"It's the same thing, Freddie. You feared going to prison and I fear loving someone and then losing them. Both of those things are fear of the unknown, aren't they?

"Margie, I feared events that were happening in the present, but your fear is of the 'what if' kind. That kind of fear could become a phobia," said Freddie as if intrigued by the concept.

Margie answered back in the same contemplative manner. "Aren't both of those fears, of the 'unknown'? What I'm saying is that fear is fear regardless of its source."

"No, well yes, fear is fear, but being locked up in jail leaves one in a position that other people will be deciding one's fate. In your case, you made a choice and became pregnant." Freddie didn't get to finish.

"Freddie! You should be ashamed of yourself. That is your grandmother you are speaking to," scolded Hannah.

"No, Hannah. Don't scold him. He's right. I didn't deliberately set out to become pregnant, but I did and I wasn't forced. So, in that sense it was my choice. I see where Freddie is going in his thinking." Margie turned back to Freddie.

"You are saying that I had a choice, but you didn't, aren't you?"

"Right! I didn't ask to be accused of murder." Freddie looked puzzled for a moment. "You didn't ask to become pregnant either, but you did choose to get with this man, since you say you were not forced. Can't you see the difference?"

"No, not really. You see, Freddie, I loved somebody and I chose to please him. In your case, you came home and found your dad dead and you chose to call the police. Didn't we both make choices?" Margie sat forward with a rapt expression.

"But I had no choice. My dad was dead, what else was I to do? I had to do something. I didn't know but what someone had broken into the house and killed him." Freddie was beginning to get defensive.

Hannah stepped in. "You two have gotten away from your original premise that fear is fear. We all have fears and some appear to be unfounded, but whether that is so or not we are still afraid. Anyway, we need to gather whatever we wish to take for I see a patrol car coming up the drive."

Margie jumped to her feet. "It's David Shortt and I still want to put on some make-up. Tell him I'll be ready in a few minutes." She hurried from the room.

David rang the door bell and Freddie went to answer it. Hannah stood waiting and pondering about Margie. *She said she loved someone and she chose to be with him. Lord if this is Hell, she's certainly paid a terrible price for loving a man who, it seems, didn't love her,* thought Hannah.

David came into the room and smiled at Hannah. "I hoped I'd get a chance to thank you for helping Keith. I can't tell you how happy it made me to find him talking again and sitting up in bed when I visited him this morning." Seeing a policeman on the verge of tears puzzled Hannah.

"Is Keith related to you, Sergeant?"

"No, but he's one of the best men I've ever met in my life. He has shielded me from danger many times since I've been on the force and has been a mentor to me in learning investigative procedures."

Hannah shook her head. "Well, you are certainly welcome, but I didn't really help him. The Lord helped him and I'm so thankful He did."

David grinned. "Okay. Then you're the angel the Lord sent to help Keith."

Margie came hurrying into the room at that moment and Hannah breathed a sigh of thanks, since she had no idea how to respond.

CHAPTER 42

WHEN DAVID ENTERED THE PARKING LOT at the hospital, Steve Hammer was parked near the entrance. He stepped from the car as Margie opened the passenger door.

"You're late. I was beginning to wonder if something had happened. Did you have any problems?

Margie looked at her watch. "We aren't that late. You said eleven forty-five and it is eleven forty-eight. Are you a stickler about time?" She frowned.

Steve looked at his own watch and then looked up with a sheepish grin. "See what you've done to me, woman. You were three minutes late and my panic button went off."

"Well then, I thank God I'm here. You would have died if we'd been ten minutes late, but I didn't put you into a panic, Steve Hammer. You did that to yourself. I'm not a clock watcher so I think you'd better learn to relax a bit."

Steve put his hands up. "Guilty as charged, but that's only where you are involved, but right now we need to hurry if we want that jew . . ." Margie put her hand over his mouth.

"Come on, big mouth. We have places to go before lunch," said Margie, grasping his arm. They turned to Steve's car, but Steve stopped before he got in and turned to David Shortt.

"You know what to do, don't you? You make double sure that Hannah and Freddie are safe."

David nodded and grinned. "Don't worry. I don't want Keith to have a relapse."

Hannah got out of the car and stood watching Steve and Margie. "They're acting like two kids with a secret. I hope they won't sneak away and get secretly married."

David's eyes widened. "I knew they liked each other, but I didn't know it was that serious. Do you really think they might do that?""

Freddie piped up. "Steve already asked me if I minded having him for a grandfather, so I think they're pretty serious, don't you, Mom?"

Hannah nodded as they reached the entrance to the hospital. "Yes, I believe they are very serious."

Nothing else was said as they rode up in the elevator. David stepped out first and looked up and down the hallway. He then stepped out of the way and allowed Hannah and Freddie to precede him to Keith's room.

When they entered, Hannah was surprised to see Keith sitting in a chair by the bedside. "Keith! How wonderful," she hurried to his side and reached out her hand.

A broad smile spread across Keith's face as he took her hand. "I wanted to surprise you and I see I have."

"You didn't get out of bed by yourself, did you, Keith?" David was astonished. "When I came by early this morning I was surprised to see you sitting up in bed. You're moving fast, but I didn't expect this."

"I had to twist some arms, but they helped me out, but only if I promised to not try standing." Just then the door opened and his nurse came in.

"Okay, Sergeant. You've performed your surprise, but now it's back to bed with you." The nurse straightened the sheets on the bed and turned back the blankets before calling for assistance.

Keith looked at David Shortt. "Take Hannah and Freddie to the lounge until I'm back in bed, will you."

David nodded and turned to Hannah and Freddie who silently followed him out of the room as a male nurse entered.

When they were seated, David said, "I think Keith doesn't want you to see how weak and helpless he is. He was always proud of his strength. He has always been as strong as a bear."

"He's still strong in my eyes, David. He is fighting so hard to get well. Most men with his kind of injuries would have given up, but he hasn't." Hannah spoke with so much pride in her voice that David's eyes gleamed in satisfaction.

"He keeps telling me what needs to be done at the farm. I'll bet that's why he is working so hard to get better. He fell in love with the farm," said Freddie with a broad smile.

"I love the farm too." Then a sad look came over him. "Dad hated the farm and I could never understand why."

Both Hannah and David noted the deep sadness in his voice and David quickly changed the subject.

"Who lives on the farm now?"

"Nobody does right now. I had a neighbor keeping it up after Uncle Jess died, but I plan to move there as soon as Steve will allow us to go back." Hannah rose to her feet and walked to the corner, which hid Keith's room from their view.

"They should have him back in bed by now, shouldn't they? I thought they only had to lift him onto the bed."

"I don't know, Hannah, but I know the two nurses that are working with him as well as the night shift team. Steve and I made sure he had safe people taking care of him."

Just then Keith's door opened and both nurses stepped into the hall and seeing Hannah looking around the corner, they smiled.

"He's ready. Come on back in. He's waiting for you."

Hannah hurried back to the room with Freddie right behind her. David made note of Hannah's eagerness. *She cares more for Keith than she realizes*, he thought as he entered the room behind her.

As soon as they walked in Keith began. "If getting out of bed today doesn't hurt me, I can stay up longer tomorrow. Today is

Monday, so if I get out each day they may let me get on my feet by the end of the week."

"Keith, I hope you aren't trying to rush your recovery too much. What's the hurry?" Hannah was now standing beside his bed.

"Hannah, I've been in this hospital, flat of my back for three weeks or more and I'm worn out with it. I never was good at sitting around and doing nothing."

"Seems to me you've been working pretty darn hard just in trying to get better. We won't sell the farm before you get out of here, so ease up a little. Mom and I want you on the farm well and strong, don't we, Mom?" Freddie didn't look at Hannah and therefore did not see her frown.

"Freddie, Keith has his own life to live. He can't work on the farm and be a policeman too. Besides, Keith has no reason to knock himself out on somebody else's farm. He wants a farm of his own, don't you, Keith?" Hannah smiled at Keith.

David had been silently watching and listening to this conversation and saw a defeated look come into Keith's eyes. *It won't be long until Keith will be strong again and everybody will see what a strong-willed man can do,* thought David.

Keith looked at Hannah and again Hannah's heart fluttered like a leaf. *What is this? The way he looks at me makes me want to shelter him and take all pain away,* she thought.

"Hannah, I love farms, but I love your farm because you are there and also because you love the farm so much. You know how I feel, don't you?"

Hannah turned red. "I know you love the farm, Keith, but . . ." She stopped for the door opened and Nick walked in.

"What's he doing here," mumbled Keith, but Hannah heard him.

CHAPTER 43

HANNAH TURNED TOWARD NICK. "I'LL BET Mrs. Hart sent you to check on Keith, didn't she?" Hannah hoped she sounded ordinary, but when he'd entered she'd gotten the same reaction as before; excitement and racing pulse.

Nick smiled but didn't reply as he walked to the other side of Keith's bed. "How are you, Keith? Mom did want me to check on you, but I wanted to see you as well since you're the closest thing to a brother that I have."

Keith smiled. "I'm glad to see you, but your timing is bad."

Nick put out his hands and shrugged. "The last time I was here it was in the afternoon and the timing was bad that time as well." He turned a beady gleam on Hannah.

"I think I have no talent for guessing about the visiting habits of people. Am I right, Mrs. Larkin?"

Hannah bristled. "Mr. Hart, if you are insinuating that I should have regular hours to visit Keith, I don't think that's your call."

Nick put up his hands. "Oh ho! The angel has horns. I'm sorry if I touched a nerve, Mrs. Larkin." Nick's voice was full of sarcasm.

Hannah turned toward the door to be stopped by Keith's loud. "No, Hannah, I don't want you to go." He gave Nick a venomous stare.

Nick stepped back from the bedside and snarled. "Oh sure, Keith, I don't have to be evicted. I'm leaving. I see you are set on letting another woman, just like Ursula, work her charms on you."

With that parting shot, he whirled and left the room.

Keith turned red in the face, trying to heave himself up, but fell back from the effort. Fearing he had hurt himself, Hannah stepped to the bedside.

"Keith, don't. Please don't get all upset. You'll ruin all the good work you've been doing to get better."

Keith's face was now white and that scared her even more. She looked around at David who was at the door. She could see that he was angry as well and didn't call him back.

"I'll call the nurse, Keith. You're in pain, aren't you?"

Keith put out his hand and caught her sleeve. "No, don't call the nurse. I'm not in pain. I'm just so angry and frustrated."

"Keith, it's all right. Nick has a problem of some kind. I don't think he is upset with you, but for some reason he doesn't like me. I don't like him either and I probably took what he said the wrong way just now. I usually like most people, but I feel funny around Nick."

Keith's eyes seemed suddenly very intent. "Feel funny? What does that mean?"

Hannah turned red. "I didn't mean to mention it because I don't know what it is and I can't explain it."

Keith released her sleeve and lay back with a sigh. "God, I wish I was on my feet. I feel so da . . . darn helpless."

"Keith, I'm sure that Nick wants to talk to you and every time he has come I've been here. I don't know what he meant about Ursula, but I assure you that I am only coming here because the doctor said it would help you. I have no charms to use on anyone and wouldn't if I could."

Keith looked sad. "I know you're not trying to charm me, Hannah. I did think we had become friends, but I guess you don't feel the same way."

"We are friends, Keith. I didn't mean I wouldn't have come to see you, but I wouldn't have been here every day if the doctor hadn't requested it."

Keith smiled. "Good. I want to be your friend, Hannah. I felt that we were beginning to understand each other. We like a lot of the same things, don't we?"

Hannah laughed. "We both like the farm, that's for sure, but I don't know what else we both like."

Keith grinned. "I've been nosey, Hannah. When I was at your house I noticed that you liked painting and I like painting also."

Hannah's eyes widened. "How do you know I like painting?"

Keith, fearing she would get upset, hesitated. "When those people broke into your house and Steve and I checked around to see how much damage was done I found your canvasses and painting supplies. I really liked your unfinished farm scene."

"You did! I've been anxious about it. I was painting from memory and I wanted to take it to the farm to finish, but never got the chance." Hannah's eyes looked sad and Keith put out his hand.

"You'll get to go back soon, I think. In fact, I have begun to believe that it was Margie they were after anyway."

Freddie had followed David Shortt out and now they both came back in. "Where did you two run off to? I saw David leave, but I didn't even see you leave Freddie," scolded Hannah.

"Mom, you were so mad at Nick Hart that darts were shooting from your eyes and I thought it best to sneak away while I could." Freddie gurgled with laughter as Hannah gasped in surprise.

"Oh that. I think I misunderstood what he meant and my reply got Nick upset."

"His reply got me upset too" said David. "I followed Mr. Hart to his car and we had a long talk. He really cares about Keith, but I learned that he thinks all women are alike and he doesn't trust them."

So, Ursula must have cheated on Keith or something since Nick accused me of being like her, thought Hannah sadly.

"I don't care whether he trusts me or not. I'm not trying to impress him and I have no charms to use on anyone. You tell him he can rest easy where I'm concerned," said Hannah.

Freddie interrupted. "David told him that in some pretty choice words, but I don't know if Nick's convinced or not. He did leave knowing that Steve is the reason you came early today."

"That should be some help, I guess. I don't care whether he likes me or not, but I certainly don't want to break up a life-time friendship." Hannah was turned toward David and didn't see the look in Keith's eyes.

"David, did Steve and Margie go to the trial this afternoon? They've been gone for hours."

As if on cue the door opened. Steve and Margie walked in holding hands. The occupants of the room stayed in place watching as they crossed the room to stand at the foot of Keith's bed.

"Somebody say something. We feel like we've walked in on a secret meeting or something," said Margie.

"Where have you been? Do you realize that Mom and I have had no lunch," said Freddie.

Margie covered her mouth with her free hand and then moved it. "Oh my gosh. Hannah, I completely forgot. I'll go right back out and get you something."

"Not just yet, love. Remember what we rehearsed." Steve grinned at Margie first, then at everyone else.

Margie sighed happily and then with a bright-eyed gleam she chuckled. "We've been out getting engaged." Steve raised their hands that had been clasped and turned them up to reveal a beautiful ring on Margie's finger and a nice ring on his finger as well.

Keith burst out laughing. "Margie did you get Steve an engagement ring as well?"

"I sure did. We're setting a precedent. It isn't just the woman who gets engaged; the man does too."

Margie wasn't laughing. "Steve said he wanted to marry me and I said I wanted to marry him. Doesn't that mean that we are both engaged?"

Hannah looked at Keith and they both burst out laughing before Keith said, "You're setting a precedent all right. What will you say if someone asks about your ring, Steve?"

"I'll tell them it's my engagement ring, of course. We spent hours deciding what we wanted and if I do say so I've got a damn pretty ring."

Keith grinned. "If the idea catches on the jewelers in town will gain a lot of new business."

"Why don't you go back to the jewelry store and ask for a discounted price since you will be enhancing their business?" Hannah asked.

"Good idea, Hannah," said David Shortt. "If I ever ask a girl to marry me I'm going to insist on a ring, too."

"What about you, Keith? Are you going to ask for a ring?" Steve gave him a narrow look.

Keith grimaced. "I don't think I'll be lucky enough to get somebody to marry me, so the question won't come up."

"Oh I wouldn't be too sure. Everybody deserves a second chance. Don't you think so, Hannah?" Steve turned his gaze on her.

Hannah turned red and stammered. "I . . . I guess. I hadn't thought about it."

CHAPTER 44

HANNAH HADN'T REALLY THOUGHT OF 'SECOND chances' until now either, but Steve's words sent the thoughts of being happy again skittering through her mind. She backed away from Keith's bed to allow Steve some space. She sensed that he wanted to talk to Keith.

Margie thought Hannah was going out of the room and she didn't want her to. "Wait, Hannah. Steve wants to tell everybody about the trial."

Hannah whirled around. "I do want to know. What happened, Steve?"

"I found it hard to believe, Hannah, but Sam Henson was responsible for your husband's death. I think we all believed that Donaldson was more of a murderer than Henson, but I guess we were wrong."

Everyone looked stunned. They had been so sure that someone had been hired to do all the dirty work.

Steve continued, "Henson didn't give your husband the Mylanta himself, but he put the poison in it. Henson thought that Bertie Briscoll added the poison, but when Jerry Willis told him that Briscoll didn't put anything in the Mylanta, Henson put the poison in it himself and sent it to Sabrina Draper."

Freddie had been listening. "You told us that Bertie Briscoll doctored the medicine, Margie."

"I heard Chief Donaldson and somebody who I thought was Bertie Briscoll talking and Donaldson asked if the Mylanta was doctored and the answer was yes," said Margie defensively.

Steve put his hand up. "Wait just a minute you two. Nobody knew about this until it was revealed today. Sabrina Draper did give the Mylanta to Bill, then Freddie, thinking it was milk, set the poisoned Mylanta out for his dad to drink and he did. Sam Henson was so devious and had it so well-planned that until today I think the jury would have had a more lenient opinion of him. He didn't make Larkin drink the Mylanta, but he hoped he would."

Hannah almost dropped into the chair near the window and turned her head so nobody could see her anguish and pain. *Poor Mrs. Henson, and that little hussy, Nicole. I didn't like her, but Sam was her dad*, thought Hannah.

"How did they learn who actually put the poison in the Mylanta?" asked Freddie with a grim expression on his face.

"Before he committed suicide, Bertie Briscoll wrote out the entire story and mailed it to his father. His father brought it to Jerome Judson who gave it to the judge," Steve explained.

"What about Chief Donaldson? He killed a woman and has been dealing in drugs and maybe white slavery," said David Shortt who had spent the day guarding Keith's room.

Steve pulled another chair over and sat down. "Bertie also put the finishing touch to Harry Donaldson's life as well. Not only had Donaldson gotten people he had charges against to do a lot of dirty work for him, he also killed a young high school student. He told Bertie about this to keep him afraid to break off their relationship."

Keith had been listening intently. "What was the jury's verdict?"

"Both men were found guilty. Donaldson 's charge was first degree murder plus all the other charges and Henson's was premeditated murder and other charges. Many of the people who had been working for them turned state's evidence to receive a lesser sentence."

"Doesn't a first degree murder conviction get a death sentence usually?" asked Freddie.

Steve grimaced. "Yes, Freddie, it usually does and I suspect this may be the verdict in both cases, but the sentencing will be held tomorrow."

Keith had been looking around the room until he found Hannah's profile silhouetted in the window. He looked at Margie and mouthed, "'help her, please."

Margie pulled her hand from Steve's and went to Hannah. When she approached, Hannah turned and put her arms around Margie and leaned against her.

"Margie, why do things like this happen? I know Bill was unfaithful to me, but he wasn't a crook. He was trying his best to find out what was going on and he did. I don't know if Sabrina Draper knew the Mylanta had poison in it or not, but she did know she was seeing another woman's husband."

Margie hugged her close. "Hannah, I loved my son, but he allowed himself to be seduced. Yes, I'm sure that Sabrina Draper was good at seducing men, but the men have to be willing. Like you, though, I'm positive that Bill wasn't dishonest in his business dealings, but who knows, maybe using cocaine would have later caused him to become dishonest."

"I guess we'll never know, Margie, but I can't help asking why. Bill was so handsome and I guess that's why I'm so wary of handsome men. I would have sworn that Bill Larkin was faithful just as I was faithful." The two women had been holding a whispered conversation, but Steve broke it up.

"Are you two telling secrets? I told everybody what I knew, but I always knew women were like that . . . you know secretive and disloyal." He grinned when Margie gave him a stern look.

The bedside phone rang and Steve picked it up. "This is Steve Hammer. Sure, here he is. Keith, Mrs. Hart wants to talk to you."

Margie looked at Hannah. "Let's go get something to eat while he's talking, shall we?"

Freddie jumped to his feet from his position on the floor against the wall. "Did you say eat? It's about time somebody remembered that they had a hungry grandson."

Steve tapped Keith's arm. "We're going to eat. We'll stop back by, okay?"

Keith put his hand over the mouthpiece. "Be sure and come back. We need to talk."

"Okay, but I may take the women home first." Steve nudged Margie from behind and followed her from the room.

In the elevator, Hannah said, "I hope I didn't cause Mrs. Hart to be upset with Keith. Both she and Mr. Hart really love him. She was so upset when we learned that Keith had been shot."

As they reached the ground floor, Hannah continued. "Nick was upset as well, so I think he really cares for Keith. Maybe I should just stay away. What do you think, Steve?"

"Hannah, all of us know that Keith started to improve rapidly when you began visiting him and the doctor asked you to come. No, I don't think you should stay away, not unless you want to see a relapse."

Hannah walked slowly behind the other three and they were several feet in front of her. *Lord, I'm so confused. I know Keith is doing much better and I know he likes for me to visit, but I don't want to mislead him. I can't tell him I feel something that I don't, but I just don't know how I feel about him. I know I treasure him as a friend, but . . . why do I get that jittery, excited feeling when Nick walks into a room? Does it happen because for two years or more I basically did not have a husband?* Hannah's thoughts were so confused that she stopped for a moment, deep in thought.

The others had reached Steve's car before they realized that Hannah wasn't with them. They looked back down the street and saw Hannah standing.

"What is she doing? She acts like she doesn't know where she is," said Freddie. He turned and walked back down the street.

Hannah shook her head and started walking again just as Freddie reached her.

"Mom, what's wrong with you? You stopped dead right in the middle of the street. Are you lost?"

"Lost! Of course I'm not lost. I was just trying to find an answer to a problem I have." Hannah looked up the street and suddenly realized that the others had been waiting on her.

"I'm sorry, Steve. I got so wrapped up in my thoughts that I just stood still for a moment. I'm keeping all of you from eating." Hannah opened the car door and looked around at the others.

"Let's go. I'm hungry."

CHAPTER 45

DURING THEIR DINNER, HANNAH AND FREDDIE learned of Steve and Margie's plans. "As soon as this case is over, Steve will be free for a while. If everything can be arranged we plan to marry and then I want to go back to Port Angeles."

"Back to Port Angeles! Oh no, Margie. Please don't move back there. I'll give you some land on the farm and you can live near us," said Hannah.

"Free land, Margie darling. Nothing like land to anchor a man," Steve chirped.

"We'll even let Steve stay there, too, Margie. Please don't move back there, but if you just want to go on a visit and will take me with you, I'm all for it," said Freddie.

Margie looked from Hannah to Freddie. "Isn't that something, Steve and I planned to ask both you and Hannah to make the trip with us, and it is just a trip. We're coming back. You could have a vacation and see your folks out there."

Steve nodded. "It was the only way I could talk her into marrying me. I know it's an awful price to pay, but she's my woman and if I have to put up with in-laws to get her, then so be it."

Margie shoved him with her shoulder. "Be serious, Steve, or they won't believe you."

Hannah had been observing the happiness and easy camaraderie between Margie and Steve and knew that she'd never had that kind of relationship. Now she smiled.

"Steve's like a little boy who's found a jar of candy and he's just bubbling over," she said, grinning at Steve.

"Yes sir-ee. You're right. I have found a candy pot and I can't wait to open the lid. It's stuck right now, but I'm going to win Miss Margie cause that candy will be all mine," Steve almost gloated as he said those words.

Margie shook her head and turned away from Steve as if embarrassed. Steve grinned.

"I first saw this woman in Port Angeles and I'm going to take her back to the very place she was standing when I picked her out for myself. She has certainly taken me on a hell-of-a-chase though."

"She didn't know you were chasing her, Steve. Had she known she might have stopped so you could catch her," said Freddie.

"No, she was too set on following that handsome son of hers. I was introduced to her at a birthday party, but she only said, 'Hello' and forgot all about me." Steve pursed his lips and shrugged, then rolled his eyes in a soulful manner. "She's a cruel woman, Freddie."

Margie turned back and looked at him. "Stop acting silly, Steve. I don't want my family to think I'm marrying a comic who makes light of everything."

Hannah realized that Steve had a happy, optimistic personality and he would always look on the lighter side of life; or at least he would take life as he found it and enjoy the journey.

"Margie, dear, lots of women would like a man who looked on the positive side. In fact, I would have loved it if Bill had been like that. God knows we see enough gloom and doom without harping on it," said Hannah.

Margie snuggled closer to Steve. "He's serious sometimes, aren't you, Steve?"

Steve grinned and put his arm around her. "I asked you to marry me, didn't I? I was dead serious about that." He gave her a smacking kiss on the cheek and Margie pushed at him.

"Steve, we're in a restaurant full of people."

Steve looked around. "They've missed their chance. We have to go. So, they'll have to kiss you some other time." Steve pushed his chair back and rose from his seat and the others followed suit.

They all left the restaurant in a jolly mood and stayed that way until they reached Flat Top Lake Village. Steve drove up to their door and waited until his passengers were out, but he didn't kill the engine. When Margie got out, he did also and came around to her side.

"I have to take David's place tonight, so I can't come in, but should you need me just dial ten on your phone and I'll be here in a few minutes." He kissed her and quickly returned to the driver side and got in. He threw up his hand and drove away.

Arriving back at the hospital, Steve took a close look of inspection around the perimeter of the hospital and then walked up the stairs to Keith's room. David was seated by Keith's bed dealing a deck of cards. The two of them were playing poker. Keith was sitting up in his bed, which had been raised to support his back.

"Well, well, well, what have we here? Who's winning?" Steve walked to the other side of the bed.

Keith grinned. "I am, of course. I always told the both of you that I could beat either of you with my hands tied behind me."

David threw down the cards and stood up. "I believe he cheats, Steve, but for the life of me I can't catch him."

Steve came and took David's seat and started shuffling the cards. "My luck is changing so I'm going to check him out."

David groaned. "Your luck may have changed, but his hasn't. He's still the best poker player in Beckley."

Keith's head jerked up. "How do you know that? Don't tell me you've been hitting those illegal poker dens scattered around the area."

"No, but I've thought it would be a good way to catch some of those crooks. It wouldn't be a very good idea though to make a raid alone, would it?"

Keith shook his head. "Promise me you won't take any unnecessary chances, David."

David patted the knee that poked up from under the blanket covering Keith's lower body. "Don't you worry, my friend, I'm not stupid. I really listened to all you taught me."

He gathered up his gear in preparation to leave, to be stopped by Keith. "David, if you have time tomorrow will you check on Hannah's house and drive down to the farm. I know she'll want to know, especially about the farm."

David nodded and went out, softly closing the door behind him.

"He's a number one good patrolman, Steve, and like a younger brother to me. I'd appreciate it if you'd watch his back until I get on my feet again," said Keith.

Steve laid the cards down. "I don't want to play cards tonight, do you?"

Keith looked up and raised his arms over his head, stretching as far as he could. "No. I want to talk."

Steve turned toward the bathroom. "Give me second and I'm all ears."

When he returned, Keith was sitting with his feet and legs dangling down the side of the bed.

"Hey, are you allowed to do that? I don't want that doctor chewing me out," said Steve.

Keith grimaced. "I don't know about sitting on the side of the bed, but I can only get completely out and sit on a chair for about ten minutes at a time. I'm so darn tired of being in bed that I hate the thought of going to sleep."

"Once you get up and back on the job you'll be like the rest of us. You'll flop when you come off an all-nighter. That bed will look like heaven." Steve pulled the chair back away from the bed and sat down.

"Keith, are you going to stay with the police force when you are well? I think you'll completely recover, but there may be some drawbacks and you could retire with a pension."

Keith grunted in disgust. "I don't want to retire and I don't want a pension. Hell . . . drat! I'm having a terrible time cleaning up my language. I didn't realize what a bad habit I have of using curse words, but I'm trying to change that."

Steve grinned. "I don't think hell is a bad word. Think about all the preachers that use it to scare people into being good. In our profession we know that they're fighting a losing battle, though."

Keith smiled. "Personally I think all of it is just words, but you'll have to admit that language without curse words is much more pleasant to the ears. Besides, I feel sure that Hannah wouldn't like it. Freddie doesn't curse and she doesn't, thank God."

Steve again rose to his feet. "Keith, when Margie and I marry she wants to go back to Washington, where she was raised, for a visit. We both had the grand idea that if you and Hannah would marry then all of us could go and make it a month-long vacation. What do you think of that?"

"That's what I've wanted to talk to you about." He heaved a long sigh. "I don't think Hannah would agree to that." Keith gnawed on his lower lip for a moment as if making a decision,

"Steve, I married Ursula when I was twenty years old and I thought I loved her, but she was unfaithful. Nick tried to tell me, but I wouldn't listen since he always stepped in when I met some girl and tried to cut me out."

"Why would he do that? Was he jealous?" asked Steve.

Keith shook his head. "I don't really know. I was always stronger than him, but as you know, he was and still is a really handsome guy."

"Yeah, even Margie says he is a heartthrob," said Steve with a sour look.

Keith pursed his lips. "Anyway, I didn't believe him when he tried to tell me where he'd seen her and who with. We actually had a fight the last time he tried to tell me and I beat him up pretty badly. When I calmed down and saw what I'd done I was truly sorry so I asked Nick if it was the truth and even though I could have finished him off he still said it was true. So, I loaded him in the car and took him with me to find Ursula. I cursed him all the way since I was so mad at him." Keith had a stricken look on his face.

"Now, I think that deep-down I believed him, but didn't want to. I had already found out that she had been experimenting with drugs and she didn't like housework, but she was only eighteen when we married and I thought she just needed to grow up. I was wrong though. Her behavior, seen with my own eyes, made me realize that I didn't love her and maybe never had. We were married for eight miserable years and but for Nick's meddling I may have still been trying to make it work. Two years later Ursula died from an overdose. She was just a caricature of the beautiful girl I married."

Keith lay back against the back of the bed. "That last time it was just like Nick said, she was in a roadhouse with the biggest drug-dealer in the area. Of course I waded in with fists flying, but the man's cronies worked me over almost as good as I had Nick and threw me out back into a pile of garbage."

Steve wiped his hand across his face. "Man, you're lucky to be alive. How did you get home?"

Keith grinned. "That damned Nick somehow got me into the car and took me to his house. We were both so beat up that Albert hired a doctor to come to the house. Luckily we didn't have any broken bones."

Steve sat deep in thought. "I knew there was something that had kept you single for ten years. You're still a young man, Keith, so why not you and Hannah. You both need a second chance at happiness."

Keith looked stricken. "I don't believe it will ever happen, but God, I wish it would. She said Nick made her feel funny and that scared me to death. Nick has a way with women, but he's seldom serious."

Steve looked surprised. "Keith, they quarrel every time they meet. I don't think there's any danger there."

CHAPTER 46

Back in Flat Top Lake Village, Hannah was also having a 'heart to heart' talk with Margie, but neither of them had any idea what was going on in Keith's hospital room.

The two women had waited until Freddie retired for the night before deciding that they wanted some hot chocolate. Really it was Margie's idea, claiming that she needed it to calm down.

"I've been on edge all day, Hannah. I'm afraid I'm making a mistake by marrying Steve, but Hannah, I'm forty-seven years old and this will probably be my last chance to have a real home."

Margie sounded so worried that Hannah put her arms around her. "Margie, I truly believe Steve loves you. I think you two are made for each other."

Margie drew in a long breath. "I realize now, that when I met Bill's father I was so hungry for love and affection that I was willing to risk the wrath of my own father. We were to be married, but he was killed in a plane crash."

Margie's voice broke and she shivered. "I loved Bill's dad, but my father was a devious devil and he made sure that I had nothing of him left."

Margie was in tears and Hannah put out her hand. "Don't, Margie. Let's talk about something else. I don't want you to be sad."

Margie smiled and rose from the chair she had taken at the table. "You're right. I asked you to drink some hot chocolate with me and instead I started blubbering."

Hannah remained seated. "I think you're going to be a lot happier with Steve, Margie, and I believe you love him, whether you think so or not."

Margie turned from the stove where she was heating the water. "I do love Steve. He's the best thing that has ever come into my life except for you, Bill, and Freddie."

When the water was boiling Margie took it off the stove and poured it into the two mugs in which the cocoa was already prepared. She stirred one of them a few times and handed it to Hannah.

"You'd best wait a few minutes. That water was boiling."

Hannah didn't try to drink. "Margie, I need to talk to somebody too and you're the only one I have. I used to talk to Sarah, but she's in Florida and I need some help now."

"I wondered when you'd decide to trust me. I may not have the answer to your problem, but I am a good listener," said Margie.

Hannah laid her spoon beside her cup. "Margie, I lived almost three years in the same house with a husband, but I didn't have a husband. Bill never talked to me, nor even looked at me, most of the time. He took the checkbook and gave me a house-keeping allowance and then complained about how awful I looked. The allowance was barely enough to get by on and certainly not enough to buy clothes or anything like that. It got so bad that I was ashamed to go out."

Margie frowned. "Here I thought that by helping him get a good job I was helping him. I'm sorry, Hannah."

Hannah reached out and patted Margie's hand. "No, you did help him and me. We bought that house on Pike Lane and Freddie had a nice home to live in. Bill was good to me and Freddie, unless he had one of his moody spells, but Freddie and I learned to deal with those. I'd say we had a fairly good marriage up until nearly three years ago. I can honestly say that three years ago my marriage ended and I've been so lonely."

"Yet, you were still faithful and Bill wasn't. From what Freddie has told me, you were a good wife and mother so you need have no regrets, Hannah. It wasn't something you did that caused Bill to stray. He did it himself and you still believed in him so I can't see where you have anything to feel bad about." Margie gave Hannah a serious look.

"You're a beautiful woman, Hannah, and you deserve a chance at happiness. Why don't you give Keith a chance? I'm sure he likes . . . well more than likes you."

Hannah sat forward in her chair. "That's what I need to talk to you about, Margie. I know that Keith likes me and I like him, but Margie, when Nick Hart walks into a room I can't keep my eyes off him. Next to Bill, Nick is the best- looking man I've ever seen and I'm afraid it shows."

"I would have thought you two didn't like each other at all. You disagree every time you meet," said Margie.

"He doesn't like me and to tell the truth I don't really like him, but still I am attracted for some bizarre reason." Hannah explained.

Both women sat silent for a moment then Margie said, "I've heard of chemistry between a man and a woman, haven't you?"

Hannah nodded. "Yes, but I always thought it was foolishness until I met Bill. Margie, I thought I'd fall out of my seat in class when I saw Bill for the first time."

"How long did that last? I mean, did you still feel like that when he died?" asked Margie.

"Lord no! I lost that the first year. It wasn't a year into our marriage before Bill started having those dark moody spells that made him a different person. Actually, I knew he had moody spells before we married, but I thought it was because his adoptive parents had died. It wasn't though." Hannah had such a sad look on her face that Margie rose and put her arm around her.

"I was so disillusioned and I blamed myself for everything that happened for a long time. Finally I took some counseling classes at Beckley College and learned that sometimes a chemical imbalance causes swings in mood." Hannah sat looking off into some other place and Margie felt like crying.

"Hannah, he must have inherited that from my father. I never had a kind word from that man, but Mama told me that at one time he was much kinder and nicer."

"Bill was good to Freddie and acted so proud of him unless Freddie crossed him, but then for a while he wouldn't talk to him or me. We learned to wait it out and soon he would be back to being nice, especially to Freddie," said Hannah, since she wanted to be fair.

Margie looked up at the kitchen clock. "Oh my, look at the time. It's twelve o'clock. We'd better go to bed or we'll never get up in the morning."

Soon the house was quiet and both women slept. Hannah dreamed that she was going somewhere with Keith, but they met Nick along the way. Nick wanted her to leave Keith and go with him, but something kept her from going. The two men began to quarrel and soon they were fighting. Hannah awoke with a start and had tears running down her face. She got out of bed and washed her face in the bathroom and returned to her bed, but not to sleep.

By six o'clock she knew that she may as well get up. She took a shower and dressed and then walked quietly down the stairs to the kitchen. She was making coffee when Margie came in, rubbing her eyes.

"I thought I heard a noise and came to investigate. Couldn't you sleep?" she asked.

"I shouldn't have talked about my problem before I went to bed. It made me have a terrible dream and after that I couldn't go back to sleep." Hannah had the coffee perking and took a seat at the table.

Margie plopped down in a chair on the other side of the table. "There's no point in me going back to bed now. I'm wide awake.

CHAPTER 47

"STEVE'S GOING TO BE IN THE sentencing session for Henson and Donaldson this morning so I guess you'll not get to visit Keith until the afternoon," said Margie when she ended a phone conversation with Steve.

Hannah had just come out of the bathroom and stood drying her hair with a towel. "That's fine with me, but I hope to God that Nick Hart doesn't decide to pay a visit while I'm there."

Margie gave Hannah a penetrating look. "Don't you want to get that excited feeling again?"

"No, I don't. It isn't a happy feeling for me. It's only an awareness that I can't explain, so it bothers me more than it excites me."

"I've heard of some men having charisma so maybe that's what Nick has. If we could find some other woman that was excited by Nick she would probably be able to give us some light on his attraction," said Margie.

Hannah grinned. "We could advertise in the paper for any woman who had been attracted to Nick Hart. I'd like to see his reaction to that."

She took her wet towel to the laundry room, so she didn't hear the doorbell and had no time to be prepared for what awaited her return.

With her damp hair hanging in wavy tendrils down her back, Hannah returned to the living room to stop abruptly at the threshold. Nick Hart was standing near the front entrance.

Nick held a nicely wrapped package in his hand and now walked toward her, smiling his devastating smile. "Good morning, Hannah. You look gorgeous, as usual."

With a racing heart and rapid pulse, Hannah smiled as well. "Good morning. I'm afraid you've caught us unprepared for visitors. I've just washed my hair and can't do anything with it until it dries."

"Don't tell me that you don't know how attractive you are with your hair looking as it does. Many women spend a fortune to get that look. Did you know that?"

Hannah's eyes widened. "They spend money to look like a drowned rat! I don't believe you."

"I doubt that, but I won't argue with you. Here's something mother sent you. She's been very upset with me for my treatment or mistreatment, as she calls it, to you. I told her that I would mend my ways, but I don't think she believes me. Anyway, she asked me to stop by here with her gift so here it is. I hope you like it."

Hannah looked wary. She didn't trust Nick and fleetingly wondered if he had purchased the gift himself. *For some reason he wants to show me up as the woman he thinks I am*, thought Hannah as she took the gift.

When it was opened, she gasped in amazement. "Art supplies! How did she know that I dabble with painting?" Hannah sat down on the sofa and placed the box on the table in front of the sofa. Taking out a canvas she discovered tubes of paint and two brushes.

She looked up and Nick was still standing. "Sit down, Nick. I'm sorry. You'll have to excuse my manners. Your visit surprised me. I haven't told anyone about my artistic endeavors . . . ."

Nick interrupted, "Yes, you have. You told Keith. That's where Mom learned about it. She said Keith told her you have exceptional talent."

"Keith found my art supplies when he and Steve were checking out a burglary at my house. Keith says he likes to paint as well," replied Hannah.

"I guess he didn't tell you that several of his paintings are on display at Tamarack, did he?"

No, he hasn't. He told me he paints, but didn't say he was that talented." Hannah was awed and pleased that his work had been accepted at Tamarack. Instinctively, she knew that Keith McCauley would never boast about anything good he did. She understood his hesitancy to 'blow his own horn' since she was like that herself. As she finished opening her package she began to relax and inspect the different colors of paint included.

Nick sat watching Hannah before saying, "I didn't think Keith had told you. He doesn't think he's much good, but he is."

At Nick's speech her head came up. "If Tamarack is showing them he must be good. I'd love to see them. He didn't say a word about his work being on display."

Nick grinned. "Keith doesn't crow about his accomplishments, but if he knew you had seen his work I'm sure it would please him. It only takes about twenty minutes to reach Tamarack from here and I'd be glad to take you if you'd like to go."

Hannah lifted excited eyes to Nick. "I'd like that . . .." She suddenly stopped. "I can't go though. I'm sorry."

"Why? Do you have a date or another engagement in the next few minutes?" Nick knew she didn't since her hair was still wet.

Hannah dropped her head. "No, but I can't go." Margie came into the room just then, talking as she entered.

"I'm sorry, Nick . . .." She stopped when she saw Hannah.

"I guess you were shocked to walk in and find Mr. Hart here, weren't you, Hannah?"

Nick interrupted. "You bet she was shocked. You should have seen her face when she stepped through that door." Nick pointed toward the dining-room.

"How were you allowed to enter? This is a gated community and without a pass nobody is admitted," said Hannah suspiciously.

Nick grinned with a mischievous twinkle in his eyes. "I drove right up to the door and nobody stopped me. Are you sure it's gated?"

Margie had quickly gone to a seat across the room. *I'm going to watch their reaction to each other and maybe I can figure out what's going on with Hannah. I think it is sort of like a crush on Elvis.*

Hannah looked warily at Margie from startled eyes. Margie saw Nick's appreciative grin and knew his manner could bewitch any naïve person and quickly said, "It is safe here, Hannah, Steve lent Nick his pass key."

"Margie, I'm trying to get Hannah to allow me to take her by Tamarack to see Keith's paintings that are displayed there, but she says she can't go. Maybe she'll go if you go with her. Are you willing? I think Keith would like it if Hannah saw his work." Nick explained.

Margie nodded. "Hannah, I do think it would please Keith, so can't we go? Nick could drop us off at the hospital after our visit and save Steve some gas and another trip."

Hannah sighed and said, "I suppose that does make sense, but I'm not prepared to go anywhere."

"With your looks, I can allow you fifteen minutes and I don't think you'll need that long." Nick's eyes were looking her over and Hannah had to brace herself to keep from shivering.

She left the room without making any comment and Nick turned to Margie. "Is she an actress? Her look of innocence has me almost convinced."

Margie gave Nick a hard, daring look. "No, Hannah is not an actress. There's nothing fake about her and I defy anyone to prove different. What's your game, Mr. Hart?"

"No game, but you'll have to admit that someone that beautiful who has been married for more than twenty years can't be that naïve and innocent."

Margie's eyes narrowed and she tilted her head to the side. "I could have admitted that until I met Hannah, but she has changed my mind. Hannah is the most sincere person I've ever met."

CHAPTER 48

MARGIE'S SPEECH ROCKED THE FOUNDATION OF Nick's mistrust in women. *Is it possible that there is one woman left who can be trusted?* He didn't have time to pursue this line of thinking since Hannah had taken less than ten minutes.

She darted in like a sprite from a forest glade, dressed in dark green pants and a lighter green top, which was loose, but there was no doubt, at least in Nick's mind, that a luscious body wasn't hidden beneath the green.

Grabbing up her purse Hannah turned. "I stopped by Freddie's room and found him involved in signing up for an online class. So, I'm ready. Let's go."

Putting out his arm, Nick smiled and said, "May I escort you, madam?"

Hannah hesitated for a moment and then took his arm, thinking his touch would send thrills up her arm, but it didn't. His arm was thin.

She found herself remembering the strength of Keith McCauley's arms when he held her after leaving the courthouse on the day Bill's infidelity had been revealed. Keith's arms had felt so secure and strong. *Oh Lord, I must be losing my mind. Why does the size of an arm make any difference?*

When they reached the car Nick seated her in the front seat and she looked around at Margie. "Don't you want to sit up here, Margie? I'm used to riding in back."

Margie had been watching Nick's actions with a troubled heart. Deep inside she felt that Keith McCauley would make Hannah happy, but Nick was certainly acting mighty smitten. *I wonder what he is up to. Always before he has been snide and sarcastic with Hannah, but not today*, she thought, but told Hannah that she didn't want to ride up front.

When they arrived at Tamarack, Hannah didn't wait for Nick to open the door. She jumped out and stood on the pavement waiting for Margie.

Nick drove on to the nearest parking spot after Margie stepped out of the car to stand beside Hannah.

"I didn't have a chance to tell you that you looked like a woodland sprite in that green. It's a perfect outfit with your hair, Hannah. I think it is the soft green top."

"I mix and match things, don't you? I'll buy a top or even an outfit and when I get home I'll realize that I had several combinations in mind when I purchased it."

Hannah's voice had that soft lilting quality that Margie had noted the first time they'd met. It had always been like that except when Margie had visited her right after Bill's death. That time, her lilting voice was filled with a heart wrenching pathos that Margie remembered for months.

Nick came back and again offered his arm, but Hannah said, "Nick, you don't need to be so courteous and formal with me. I'm a farm girl, remember." She laughed and started walking toward the entrance.

Once inside, Nick led the way past the many craft booths, the coffee kiosk, and the restaurant, where Hannah noted delectable looking ice cream was displayed and then on past the book area. She wanted to stop at each area and look, but knew that Keith would be waiting. Finally they came to the paintings and a picture of an older lady sitting in a rocking chair caught her attention.

"Oh Margie, isn't this beautiful? That looks like the picture of my grandmother, Sarah. The picture always hung over our fireplace. I wish I still had it, but Cam asked for it when he married and Dad gave it to him."

Nick was standing beside Hannah. "That's one of Keith's paintings, see," he pointed to the initials s k m in the lower right hand corner.

"His name is Samuel Keith and when we were in school the teachers all called him Samuel. He didn't like it and he'll be upset when he learns that I've told you." Nick grinned mischievously.

"Our Keith doesn't want to leave any kind of negative impression with you, Mrs. Larkin. Did you know that?"

He's trying to make me angry and I don't know why, she thought and so she answered light heartedly. "Well, that shouldn't be a bad impression on anybody. I like Samuel for a name. It has character."

"It seems to me that you like a lot about, Keith. Am I being presumptuous in my thinking?"

Hannah had been walking along in front of the other pictures by Keith and was only half-listening. She turned and realized that Nick had said something.

"What? Did you ask me something? I was so interested in Keith's choice of color and his brush techniques that I wasn't listening."

Nick looked at Margie and rolled his eyes. "That's a first. Women usually pay attention to me when I'm talking." He sighed as if deeply hurt.

"I like painting and love to study the artist's approach like this . . . Oh, I'm sorry. I know that unless one loves to paint my enthusing about techniques can be very boring. Please tell me what you asked and I promise to listen this time."

Hannah smiled at him and he returned the smile, but this time his smile got no reaction from her.

"I just observed that you seemed to like lots of things about Keith and wondered if I was wrong," said Nick.

Hannah was looking at the painting in front of her again and without turning she said, "Yes . . . Yes, I do like lots of things about Keith. He's dependable, strong, kind, and very talented. What's there not to like?"

Margie grinned with relief. "Nobody will try to refute that, Nick. I've noted all those qualities about Keith myself."

Nick looked at his watch. "If I don't take you on to the hospital, Keith will no longer be a friend of mine and may not be anyway. He doesn't like me to be around you, Hannah."

Hannah turned startled eyes toward Nick. "Why? I thought you two were like brothers."

"Competitive brothers or at least I'm competitive. Keith seems to always know what he wants and I'm never sure. I usually try to wrest what he wants away from him, but he's always forgiven me." Nick looked at Hannah in appreciation and sighed.

I promised Keith I'd not move in until he was on his feet and I won't, but I'd certainly like to, he thought as they walked back toward the entrance.

Nobody talked much on the short drive to Raleigh General Hospital. As Nick pulled to a stop at the entrance to the hospital he said, "I'm sorry, ladies that I can't come in with you, but I have a business meeting in about fifteen minutes."

Both women got out and thanked him for taking them to see the paintings. "I'm going again when I have more time to spend studying the art work there," said Hannah and stepped back to wave as Nick threw up his hand and sped away.

CHAPTER 49

WHEN THEY ENTERED KEITH'S ROOM, HE was standing by his bed, but a nurse was on the other side. Hannah stopped as her eyes widened in amazement. She smiled happily and walked toward him.

"Keith, how wonderful. Is this the first time you've been on your feet since the accident?"

Keith grinned. "No. I've been sneaking up, but holding to the side of the bed. I didn't want to do something to set me back."

"That's smart, but I see that a nurse is stationed here. I'll bet they knew you were doing this and are afraid to trust you."

Keith looked at the nurse. "She caught me this morning, Hannah, but since I wanted to surprise you they agreed to allow me to stand when you walked in."

Hannah was puzzled. "How did you know when I'd be here? Steve didn't bring us today."

"I know. Steve told me that Nick was bringing you and I knew what time you left the Village, but it's taken you longer to get here than I expected."

Margie turned startled eyes to Hannah. "I'll bet Freddie told Steve that Nick was bringing us here today. I know I didn't."

Keith smiled. "You're here and that's what counts. What time did Nick pick you up?" He looked at Hannah.

Hannah shook her head and turned to Margie. "Honestly I don't know what time. I do know it was before lunch. We went to Tamarack so what time do you think we left the condo, Margie?

"Whose idea was that? I mean who wanted to go to Tamarack?" Keith seemed uneasy.

Hannah could sense it and didn't know what to tell him, but decided he wouldn't be upset because Nick wanted to show her his paintings.

"Nick wanted me to see your paintings and I'm glad he did. Besides, we didn't quarrel today. Actually he was really nice for a change," said Hannah, thinking Keith would be pleased.

Instead Keith scowled. "I figured he would be." Noting Hannah's worried look he quickly added, "He told me that Minnie had been really upset with him about being so rude to you."

Hannah smiled and looked at Margie. "Oh, so that explains it. Margie and I wondered why he was being so nice and friendly, didn't we, Margie?"

Margie raised her eyebrows. "Oh yes, he was a pure Sir Galahad today."

Keith grimaced, but made no comment, and then the nurse stepped in. "Sergeant, I'm afraid your time is up and you'll have to go back to bed."

"Can't I just sit in this chair for awhile? If I get tired, I promise to call you and go back to bed," said Keith.

"You can stay there for fifteen minutes, but no longer." The nurse was very firm in her statement and Keith nodded.

Margie and Hannah moved out of the way and Keith who was dressed in pajamas sank into the chair. He frowned when he first sat down, but then seemed to relax. The nurse nodded and left the room.

"Keith, why haven't you told me about your paintings? Those on display at Tamarack are beautiful?" Hannah gave him a stern look as she continued, "Nick seemed so proud to show us your work and I can understand why. After seeing your work, I'm ashamed that you found my meager attempts at painting."

"Meager attempts! My God, Hannah, you have a depth to your work that I haven't been able to master. Who taught you?"

Hannah smiled. "Nobody, but I took some art classes as electives in high school and then did the same in college. Mostly I have been experimenting and wasting a lot of paint."

Margie saw that the two of them would never know she'd left and decided to go to the lounge. "I'm going out in the lounge, in case anyone is interested," she said as she quietly closed the door.

Keith stayed up twenty-five minutes and they talked about everything on earth. Painting flowers began the conversation and wound through family, genealogy, schooling, careers, children, and parents. When the nurse opened the door and came in they were both disappointed.

Hannah walked out to find Margie while the nurse was getting Keith back in bed and situated comfortably. She found Margie and Steve talking like an already married couple who were very content with each other.

"Why didn't you come back in, Margie? Keith and I talked about everything. You know, I'm finding we have a lot in common," said Hannah as if surprised.

Steve grinned. "If you had asked me, I could have told you that, days ago."

"Next time I want to learn something I'll ask you first, Steve, and save myself a lot of trouble," said Hannah, with her dimples going in and out ready to laugh.

"Oh ho, she has you figured out already. I hope she doesn't tell everyone what a 'know-it-all' I'm planning to marry," said Margie.

"Hey listen, there's no need of both of us worrying our heads with knowledge. I don't mind telling you anything you need to know," Steve said, feigning innocence.

Margie punched him on the shoulder. "Hannah, do you think I can stand this man on an everyday basis?"

"It'll be hard, Margie, but I think you're strong enough to handle it. You may have to come visit me really often, though."

"Oh no, you don't, Miss Hannah. You're not dragging my wife away from my side. If she comes I come too, so two or nothing." Steve got to his feet. "Let's go check on Keith. He'll think we all went home."

Hannah looked at her watch. "We've been here over an hour already so we can't stay much longer."

Steve grasped her arm. "Wait just a minute, Hannah. We need to talk." Steve paused a moment.

"I think Keith will be allowed to go home in a few more days, but there's nobody there to take care of him. What if we could get Keith to go to the farm? Could you and Margie take care of him through the day? I'd come out and be there at night if you'd agree to do that. What about it?"

"I thought you said it wasn't safe on the farm. Do you know something that we don't?" asked Margie.

"Nothing except that all the people Keith and I had arrested for being involved in one of Henson or Donaldson's scrapes is now serving time or is out on parole and don't pose any danger. Of course, during the day, Freddie and Keith will have access to weapons and I'll be extra at night. I talked to Jerome Judson and Judge Wilson today and they seem to think the danger to you and Margie is past."

"Whew, that's good to hear. When can I go home?" asked Hannah.

"Which home do you mean? Are you meaning the house in town or the farm?" Steve stared intently as if fearing what she would say.

Hannah's eyes widened. "Why, the farm, of course. That's my home." Hannah smiled widely and continued. "I'll have to pack up everything in the house on Pike Lane and then get a realtor to sell it, I suppose."

They had now reached Keith's room and had to stop talking about going home until something could be worked out. As they entered the room, they saw that Keith was on the phone. He put his hand over the speaker and motioned with his hand to come in. He abruptly said his good-byes and ended the call.

"That was Nick. He asked if you wanted him to drive you back to Flat Top Lake Village and I told him no. I'd rather you'd call a taxi if Steve can't take you."

This has to stop thought Hannah and walked over to the bedside. She stood looking at Keith so intently that he finally said, "What? Why are you staring like that?"

"Keith, I want to know why you don't want Nick to be friends with me. I don't think you want him to be rude to me, but you don't want him anywhere near me either and I want to know why," said Hannah in a stern voice.

Keith was silent for a moment and then blurted, "I'm jealous."

"Jealous! Why? I'm not going out with Nick or anything like that and besides you don't own me. I can be friends with anyone I want to be friends with." Hannah was getting angry and Keith knew it.

"Hannah, don't get angry, please. There's a story behind my jealousy and if you knew it I think you'd understand."

She stood still as a mouse with her thoughts in a jumble. "Okay, I'll take your word for it, tonight, but I need to hear that story. I'm not going to be a 'bone' that you two squabble over and I'd tell Nick the same thing. That's something for you to think about for right now."

Hannah turned to the door, but looked back and said, "Good night, Keith."

His 'good night' was soft as the others followed Hannah out the door.

CHAPTER 50

THAT NIGHT THE TWO WOMEN AND Freddie stayed up late. At first, they decided to go to the house on Pike Lane, but then Margie said she needed to pack up what was left in her apartment.

"Do you have an unused building at the farm? I need some place to store my furniture, if any of it is worth saving after the break-in," said Margie in a sad voice.

"What about that tool-shed that Papaw kept his tools in? It could be cleaned out for Margie's furniture, couldn't it, Mom?" Freddie had an excited look on his face.

Hannah looked at Freddie. "It's probably full of snakes, rats, and God knows what else. I haven't been in that building in years." She smiled at the memory of the playhouses she once built inside that shed.

Margie laughed. "We can let Steve clear out the snakes and rats, but I'll sweep down cobwebs."

Hannah laughed gaily. "Yes, let Steve do that, but we still haven't decided where to start. Are we going to your place first, Margie?"

Margie sobered. "Before we decide on anything else you have to decide if you want to take Keith out to the farm, don't you?"

Freddie's eyes lit up. "Is Keith well enough to leave the hospital?"

"Steve seems to think he will be released soon, but he needs somebody with him. There's nobody at his house and Steve asked Hannah to take him to the farm. He says Hannah and I could keep an eye on him, until he is completely recovered," explained Margie.

"You're going to take him to the farm, aren't you, Mom? He did a lot for me and now he needs help. I don't see how we can refuse," said Freddie in a determined voice.

Hannah nibbled at her lower lip in indecision. "I want to help Keith, Freddie, but I don't want to leave the wrong impression with him. I'm not ready for a relationship with Keith or any other man and he might think this move means more than it does. That's the problem."

Freddie rolled his eyes and looked at Margie. "He's not going to think that, is he, Margie? Sure he likes you, Mom, but I'm sure he knows you're not in love with him. You're not in love with him, are you?"

"No-o-o, I'm not in love with him, but I really like Keith. I just honestly don't know how I feel and I don't like to feel pushed," said Hannah.

Freddie jumped to his feet. "Why do women make such a drama about everything? Just talk to Keith about it. He's a really up-front guy and he'll listen and give his honest opinion. Keith likes honesty above all things."

Hannah look startled. "Freddie, a woman doesn't talk to a man about how she feels about him. He'd think I'd lost my mind."

Freddie shook his head. "Women are so irrational. That's why there are so many divorces in this country. Women want to clothe all their ideas in illogical jargon."

"Freddie, they do not. I've never known a woman to tell a man that she likes him, but doesn't love him unless he's proposed." Hannah looked at Margie and raised her eyebrows.

"Margie, did you ever hear such foolishness in your life? I don't know where Freddie gets his crazy ideas."

Margie sat forward on the sofa as if fascinated by Freddie's idea. "I don't know, Hannah. I think maybe we women don't think like men and Keith just might understand. It may not be a bad idea to just lay it out to Keith and see what he says."

"I'm shocked, Margie. Surely you're not agreeing with Freddie. I can't tell Keith I like him, but I feel funny around . . ." suddenly remembering that she had never told Freddie about her reaction to Nick, she didn't finish.

Freddie gave Hannah a disappointed look. "Mom, surely you don't want Keith to go home to an empty house. He's not able to cook or anything. I've never known you to be cruel, but that would be cruel."

Hannah threw up her hands. "Okay, Okay, Freddie. Keith can go to the farm and if he gets the wrong idea it will be your fault."

Freddie got up and put his arm around Hannah's shoulders. "Thanks, Mom. It won't be too much trouble. Margie and I will help, won't we, Margie?"

Margie kissed Freddie's cheek. "You're a good boy, Charlie Brown. I think I'll keep you."

Before they went to bed they decided to enlist Steve's help in packing Margie's things up and hiring a moving van to deliver them to the farm. "We'll have to get help in cleaning out that shed before we do that, though," said Hannah.

The next morning Hannah was awakened by a knock on her door. When she called, "Come in," Freddie cracked open the door and stuck his head inside.

"I called Jim Talbot and he'll start work on the shed today. He said he'd clean it out, check the roof, and replace any broken windows. I hadn't thought of that, but Jim said if it leaks everything will get ruined. He's a good carpenter and he promised to have it ready by day after tomorrow."

Hannah smiled. "You sure are an eager beaver. You've done a lot of work and I'm still in bed. Now go away so I can get ready for work as well."

After breakfast, Margie called Steve and soon they all trooped up the steps into Margie's apartment. It hadn't been touched since the vandals broke in and it was hard to decide where to start.

The efficient secretary in Margie took over and soon people were assigned to certain tasks. At one o'clock Freddie came into the kitchen.

"Do you pay laborers or feed them? I'm hungry."

"So am I," said Steve as he walked in from the outside. "I've filled that dumpster. We'll have to haul that off before we can get anything else in it."

Margie grinned and stood back with her hands on her hips. "Well, for gosh sakes, we can't have our men die of hunger can we? Steve, you and Freddie go down the street to that Pizza Hut on the corner and get us some food. I want a large sweet tea and so does Hannah." Margie looked and Hannah who nodded happily.

Finally by three o'clock every room was stripped. "We can hire a cleaning service to come in and spruce it up." Steve clapped his hands together.

"There, we don't pay rent on this place any more, Margie mine. We have other fish to fry, don't we?

Margie grinned and put her head on his shoulder. "That we do, handsome, that we do."

Hannah came out of the bathroom where she had tried to clean some of the dust and grime from her hands and face. "Steve, you need to call Keith and tell him we won't be there today. If I don't get a shower I wouldn't be admitted anywhere."

Steve assured her that the call had been made and that Keith understood. "I told him that you wanted to take him to the farm when he was released."

"What did he say about that?" asked Hannah.

Steve grinned. "At first, he didn't believe me, but when I convinced him it was true he sounded like a kid at Christmas."

"If we get him better over there he'll have to work seven years to pay us back, won't he, Mom? Freddie acted more excited than Hannah had seen him act since Bill died.

Margie looked at herself and Steve. "Lord, we are all dirty as the chimney sweeps in the story of Oliver Twist. Let's go back to the condo and get cleaned up."

CHAPTER 51

FOR THE NEXT THREE DAYS HANNAH, Margie, and Freddie worked along with two boys and one girl that Steve had hired. They cleaned the house on Pike Lane and called a Real Estate Agent.

"I know it appraised for $150,000 but lower the price if you don't sell it in a month," said Hannah, since she never wanted to live there again. Steve had hired movers to take all the furniture to the farm and Jim Talbot and his son helped unload and carry the furniture into the house on the third day.

Inching her way between pieces of furniture to reach the kitchen, Hannah felt the happiest she had in two years or more. *I'm really home* she thought as tears threatened to break though the barrier she had erected when others were present.

Steve shifted pieces of furniture and also made it to the kitchen.

"Freddie says that gas station on Route 16 makes really good hot dogs. Margie and I are going to drive out there and buy our dinner. Is that all right with you?"

Hannah turned to look at him. "You have dirt all over your clothes. Are you going out like that?" Margie walked in from the shed where she had gone to check on her furniture. Steve and Hannah erupted into gales of laughter.

Margie's face was streaked with dirt and something with a reddish-purple look. "Princess Minni-ha-ha, has her war paint on, don't you, dear?" Steve pulled her into his arms and kissed her.

"I love you anyway, but that red-purple stuff certainly isn't strawberries or blueberries. What is that, Margie?" he asked and ran his finger down her cheek. He held up his finger with the same hue on it.

Margie's mouth gaped open and her eyes blared. "Did that come off my face? I don't know what that is." She darted to a mirror hanging above the sink.

When she saw her image reflected she laughed until tears ran down her face. "I saw some dark blue berries on a bush beside the shed and I crushed some with my fingers," she held up her now stained hands. "Will it come off?"

Hannah started laughing again and yelled, "Freddie, come here. Come see where you got your penchant for squishing everything you see. Your grandmother does the same thing. Look at her. She's been into pokeberries."

Freddie appeared in the door, out of breath. He stood in awe-struck disbelief. "Grandmother, what purple cheeks you have and Oh grandmother, what purple hands you have," he chortled and doubled over with laughter.

Needless to say both Margie and Steve had to clean up a bit before going shopping for food.

Nothing was moved that night except for shifting the furniture enough to get to the sofa, which was to be Steve's bed that night. Hannah lay in her upstairs bed and listened to the whippoorwill call from out near the barn and silently thanked God that she had finally come home.

As they ate breakfast the next morning, Steve said, "We can work until one o'clock and then we have to go see Keith. He's been walking up and down the hall and he thinks they will release him today or tomorrow."

"Where are you going to put him, Hannah? Should he go upstairs?" asked Margie.

Hannah shook her head. "I don't know. Steve, what do you think? Dad and Mom's old room would probably be the best for him since it is bigger, but can he walk up and down stairs?"

Steve chewed and swallowed. "Don't know, ma'am, but I'll sure as Hell find out." He pulled out his phone and pressed the button for Keith.

After their greeting, Steve asked how he was and if he was walking better. What Keith said couldn't be heard but they did hear Steve's part.

"Slowly but surely, you say, but what does the doctor say?" asked Steve and looked at Hannah, giving her an a-okay sign.

"He did? When did he say you could go? Hannah has a room prepared for you if you can manage the stairs. Can you get up and down stairs?" Steve sounded excited.

When Steve hung up he turned to Hannah. "He can use the stairs, but the going will be slow at first. He's being released tomorrow and he is really excited."

"I'm not going to the hospital today since he'll be released tomorrow. This mess has to be straightened out or he won't be able to get in the house," said Hannah.

Steve pushed back from the table. "I think that will be fine, but I'm taking Margie with me. Can you get Jim Talbot to help Freddie heave this furniture around?"

Freddie pushed his plate back. "I've already asked him and he'll be here around nine o'clock. I told him to bring his wife with him to help Mom."

Soon Steve and Margie pulled away from the farm, but Hannah was so busy she didn't even know when they left. Most of the furniture was shifted into the various bedrooms and some pieces were to be used in the living room. Hannah had sold several pieces of furniture from the house on Pike Lane since she didn't need it on the farm and didn't have room for it.

The living room held a nice mixture of period pieces and antiques, all in good shape. Hannah stood looking around the room with a critical eye. "I should have had this floor redone before we moved back in, but it's too late now," she said aloud, thinking Freddie was in the room.

"It looks really nice as it is," said Nick Hart's voice and Hannah wheeled around with wide staring eyes.

"You scared the life out of me. What are you doing here?"

"I came to see how you are doing and if you needed any help. I didn't mean to scare you. I'm sorry. I should have called, but you don't have a working phone out here, do you?" he asked.

Hannah knew she looked bedraggled and unkempt and that embarrassed her. He had certainly chosen a bad time to visit. She turned toward the sofa and motioned.

"Have a seat, Nick. Would you like a drink or coffee? I believe there is still some in the pot."

Nick walked over and sat down as he said, "I'd like some coffee. According to Keith, you don't drink alcoholic beverages. Is that true?"

Hannah turned to get the coffee as she said, "Yes, that's true. I have never acquired the taste for alcohol. How do you like your coffee?"

"Black, please." Nick sat looking around in appreciation. "How old is this house, Hannah?"

Hannah returned with the coffee and after passing it to Nick, she sat down on the arm of the nearest chair. "It was built before World War II started, so I think it is a little over eighty years old."

"It looks solid and anchored. Driving down the road I could see the house from a distance and it makes a pleasant view. Whoever built it must have been a good carpenter."

Hannah smiled. "It was built by my great grandfather and Dad always said that he was a skilled builder."

Nick's eyes roamed around the room and the edge of the staircase leading up from the hallway. "How many rooms are there in all? It looks almost majestic in its simplicity."

"Thanks. I always felt it was a palace, but then most children feel like that about their home if it is a happy one, I guess."

Nick put down his cup and rose to his feet. "Mom feared you were working too hard. She insisted that I come out and check on you. Have you had any help? You couldn't have possibly done all this without help."

Hannah grinned. "I could have, but not in three days. I couldn't have gotten it all done without the help of Margie, Steve, Freddie, and the Talbot family. We've all worked from morning to night until today."

Nick smiled that devastating smile, which still made Hannah's heart lurch. "You have dark circles under your eyes, which usually makes women look used, but not you. You look like an innocent fairy sprite. How do you do it?"

Hannah turned red. "I don't know what you mean. When one works hard and doesn't get much sleep they usually get dark circles. I'm worn out, but I think we're ready."

Nick sniffed. "Um, um, what is that delicious smell? I got a whiff of it as I came in."

"It's a beef roast I'm baking for dinner tonight," said Hannah.

"You're preparing a welcome home dinner for our friend, Keith, aren't you?" Nick turned his gaze upon her as if he didn't understand her.

Hannah rose from her perch on the chair arm and said, "Yes and I need to go check on it right now. Make yourself comfortable."

"Did you ask Keith to come here and convalesce? Mom thought he would come to us. I drove out to the hospital and he was all dressed and waiting on Steve to bring the car for him. He told me he was going to live here while he is completely recovering."

"Yes, Nick, he is going to recuperate here with me, Margie, and Freddie to help him and I didn't ask him to come. However, I did invite him if he wished to come. Is that an issue with you?" Hannah asked defensively.

"Are you in love with Keith, Hannah? I don't believe you are. I think you know very little about men and because Keith has been nice and helpful you are confusing that with love," said Nick.

Hannah turned red with anger and confusion. "How I feel about Keith is none of your business. You don't know me well enough to be interpreting my feelings, either."

Nick had stepped closer to her as she gave this speech and suddenly he swept her into his arms and kissed her. His lips were wet and Hannah was surprised that she found his kiss repulsive instead of heart stopping as she had assumed it would be. She shoved against his chest and when he stepped back he received a resounding slap to his right cheek.

"Who do you think you are, Nick Hart?" Hannah's face was now deathly white, but her eyes were blazing. She walked to the doorway and motioned him out.

Nick sneered. "You haven't been kissed much either, but you can't fool me. I know your kind. You'll put on a big act until you get what you want and then it's over. I'll not let you get your claws into Keith, though. He's like a brother to me."

"I'm asking you to leave, Mr. Hart, and I'd rather not see you again, but I won't stop you from visiting Keith. I only ask that you let me know when you plan to visit." She was thankful when a horn sounded from the front lawn.

CHAPTER 52

HANNAH WALKED TO THE EDGE OF the porch and didn't realize that Nick had come to stand beside her. Keith McCauley, the passenger in the car realized it, though, and quickly opened his door.

Margie turned and seeing the angry look on Keith's face she gasped.

"Keith, wait. You'll hurt yourself." She jerked her door open and lurched from the car to grasp Keith's arm as he started toward the porch.

Hannah, sensing that something had agitated Keith, glanced sideways and saw the secret smile on Nick's face. She turned to glare at him.

"You're a devil, Nick Hart. You don't love Keith like a brother and I doubt if you know what love is," she snapped as she quickly went down the steps. Once on the ground, she hurried to meet Keith and impulsively threw her arms around him.

"Gosh, you look good on your feet, Keith," she said in a muffled voice for Keith's strong arms had enfolded her and suddenly 'home' took on a deeper meaning. She tilted her head back from his chest and Keith looked down at her.

His eyes held so much love that Hannah's eyes shone with delight.

"Oh Hannah . . ." began Keith, then beyond his determination to 'make haste slowly,' he found himself kissing the woman he loved better than anything on earth.

Keith's kiss wasn't wet . . . his kiss was . . . Hannah stopped trying to describe the feeling that swept over her and found herself returning the kiss.

Again the scene was a *tableau vivant* for several minutes. Suddenly breaking into a merry laugh, Margie said, "Well, that is certainly a nice welcome, Keith."

Keith raised his head revealing an awed sense of wonder, but he didn't release Hannah from his embrace. He smiled and Hannah thought it the most beautiful smile in the world.

"Wow, Hannah, would you mind repeating that?" he asked with a mischievous gleam in his eyes.

Steve stepped up. "Hold on there, Champ. The doctor said you were to come home and rest and a little more of that and you won't rest, that's for sure."

Hannah turned rosy and buried her face into Keith's chest. Margie nudged Steve in the side.

"Leave it to Steve to ruin a beautiful moment." Steve looked at her in shock.

"I'm trying to take care of him, woman. He has to get better if we want to have a double wedding, don't he?"

Margie gave him a startled look and shook her head. *If he puts new doubts in Hannah's mind I'll do him an injury*, she thought as she saw the bemused look of delight on Hannah's face.

A stunned Nick came off the porch and stopped in front of Keith. "Well, Bro, I think maybe you've won the real thing and I'm beginning to think I've been wrong." Keith acknowledged his admission with a nod and Nick went hurriedly to his car and drove away after throwing up his hand in farewell.

Those present watched Nick drive away without comment, but were glad for the arrival of Freddie, which filled the awkward silence. Freddie wasn't even startled to see his mother in Keith's arms.

His first question was, "Steve was today the end of this long, long, tangled tale we've all lived through?"

Steve sighed. "Yes, and thank God it's over. Harry Donaldson is sentenced to death and the leader of the gang that shot me and Keith, was a man named Beano Darling. He was a crony of Donaldson's and had escaped from prison where he was serving a life sentence for a prior murder, so he'll end up on death row as well."

Steve gave Keith an understanding look. "I think his intent was to kill the two men Keith and I held, as well as the two of us. Donaldson hired him out of hate of the police and revenge on me and Keith and Darling hated police anyway, so he didn't need much encouragement. Lucky for me, my man was big and heavy. He took the bullets I would have received."

"What about Sam Henson?" Freddie asked. "He should have gotten the death sentence too."

"The jury felt that since he hadn't actually committed a 'hands on murder' he should serve a life sentence, but with the option of parole after twenty years and good behavior," explained Steve.

Margie's lips were pressed in a hard line. "They got what they deserve, I guess, but I don't have much room to talk. With enough provocation nice people can act in strange ways. I know that as a fact."

Steve pulled her close and smugly said, "Yes, love, that's true, but sometimes bad things pave the way for a lot of good.

The five people gathered in front of the house were all talking at once, but Margie put a stop to that.

"Steve, for heaven's sake! Stop talking and get Keith in the house. He can't just get out of a hospital and be left to stand in the driveway all night."

Steve looked startled and then grinned as he took Keith's arm. "Well gosh, I don't see why not as long as Hannah will stand with him. We are all so relieved that things have turned out as they have that we just can't stop talking."

Margie smiled at Hannah. "I thank God this terrible ordeal is finally over."

Hannah, still standing in Keith's encircling arms, couldn't believe this happy feeling was real. She carefully pulled Keith's arm around her shoulders on the other side from Steve and they began the slow walk to the porch.

Margie hurried ahead ready to help them get Keith up the steps if needed. As they reached the steps Hannah looked up with a smile on her face.

"Yes, Margie, I certainly do thank God it's over. My life was in such a mess and if I hadn't believed that God has a purpose for each of us I don't think I could have survived."

They let Keith stop to rest when he stepped onto the porch and Hannah stepped from under his arm. "For a sick man you still have a heavy arm, Keith."

Hannah arched her shoulders from left to right. "I sure hope God lets me know what my purpose is and I also hope I've been given a second chance at happiness."

Keith's grasped her hand. "Maybe we've both been given a second chance." He bent down and kissed her cheek. "I pray that God is giving us our chance together, Hannah. I love you more than life itself."

SHORT BIO

ADDA LEAH DAVIS IS A MCDOWELL County, West Virginia native who has now lived in Russell County, Virginia for more than twenty years and dearly loves the entire area. She is a retired elementary school teacher and counselor.

After retirement from the school system she wrote for two newspapers in McDowell County, started an oral history theater group, was Director of Economic Development in McDowell County for six years.

Mrs. Davis has presented workshops on oral history, community development, leadership, and writing. She is energetic and enthusiastic about any project she starts and about life in general.

Davis is the author of fifteen books; **"Fantasy Stories of the Life Cycles in Nature (Making Science Enjoyable),""Here I Am Again Lord, Landon Colley, An Old Time Primitive Baptist Universalist Preacher," "Caleb's Song," "Golden Harvest Workbooks for Grades 1, 2, and 3," "Abigail's Redemption,"** and the **Lucinda Harmon Saga** which includes; **"Lucinda's Mountain," "Jason's Journey," "The Beckoning Hills,"** and **Farther Along**. She has just completed the third book in a mystery series titled **The Untangling Tale** and includes **"A Fatal Love of Place," "A Fatal Web of Deceit,"** and **"Fatal Choices and Second Chances."**

When first leaving her life in West Virginia she was devastated, but today, Davis will tell you that hearts, like love, can expand as hers has because she now loves Russell County, Virginia and the entire area. The many friends and fellow writers that she has been blessed to meet and learn to love, attest to this knowledge.